BONE
WHISPERS

Rosalind Brackenbury

coffeetownpress

Kenmore, WA

coffeetownpress

A Coffeetown Press book published by Epicenter Press

Epicenter Press
6524 NE 181st St.
Suite 2
Kenmore, WA 98028

For more information go to:
www.Camelpress.com
www.Coffeetownpress.com
www.Epicenterpress.com
www.Rosalindbrackenbury.com

Cover design by Scott Book
Design by Melissa Vail Coffman

Bone Whispers
Copyright © 2024 by Rosalind Brackenbury

Library of Congress Control Number: 2023945716

ISBN: 978-1-68492-145-4 (Trade Paper)
ISBN: 978-1-68492-146-1 (eBook)

For my brothers
and for MJD

"It is memory that solders together the processes, scattered across time, of which we are made. In this sense, we exist in time. It is for this reason that I am the same person today that I was yesterday. To understand ourselves means to reflect on time. But to understand time we need to reflect on ourselves."

—Carlo Rovelli, *The Order of Time* (2017)

"We are all governed by what we were as children."

—Michael Ondaatje, interview in *BRICK* magazine (2007)

PART I
FORENSIC

ONE

YESTERDAY I WAS AT HOME IN OUR HOUSE in upstate New York, packing a bag, preparing to leave for England. Today, I'm back where it seems that I have always been. Halfway across the Atlantic, I slept briefly, the blue night shut out, stars and planets invisible, portholes shuttered, screens flickering, the curve of the earth unseen as if everyone had lost interest in its existence. I felt, waking, like a fish floundering on a rock, though I used to take this flying business in my stride. Now I am slightly nauseated, aching, my skin raw and eyelids dry, dragging my luggage after me. One day, as my friend Paula keeps on suggesting, I will treat myself to business class, and have room to stretch out and sleep.

I'm back in Dorset this summer to see to repairs to the house that was my maternal grandmother's and is now mine and my brothers'. The road from the ferry winds between hills and dips, moorland covered in heather, bracken and small wind-blasted trees, where wild ponies and cattle wander and graze and there is no other road. The village is on a peninsula, in the southwest of England, where the waters of Poole Harbour and the English Channel surround it on three sides, and there's one road in from the landward side. You reach it most easily on a car ferry and you leave the 21st century behind. The land looks as it did when I was a child, and probably close to how it looked in Thomas Hardy's day, when he wrote his Wessex novels about this part of England that he loved. I am at home here—it was the place for dozens of childhood holidays and visits to my grandmother, the place to return to after school was ended, the place to come to with student friends, and then as an adult.

The bus bumps down off the ferry and I look out of the window as it seems to topple between hills, taking the curves and dips of the narrow road, and time falls in upon itself in layers, all the years, all the memories, all that I have brought with me, all that makes me eager to arrive, and always has. The trees have grown taller, yes, and the hotel has been painted, and two of the shops in the village have closed, and the elm tree at the heart of the village died years ago, and most people I knew here are gone. Yet I ring the bell, get off the bus at the same almost invisible bus stop, and heave my bag down, thank the driver and set off by foot up the road that leads to the house, uphill, facing into the setting sun, tired from my journey and older than I ever was, and drag my bag behind me, feel the weight of my back-pack on my shoulders, put one foot in front of the other, and at last, arrive.

The house was built in the 1930s and so is neither old nor romantic. I remember how, when my grandmother first bought it, I was disappointed that it was not like Manderley in *Rebecca*, a brooding mansion on a cliff. It's foursquare with symmetrical windows and a wooden veranda running along its front, its pebble-dashed walls are covered in Virginia creeper now, and it has a look of emptiness and disrepair. None of us has been here for a year or more. Houses decay fast when nobody lives in them. The grass is a foot high, dry as hay, sown with moon-daisies and yellow wort. The hedges are strewn with nets of bindweed and tangled honeysuckle, and are grown taller than a man.

So much to do, if I've a mind to do it—we are wondering if perhaps we should sell it, as we come here so seldom. I take my key to the side door and let myself in, as I have a hundred times before.

WHAT I HEAR IN THE VILLAGE SHOP later this same day stuns me, and I can't put it all down to jet-lag.

"Nessa, are you all right?" Eric is asking a little anxiously, as if afraid I may faint. I knew his father; the family has kept this shop since I was young. He leans over the counter towards me, puts out a hand.

"Did you say what I thought you said?" I feel a little dizzy, it's true.

"Yes, sorry, was it a shock? I thought I should let you know—so that, you know, the yellow tape, the excavations, you knew what was going on."

I'm simply here to pick up a few groceries when I hear what Eric's telling me. *Human bones have been found, where sand and rock covered them, at the foot of the cliff on the near beach.* I've been picking up milk, eggs, cheese, bread, wine in my basket—but now he has my full attention.

Eric looks like his father—tall pale men, prematurely balding, with gentle manners. "Yes, it's been a strange time. We're not used to this sort of thing, here."

"I'm okay, thanks. Just a bit tired, I've flown in from America. You said they found human bones?"

"Yes. Just last week. Everyone's talking about it. Cops were in and out of here like dogs in a butcher's doorway."

"Do they know who it was?" He looks surprised. Most people must ask: was it a murder or an accident?

"No. I heard they think it wasn't a recent death. They've taken the bones away, you know, to be analyzed. You can find out a lot these days. It could've been from a cliff fall, years ago."

Erosion has been going on here steadily over the years—the whole coast is being gradually eaten away. The shape of the land alters with the tides. Cliffs crumble. Animal bones, fossils, lost implements, fragments of houses, gardens, the places where lives took place—anything can come to light. Plates and cutlery, tools, even musical instruments. But human remains?

"There were all these police cars parked all over the village—just a few days ago. Like I said, they were in and out of here, asking questions. Nobody I know had a clue."

"Where was it, exactly?" I hear my own voice, a little hoarse, the way it is when you haven't spoken for a long time.

"Out by Redend Point. Near where the pill-box is. You know? Just before the point, where there was that fall years ago. It was before the bulldozer cleared everything out and flattened it. Bloke got out to have a smoke, stopped the machine. Saw the skull, then some bones. The cliff falling on her had smashed her up, she can't have been whole."

The immaculate chain of a spine, the links of wrists, the tiny tail-bones that none of us need.

"Was there much in the paper about it?"

"Take a look. This week's Gazette has just come. They think she'd been there some time."

"So, they are sure it was a woman?" I ask.

"Well, yes. Easy enough to tell, I suppose. You know, the size. The pelvic bones. Then they look at dental records, to find out the age. She was only in her thirties, it seems."

It shocks me to hear about the investigation of some unknown woman's pelvic bones, made obscenely available to the public eye. Bones are a private matter, veiled throughout our lifetimes in flesh and skin. Nobody should be seen this naked. I think of the X-ray I was once given after a fall from a horse, that ghost-picture of my own pelvic arch that I had never before seen, but that I still keep in a drawer at home, a secret image of an invisible part of myself. To see my own bones floating in darkness on that negative—well, it makes me feel barely anchored to my life.

THE VILLAGE SHOP IS FULL OF ALL THE THINGS that anyone might need on vacation: from sun umbrellas to malt whisky, through a dozen kinds of sauce to potatoes heaped in a box, local cheeses, post-cards, newspapers, bath salts, apple cake. A tall middle-aged man has come in and is standing close behind me. He clears his throat, as if what he has to say is more important than our conversation. Clean jeans, a Barbour jacket, checked shirt—I know the type. He wants to pay with a card for a bottle of single malt and some local cheese and *The Times*, and he's in a hurry and reaches past me, pushing me to lay them on the counter. He clears his throat, and asks, "So, the cliff path is safe now? No more cliff falls to worry about?"

Eric says, "You can't be sure of it. But they've fenced the edge, most of the way. You just have to watch your step." He rings up the man's bill, closes an eye just slightly to wink at me. I remember him as a quiet child, playing at the back of the shop, probably listening to customers, his father standing where he stands now. The village gives newcomers a wry look, still.

The brisk man with the Glenfiddich and the Dorset cheese leaves, the paper under his arm, pulling close to heel the enormous dog—a great Dane with sad waiting eyes—that was tied up while he shopped. He's given me, without realizing it, the space to draw back, calm myself down; to stop imagining an unknown woman's pelvic bones.

"That's the new owner of the old Vicarage. London people. They come down for weekends." Eric's voice only suggests criticism.

"Ah. So can you get to the beach, do you know?"

"When the police were down there, nobody was allowed through. The dozers were there clearing away the rubble ready for the tourist season. But I think you can get through. So, are you here for the summer, Nessa?"

"A couple of months." My voice is stronger, I'm easy with him now, this is casual, it's chat, it's what you do in a village shop. "My husband's coming to join me. The house needs a lot of attention. Nobody's been there for more than a year."

"Yup, winter's hard on an empty house." If he's making a quiet point about second-homeowners, I let it go.

"I've some work to do, too. Writing. It's always a good place to get on with it."

I want, urgently now, to go and see where the cliff fell, where the bones were found. "Can I leave my bags here for a few minutes? I want to walk down and have a look at the beach."

"Of course." He stows them behind the counter, beside bags of cut kindling, under the rack of newspapers.

YELLOW-PAINTED BARRIERS BLOCK OFF THE WAY down to the beach and there is still a sign: No Access. I slide past one end of the barrier, against the scratch of thorn bushes. Some big machinery has been this way: the bushes at the side of the ancient track are sliced and mangled, the earth underfoot torn up. I go down towards the opening, where trees curve overhead and you see the sea as if in an oval frame. I turn left and walk along the beach towards the cliffs. It's low tide and the rocks are bare. There seems to be nobody about. I see the yellow bulldozer, the smaller back-hoe. The maw of the bulldozer tipped against the cliff. Sand flattened now where it was roughly dug. Hills of rubble, from where the cliff fell. I tread carefully, looking to see if there is anyone. Just the machines, as if they have been stopped in mid-movement. A frozen slice of the action, a snapshot of what was. Where the cliff had fallen in, where the rubble had been cleared, a woman's skeleton came to the surface only days ago, was nearly ground under, only just saved by the bulldozer operator who stopped his machine and stepped down to smoke a cigarette, and saw what was in front of him.

The bones have all been removed, of course. Do they put them in a box? How do they handle them—gloved, careful, matter-of-fact? How do you pick up a human skull? I imagine the pathologist, the forensic experts. Like patient archeologists with their fine brushes, or the geologists who pick fossils from shale just up the coast from here, they'll have sorted them from rubble—a vertebra, a fragment of collar bone—bones that may look by now like the sandy rock itself.

"IN PREPARATION FOR NEXT YEAR'S 75TH anniversary celebration of the D-Day landings, the smaller beach known as South Beach has been cleared of the rubble from a long-ago cliff-fall. The beach was used as a practice area for the invasion of Europe in 1944. The partial skeleton of a woman was found in the rubble. Tests are being performed at the University of Southampton to discover the age of the bones. They are not thought to relate to a recent death. Police at the site said that a murder investigation was not being considered."

I walk back to the house slowly, taking my bags and the paper with me. A story, like a human skeleton, has to be pieced together in order to make sense of it, I know that. But sometimes you do not want the whole story. You'd prefer the pieces to lie where they were left, out of sight.

Two

I'M BACK HERE FROM AMERICA THIS SUMMER, as I told Eric, to see what repairs are needed in the house that was my grandmother's and is now ours, my brothers' and mine. I also have an essay to finish for a book that's coming out next year. On account of an article that I published in an academic journal in the late 90's, I've been asked to contribute to a book of essays to be published by Columbia University, where I used to teach political theory. It's to be called "Democracy At Risk: Fact and Feeling in the 21st Century," and the deadline for contributions is at the end of October. I'm reluctant to begin on it, while knowing that I must.

First things first, though—our house. It has been empty for more than a year, and it smells of locked-in air. There are dead flies on its window-sills and dust in every corner. Spiders' webs in the larder. Brown stains in the bath tub where a tap has dripped. A mattress to turn and beat, before I can make the bed. Kitchen taps that shoot discolored water out before the flow turns clear. The kitchen window with the cracked pane, damp coming in. And silence, to break open with music on the radio, staleness to dispel with windows flung open to let in the air. Memories waiting in every room. Childhood, youth, maturity—and now, approaching age. Why come back here when I could be in a comfortable writing retreat in America to work on the chapter I'm supposed to write, being fed good food, given a clean room and a desk to write at, and the company of others?

This house is not old in the way of old English houses, but it has all the lapses and weaknesses of an old person whom nobody touches. It has sat empty through winters, deprived of a loving or at least active hand. It has no charisma but it has a soul. You can hear it sigh as the air moves through. The creak as I tread the top step of the stairs is surely the sound of its return to life. The smell in the hall must be partly of winter damp—yet surely it always smelled this way? The cupboard in the hall breathes out old raincoats and wet wool. The glass-fronted bookcase—my grandmother's furniture is much older than the house is—opens with a whiff of unread books. I sniff the cracked-open pages of a book published in war-time—*Peace with Bandits?*—the smell of utility, cheap paper. Then I pull out a mildewed leather volume from the collection of Hardy's novels, *The Return of The Native*, one of my favorites, to read before bed. The sitting room, its windows looking over the moor, has the same worn carpets, and a mouse or moth has nibbled at their edges. The fireplace has logs in it—how long have they been here? The chair where Gran used to sit with her evening glass of whisky, watching for us children to come home—well, it's still there, still facing that way, and its cretonne loose-covers are only slightly more dilapidated than they ever were. I walk about opening windows. Moths come in, smudging the pane, and batter at the lamps. I close them again. I'll buy mouse-traps, moth deterrent, window cleaner, furniture polish. Call someone about the gutters, on account of the stains running down the outside walls. Find a plumber. Get the roof checked. And so on.

Across the road, the trees have grown. The oak at the corner spreads green branches wide across the sky. All the bushes and scrappy little hazel and birch trees at the roadside have grown into mature trees. The view is sliced vertically, so the blue of the harbor dazzles between the trunks. I lean from an opened upstairs window to look out—and there it is, the familiar view, the line of the hill unchanged since childhood, sixty years of history condensed into trees' height, a redisposition of heather. The ferry on its slant journey back across the harbor entrance to the mainland. A white yacht crossing in front of it—steam gives way to sail. Windows glint on the mainland shore. Evening stretches into a long-drawn twilight, the whole sky striated, afire, and finally drained of color, absence of light that precedes a gentle dark.

Downstairs, Radio 3 for some music—polite English announcer's voice, sharpness of Bartok. I've turned on water, electricity. My grandmother surfaces in me, she who was younger then than I am now. Everything repeats: movements echoed through ages, through history, actions of women, warming, airing, opening up a house. As if we all live and die in a long line, our moves predictable. The most you can hope for, dying, is surely not to be anonymous, to be known, to have a name. It's why I need to know who she was, that woman they found, before she became just scattered bones. I feel a shiver go through me, though the evening is warm.

The house reminds me at every turn: pay attention to me. I'll call Bruno, my husband, who will tell me, of course, that I can get someone in to cut grass, fix things, even clean. It's what you do in America. It's still only morning now in California, he may be out with his family, or eating brunch. I've felt it before, when you talk to someone in a different time zone, you have to explain to them, this is happening, that is going on, the sun is up, or sinking, it's lunch time, or, I've only just got up. As if you did not normally spend days and nights together, not even having to notice these things. As if suddenly preambles are necessary, the little anxious checks. Now that I want to talk to him, I mind that I can't—it feels urgent to tell him about the bones, my frisson of alarm, my sudden need for music and wine, and there is nobody else who will simply listen, and understand. I leave a message: I'm fine. Call me, but not too late.

Outside the house I stand at the edge of the uneven gravel road studded with rocks, just as steep and pitted as it was fifty years ago.

There's the moor opposite, new shoots of birch and gorse grown up since a last heath fire that left a blackened scar. Here, I'm ten and twenty and thirty as well as the age I am now. Here time may as well not matter. The Beaker people lie buried, chieftains laid under their quilts of earth, high on Ballard Down. Druids worshipped in the oak woods. Vikings sailed in for a last sea battle. Saxons built a small church. Normans came from France and built another, stone, indestructible. French stone-masons crossed the Channel to carve the faces peering down from the capitals. People bred horses and cattle, drove them to market, came home to cottages with peat and furze fires burning, smoke curling above thatch. Generations, dozens of them, born, living, dying unrecorded. Anonymous lives, working people, women, children dying in childhood—become bones, become dust.

I'll make a list. Not of successive generations, but of everything that needs to be repaired. Window sills that are rotting, windows that will not shut, handles that fall off doors, leaks, taps that drip. Tonight, I'll drink my wine, eat something, maybe try Bruno again later, and at last fall into the deep pit of jet-lagged sleep, when the body simply takes over from the anxious mind. I'm more concerned than I was when I was young about the state of my body; its sudden aches, its unprecedented fatigues preoccupy me more than any worries I once had about its beauty. The flesh is falling away, no doubt about that. Wrinkles and folds appear. My own bones come rudely to the surface. Perhaps that's why it disturbs me to think of a woman buried under sand and rock, her whole body dissolving until its broken skeleton is all that is left, and no story allowed to her, no recorded memory—no history. No name.

I open a bottle at sunset, a too-warm Cabernet, earth-tasting. A glass of wine to make me feel less alone. A glass to raise to Bruno, my dear but absent husband, to time past and present—and to myself, to give myself courage to begin on what I have to do.

After dinner, I touch in Bruno's cell phone number once again. His day in California is still young; the whole of California seems so young, from here. He's not answering his phone. He's having a nap, doing something sociable, something else. He's in a pool, at a bar, watching a movie. This hurts for a moment—where are you, aren't you waiting to hear from me? Perhaps he doesn't even exist. Perhaps I invented him. Perhaps he is still out there in the future, waiting for me to knock at his door. I leave another text—I'm here, I'm fine, the journey was okay. Like tucking a note into a bottle and throwing it out to sea. So near and yet so far. This present moment, here, and then that other reality across the Atlantic that is fading already, hard to imagine; intimacy, ease of access. I'm more exhausted, more febrile than I realized. My husband being out of reach has shaken me—I'm so used to having him there. Where is he, that he hasn't taken his phone with him? I'm not tuned to uncertainty where he is concerned, I take him for the rock, the anchor that he usually is. But tonight, I'm ill at ease and even annoyed, that he is not responding. Of course, the point of traveling alone is to be alone, and I wanted it, this journey back to my roots—but something has shaken me loose, and I need to hear his voice. For him to be present, even in a place and time-zone that are this far from where I am; with me in a life that was mine long before I knew him.

THREE

I WAKE WHEN YELLOW LIGHT HITS THE WALL at four-thirty. In summer here, the nights are short and the sun comes in like a flashlight. I make tea, then go down to swim, wearing the old swimsuit I left years ago in a drawer here and a denim shirt of Bruno's, a pair of shorts and my sneakers. I walk down the road, eager and alert now in spite of my dreams. The village is still asleep, the shop closed, only the clock at the village hall striking the hour. The barrier is still up—must have been hastily put back in place yesterday, once the machinery had come through. The path is cratered with huge tire-marks, as if a tank had passed. At the end of the sunken way towards the beach, the sea is mirror-calm, holding the pale waking glow of the sky. The tide is high when I arrive, the beach a narrow strip. The flattened sand under the cliff is today like a chest after a mastectomy, indicating only absence. I walk along to the upturned dinghy that lies tipped under the cliff, leave my clothes draped across it, and cross sharp stones to enter water that holds my ankles in its cold grip, then rises up to circle knees and thighs. I throw myself in, gasp out loud and go under and come up swimming, water in my eyes and ears. Down the beach I see through the blur of water two people wade in like long-legged birds, she in a one-piece cover-up, he in old-fashioned Speedos, stumbling

hand in hand. We all strike out towards the horizon with our careful breast-strokes. The ripples spread widely, intersecting far out.
Their two dogs wait at the shoreline, waiting for a call to summon
them rushing and splashing into the shallows, to swim out, ears
floating, muzzles lifted as they make Vs in the water. The world
seems to have been cleaned in the night.

It's hours yet before the families with their bags and awnings,
chairs and picnics, will begin to arrive to stake out their territories,
mark out the sand, hammer in tent pegs, their canvas wind-break-
ers letting them turn their backs on everyone else. It's how the
English colonize a beach: first you stake out your territory, defend
your space, then set up your furniture, sink down into your chair
and open the tabloid newspaper you have been waiting to read,
the same one read all up and down the beach with its black doom-
announcing headlines an inch high. Someone always used to make
tea on a camping stove, but now there's Pete's Café, a coffee-and-
sandwich stand at the place where the path comes down to the
beach that lends out deck-chairs and makes tea and coffee on the
premises as well as, interestingly, halloumi sandwiches, and paella
on Friday nights—bring your own bottle. The stall is still closed
for the night, the striped deck-chairs stacked, the sand damp and
unmarked.

I swim out towards the moored boats, turn and swim parallel to the shoreline, then face at last in towards the shore, looking
at the cliffs from the water, across distance. There is the concrete
gun emplacement. You can see it clearly from here on its sandstone summit among the lopped trees. There are the stacked fallen
trunks along the beach, the raw place where the excavation was,
the reddish sand that falls still in its slow perpetual trickle. The
land is falling into the sea. The shape of the coastline changes
slowly over centuries, and then more sharply. Everything speeds
up—land goes underwater, sea advances, what was solid becomes
liquid, what was certain, unsure. In the water, this feels unthreat-
ening; I am part of its easy element as it encroaches, I'm on its side.

The place on the cliff where the rubble of sand and rocks has been recently cleared is from this vantage point a diagonal stripe, pinkish, paler than the rest. The cliffs here are of the same striated red and yellow sandstone as on the Isle of Wight, just across the water. I scramble ashore, hobble over stones on to the firm sand at the high-water mark. Brown bladder-wrack and green salad-like transparent weed stripe my feet. The white chalk cliffs of the headland recede behind me. The swimming couple have come ashore, followed by dripping dogs who shake themselves all over their towels. They pick up their clothes and go back up the path. Sunlight spreads down the beach. I know it will be a hot day.

At the point ahead of me, the tipped gray concrete cylinder of the pill-box sits skewed at the bottom of the cliff, its dark eye still gazing out to sea. Everything erodes, except this relic of the long-ago war. Cliffs have changed shape around it over the decades, trees are now growing out above it almost horizontally, chestnut, hazel, holly, birch. Directly above me, invisible on account of undergrowth, is the look-out with its gun emplacement, visible when you are out at sea, but not from this close. It's just history, just a relic. I stand and stare up. There is a new notice nailed to wooden posts, solidly stuck in the sand: "*Beware Rock Fall. Dangerous even at Low Tide. Stay away from Cliff.*"

Rocks go on falling, the cliff goes on sliding, whether anybody is here or not. Geological change happens, seen or unseen. The sea gnaws at the land's edges until they fall away. I walk back in my wet swimsuit, towards my small pile of clothes on the upturned boat. I am just a pair of bare feet leaving prints that vanish on hard sand, instep then toes. A pair of eyes, a cheek turned to the wind. A sea-creature—until I'm under the cliff again and the place where they found her is suddenly close.

It was a woman. They were a woman's bones. But what, if anything, has that woman to do with me?

I hear my cousin Anabel's voice in my head, from all those years ago. *Nothing, Nessa. You saw nothing. You were not even there.*

SINCE I CAN'T REACH BRUNO AND WANT TO TALK to somebody, I call Paula in London—my old friend and former editor, she who has been urging me to fly business class and take better care of myself generally.

"So, Nessa, good, you made it! You could have come here, slept off the jet-lag."

"Well, I thought I'd better get here. You know? And, I hope you'll come and see me, when you have time?"

"I do have a lot on. Everybody has books coming out at once. Maybe in a couple of weeks? How are you, are you okay?"

"Just tired. I don't know which way up I am right now, but I'll get over it. I have this chapter to write, and the house is a mess."

"Well, there's no rush, is there? Sleep, darling; eat, go for walks, sit in the sun, if you can bear it. I don't know when we've ever seen so much sun. And of course, come and stay when you've had enough of solitude."

"Oh, I will. But an odd thing happened; they've just found some bones on the beach here, they were dug up by a bulldozer, and it's made the whole place feel—well, different. Like a crime scene."

"Sounds a bit spooky," she says, "But these things do happen. Now, get some rest! I'll see you soon."

A bit spooky. Well, yes. But the anxiety that sits just below my breast bone each time I think of it is about more than that. I feel as if something or someone is coming towards me, and I don't know who, what, or why.

LATER THAT EVENING, I SIT AND SKIM THROUGH the album of crinkle-edged black-and-white photographs I find in the bottom drawer of my grandmother's desk in the sitting-room. Here we all are. Anabel, my older cousin from London, Jean-Ann, Patrick, me. The caption in my mother's handwriting is *Summer 1952*. Somebody captured us that first time here as we stood in rows against the hedge, posed around my father's car, played with a dog somewhere, grimaced against the sun on the beach. Children in the clothes of the mid-century, in those sandals we wore, those wool swimsuits, those off-white canvas shoes that had not even begun to look like real sneakers. This was us, frozen by the techniques of another time, in a medium nobody uses or even recognizes these days, stuck in an eternal past in an album in a drawer that nobody has opened for years. We are a part of history, a scene from the distant past; and yet we are, most of us, still alive today. Patrick, my younger brother, lives in New Zealand, Anabel in the north of Scotland, I went to America. Only Jean-Ann, my friend from school, died young.

I let the album rest open against my legs and close my eyes. I wish now that I had come here with Bruno, instead of thinking that I could get on with some work as well as clean up the house, call the plumber and the electrician, make lists of what needs to be fixed. With him, I could have pointed us out, laughed, made a joke of our out-of-date clothes, our willingness to line up and clown as somebody took our pictures. In the age of selfies, we look like amateurs. And he, the photographer, would have noticed the grain of the print, the faded edges, the way nothing, unless you prepare it for lasting, can last.

HE PICKS UP HIS PHONE AT LAST and I breathe out with relief. "Ah, you're there." I'm on my way to bed, but it's a bright Californian day where he is.

He says, "Honey, you sound strange. Are you okay?"

"Yes, I'm fine. I called you when I arrived, but you weren't answering." I don't say, where were you? How can you not have been available?

"I'm sorry. I don't always hear the phone when the kids are making a racket. How are you? I have been thinking of you, ever since you left."

"I'm fine," I say again. "I'm swimming, walking, it's hot, imagine that, in England, and everybody's behaving as if the sun has never appeared here before. Anything over twenty-eight degrees is a heat-wave."

"What's that, about eighty?"

"Yeah, I guess." With him I become more American, detach myself from the person I used to be, when I came here with my family, then with my first husband, Roland, and other friends, and then after my divorce, alone.

"Getting much work done? How's the chapter going?"

"I haven't really started. There's a lot to be done to the house—and it's kind of overwhelming, actually."

"Well, I guess you'll have time before I come and distract you. How is it to be back in the old country? What about Brexit?"

"Oh, God. I haven't read a paper since I got here, except the local rag, and I limit Radio 4 or I'd listen to it all day. But no, the country is taking itself apart, it's awful. I try not to think about it, since I can't even vote. But it's gone mad. Everyone in Europe thinks we're completely crazy."

"Can't be worse than here," he says.

"Don't let's talk about all that. How are you, sweetheart?"

Like this we move back into the everyday of the widely different places we find ourselves in, across a world of space and time that spins us in its wake. He tells me—the grandchildren, pancakes, a visit to the Science Museum, seals in the Bay.

"They found some bones here," I tell him, because I have to. "Just before I got here. On the beach."

"You mean, human bones?"

"Yes. A woman. I can't stop thinking about it."

"Nessa. Why? Don't get nervous there, all on your own."

"You know, seriously, it seems so strange, that she should be found just now. The cliff fell on her, long ago, people think. And she's only just been dug up."

"I guess it happens. Stay away from the cliffs, okay?"

"That's what all the notices say."

I NEVER TOLD HIM MUCH ABOUT THAT first summer our family spent here after the end of the war—not out of wanting to hide anything, rather that when you have lived together as long as we have, there's simply too much past to recount. The time for confessions and anecdotes passes, after the first times of urgent discovery. When I moved to the US, I threw out all my old diaries, gave heaps of clothes away, consciously discarded the person I had been—or so I thought. Every immigrant cuts his or her life in half, picks up only what is useful, or easy to carry, to the new country. We are all pretending to be half of ourselves—our lives are made up of the before and after, but the cut is never clean, I have learned, and certainly not painless. Bruno, child of Italian immigrant parents, guesses at this, respects it, but does not ask me much about my earlier life. It's a form of tact. A form of loneliness, too. When he comes here with me, he's the exotic foreigner, the friendly American. Nobody even asks him where he comes from, that peculiarly American question that begs only a simple answer. He's my American husband, and that's enough.

I want to show him these photographs when he comes, and present him with the girl I was at ten, eyes narrowed at the camera, hair wild, knees bony under shorts or bird-legged and flat-chested in a sagging swimsuit. Young Nessa, never alone, always with cousins and brothers, one of a now scattered tribe. Myself. My young self, at a time when my life was forming itself into patterns I was unaware of, and could not control.

I TRY A MORNING SITTING AT MY GRANDMOTHER'S DESK, where my laptop waits, to write my chapter. On the strength of an article on David Hume and the Scottish Enlightenment I had published in an academic journal, analyzing the balance of reason and emotion that he posited more than two hundred years ago, I've been— to my slight surprise—asked to contribute to this book on thought and feeling in the age of unreason. It's to be published by the university press at Columbia, where I used to teach political theory before I retired. In the age in which I live, I'm thinking, unreason certainly appears to rule. What has happened to the ideals of the Enlightenment, that intellectual renaissance that claimed reason as the guide to human endeavor, transported to America by Thomas Jefferson and the founding fathers of the country I live in? I don't feel like writing it—yet here it is, my assignment. The editors are waiting for my few words to clarify the world to history professors and the handful of students who may read me, while the prophets of unreason rage on regardless. I look up, and out of the window, to the line of the moor and the cloudless blue of the sky and know that I can no more stay indoors to do my homework now than I could when I was ten years old. By noon I have written three sentences, ones that will probably have to be deleted. Hume and Jefferson can wait, for another day at least, and I tell myself that my thoughts will fall into place as I walk out of doors. They often do.

I'm already on my way out, when the house telephone rings on its insistent double note, and goes on ringing—no voice-mail here. I pick it up. The plumber. He'd had my message that I needed a leak fixed. Would this afternoon work? He could come when he's finished another job in the village. Do I know if it's the ballcock?

"I pulled up the ballcock but the water's still running from the downpipe."

"Ah, right, I'll be there after five. Can you turn the water off? There's a hose-pipe ban, with this drought."

"Sure. I'm going out. I'll do it before I go." I go to the cupboard under the stairs.

"That'll be grand. I may bring my little boy with me; I'm picking him up after school."

I go to the cupboard under the stairs, wrench the iron handle around till it's parallel to the pipe, remembering my father doing just this. No water for the day—oh well. I clap on an old hat, fill a water-bottle to take with me, rub sun-block into arms and face. I leave the back door open in case the plumber comes before my return, and set out to walk in the growing heat of early afternoon, up the steep path that leads on to Ballard Down, the long hill that rises behind the village and forms the flint and chalk spine of this peninsula.

The grass is worn away, bleached where it still grows; there's little for the grazing cows to eat. A new calf struggles to its feet on the summit, its mother nosing dry ground for nourishment as she lets it butt and suckle. The world up here is blue and windy. Once you have scaled the summit, the way is downhill, towards the cliff edge, where the white teeth of the cliffs go all the way down to the beaches far below that can only be reached from the sea. Here are deep caves in rock, once used by smugglers as they brought brandy and tobacco over from France, avoiding the Customs and Excise men. The coast of France—Normandy, the Cherbourg peninsula—is just across the water from here. There are caves, used by smugglers over centuries, that you can only see from a boat as it comes in closer to shore, skirting the danger of hidden rocks. A coast of shipwrecks, hard to land, where to pull a boat up the shingle would risk a sudden wave, a tug of current, washing you back out to sea. A hard coast to invade, as the Vikings found when they were defeated in Swanage Bay, as Napoleon discovered, and Hitler had to admit, neither of them seamen, both of them scared off by the force of water. Here, as all the way along the southwest coast of the country, people watched for the approach of Philip II's Armada, with bonfires set to be lit on the cliff-tops, a chain of information passed by fire; here they kept watch for signs of an invasion by the French under Napoleon, and later built the concrete shelters and look-outs that would enable them to spot and fire on approaching Germans, should the invasion, as many thought it would, come by sea.

In another lifetime, at nineteen, I walked up here with Ted. Who was that girl, and what did she want? What did she give away too soon? And he, what became of him? I'll probably never know. We were so young. A young man, a young woman, an afternoon walk up this same hill before any of the parameters of my life seemed set for me. Do we have choices, really? Or are our ways set by the moves we make before we are old enough even to know what our choices are?

Ted. I wonder if he is even still alive.

THERE ARE FIRE RESCUE AND PREVENTION trucks today, up on the crest of the hill where I have never before seen a vehicle. Men in yellow helmets lean talking together as they roll in a long black snake of hose. Yesterday there was a fire; I can still smell it on the wind that comes in from the sea. Part of the wood on the cliff path burned last night; they have just succeeded in putting it out. It's too dry: the land, the gorse, the stunted trees are tinder. I think, *California, Portugal, Greece.* The men say, "You can go ahead, you'll be all right. We have it under control." There is still the charred edge to the grass, and bare black gorse like charcoal sticks, and the smell is sharp.

Fires burn along the top of Rainbarrow in *The Return of the Native*, the book I pulled last night from my grandmother's bookcase in the old leather-bound edition—leather doesn't do well in damp houses, so the cover is black-spotted, and the pages have curled with damp and dried again. I read the first pages again in bed, hunched under a single sheet, with moths batting at my lamp. It starts with the land, and its fires—controlled fires, bonfires not conflagrations, people crouched around their own fire, feeding it with furze—that was the fuel here then. It's Eustacia Vye's fire that draws Wildeve in out of the darkness. In Hardy's day, the fires were deliberately made, carefully tended, signaling desire.

The random fire on the hill is the latest local event: perhaps it has made people forget about the bones dug up on the beach. I go on down the path, down to where the white columns of chalk called Old Harry and his Wife jut up from the sea, and the seabirds swarm. Here the cliffs are tall, the drop vertiginous. Water foams up at the rocks a hundred feet below. A boy flying a blue kite is pulled off the ground a foot in the air, and his sister catches him and pulls him down, and they both roll on the turf, and the kite collapses. Blue and white and buoyant in a blue and white sky and then tangled and deflated like a paper bag.

People are crowding up to the cliff edge today, taking selfies, proud of the fact that they teeter at the very break-off place of the land, exhilarated by their own daring. I pass the path branching off through the bracken that leads, I know, to the very edge: sudden and sharp. It's always been there. People have always wanted to peer over, even imagine danger. I can't go there, not even to look. The land remembers what happens, even if the people do not. Maps don't show paths like this, just mark where the land ends. Now there are hardly any maps—not like the folded Ordnance Survey maps our father had, all neat in a drawer, to be folded like concertinas along their worn creases each time you put them away.

I walk on, thinking that the maps are inside us now. We have had to memorize them and let them go.

At the farm tea-shop on the way home, I go in for a cup of tea and a scone, partly on account of no water in my house, partly because I want to ask somebody else my question about the bones found on the beach. A woman brings me my tea-pot and milk jug, my plate of scones and cream; lingers, waiting to chat. There is nobody else in the tea-room. "Visiting, are you?"

"Yes. I've come over from America, but I grew up here. I was here when I was young, for summer holidays. Our family had a house up on the moor road—we still do."

"Ah, the place hasn't changed much. Been up on the hill, have you? I heard that the fire up there burned most of the night."

"They had put it out, when I got there. It just smelled of smoke. There was a big burnt patch on the other side, where the path goes down."

"Aye, it's been too dry, that's for sure. Never known a summer like it."

"This building used to be part of the farm, didn't it? I remember there being tractors, harrows, things like that."

She gestures towards the framed photographs on the wall—the horse teams, the ancient buildings roofed with thatch. "Before my time. But yes, it was a working farm."

I bring out my question, the one that nags me. "I heard they found a skeleton on the beach. Did they find out any more about it, do you know? It seems an odd thing, to find it after apparently quite a long time."

"Well, it was where the cliff fell in, see, that's why nobody found it before. The cliff's been falling gradually since, oh, the last war probably. But they wanted to clear the beach so's to let people see where they did all that for D-Day, you know, the mock-up, practice for going into France, wasn't it? The anniversary's next year, seventy-five years. It would have been in my Grandad's time. Do you want some jam with that? I've some home-made strawberry."

I nod for the strawberry jam—if I'm going to eat scones and cream, I might as well go the whole hog. She fetches it, parks her behind against an antique dresser that stands against the wall. "Nobody knows who it was. The cliff must've just fallen on someone when they were walking there. Funny that nobody was reported missing at the time."

"Perhaps these days, they would have been."

"Probably. Well, enjoy your tea."

When she comes back to clear the tea things away and I thank her and give her my six pounds, she says, "They did say that it may not have been an accident. I did hear that."

"The fire or the cliff fall?" I ask.

"I meant, that woman's death. Though you can't be sure about fires, neither. There's some idiots still throwing cigarette ends around."

"But they are not treating it as a murder case, I heard." I hide my question in a careful statement.

"There probably wasn't any point.," she says. "Seems like she's been there a long time. But no, I remember when I was younger, there was some talk of a person disappearing, a visitor to the village, and nobody knew what'd become of her. There was a man taken to hospital, died there, I heard. Hit on the head by a falling rock. It's dangerous, always was, going too near the cliffs, we all knew that."

You saw nothing, Nessa. You weren't even there.

"And you think he wasn't alone?"

"I dunno. People talk, you know. Village gossip. It isn't always true."

"Well, thanks for the tea. I'll come again."

"You came from America, you said?"

"I've lived there a long time. My husband's American."

"My word. Long way off, America."

I agree, and am about to go on my way. As I move towards the open door of the building that used to be a cow-shed, she says, "They do open up cases, though, don't they? Remember, there was that young woman, estate agent wasn't she, who got murdered in a house she was showing, and nobody ever found her body, but now they think they have. In London, it was. Seems like once you have a body, or a skeleton at least, you can find out a whole lot more."

"I suppose you can, yes. Well, thanks again for the tea."

Outside, the sunlight seems astonishingly, even cruelly bright.

FOUR

THE PLUMBER HAS HIS VAN PARKED across the road when I return, its rear doors open. Joe Hardcastle, Plumbing and Small Works. The back door to the house is open, and a child in school uniform sits on the step eating a sandwich.

Joe himself comes out, spanner in hand, his sleeves rolled. "Mind, Joey, let the lady through. This is my little boy, Joey. It's my day to have him. Hope that's not a bother. Anyway, I've fixed your toilet, the tank was blocked, the downpipe was half seized up with rust. If it happens again, let it run, pull up the ballcock like before and wait a few minutes, and it should stop."

"Thanks. Do you want a cup of tea?" It used to be customary in England to offer workers a cup of tea when they came to your house. I wonder if it still is.

"No, I'm all right. We had our snap, didn't we, Joey? He's always hungry when he gets out of school; I don't think they give them enough for their dinners. And we had our tea. It's a hot day for a walk, though. Did you go far?"

"Up on the hill. They've put the fires out, I saw."

"Yeah, that was the second time this year. First we get fires, then we get a body on the beach. Heard about that, did you?" He begins packing his tools away in a plastic box. The child Joey pushes the last of the sandwich into his mouth and stands up. His gray school socks wrinkle at his ankles.

"Yes. The lady in the tea-shop at the farm was telling me."

"Seems like they're not sure if it were an accident. Could've been done on purpose, is what they're thinking."

"Really?" I'm a little ashamed to be so obviously interested. If he had not mentioned it first, would I have brought it up?

"Well, I don't know for sure. Guess we'll know in time. But if she was done in, it was a long time ago."

We say goodbye, and I tell him I'll call if I have any more trouble. I've a hunch that the whole plumbing system—lead pipes, toilets with high cisterns and ballcocks to be pushed up—will need to be replaced. But not now, and not by me.

A village this size needs its gossips, I see—and I'm glad of them. I'm only going to find out more by talking to people as casually as I can. But there is no solid news, nothing that can be called a fact. Perhaps the next edition of the Gazette will have an announcement, perhaps not. As Joe Hardcastle said, murder or accident, it all happened a very long time ago.

I go out of the house the next morning after my breakfast of toast and coffee with Radio 4 for company—the pro-and anti-Europe argument, John Humphrys cross-questioning some lying politician until I can't bear it any more. I listen like a good householder for the faint trickle from the toilet, that seems to have stopped at last. I take out the rubbish to the bin in the alleyway and hear a whinny from the field across the road. I cross the road, the empty kitchen bin in my hand. A horse breathes loudly on the other side of the bramble hedge, there's a stamping of hoofs. A van is parked there, and two ponies stand beside it, munching hay. A young man sits on the step of the van, rolling a cigarette on his blue-jeaned knee.

"Hello," I say. "Lovely morning."

He nods. The scene is so directly taken from the book I am reading that I can hardly believe that the man and his van and ponies are real. There's a character in *The Return of the Native* called the reddleman because he sells reddle, the dye used to mark sheep, at local farms. He is red from his own dye—hands, face, clothes. His real name is Diggory Venn, and he is quietly in love with Tamsin Yeobright who is promised in marriage to another man—the same Wildeve who flirts with Eustacia Vye beside her bonfire. He listens, sharp-eared outside houses, hidden with his van and his ponies behind hedges and hayricks, watching who passes by. He watches, waits. The reddleman is hidden at the heart of the book, yet he is central to it because he knows what is going on. His eyes are the eyes of the heath itself, Hardy's great Egdon heath; his voice is that of the earth. Can the land have a voice? Hardy says so.

Now I seem to have met him—or his modern equivalent.

My reddleman is not red, but tanned, with cropped hair, wearing a T-shirt, jeans and boots. "Morning. Yeah, it's nice this early. Gonna be hot again later, though."

The morning hums around us. Bees are working in the buddleia and honeysuckle. The ponies put up their heads, ears pricked, then go back to munching hay. They are honey-colored, broad and solid with short legs and shaggy fetlocks and manes.

"I heard your horses. What are you doing? If you don't mind my asking."

He says, "I'm here to clear the bracken, so the heather can grow back. They used to use chemicals, herbicides, but they don't do that anymore. I drive the ponies with this little machine here. It cuts the bracken and gorse so the heather has a chance to grow. It's a slow-grower, heather, and the bracken comes up fast, see. Today I'm working on this part, between here and the rock."

"They look very strong, your ponies. Where are they from? Not around here?"

"They come from Comté in eastern France. They're French."

"Where the cheese comes from."

"Yeah. And the machine they pull, I made it myself."

It looks like a small harrow, with wheels. "And the harness?"

"It's Amish. They know a thing or two, the Amish. I get it from them in America. Off the Internet."

"So, you're quite an international set-up."

"You could call it that, yeah."

He's not red, and his horses and harness come from France and America, but he's young, he's itinerant, and he's doing a job that used to involve spraying chemicals but now has more than a hint of Hardy's century about it.

He tells me, "It's all part of putting the place back to the wild. Those fenced fields, down by the harbor—they've taken down the fences, so the heather can grow back. And the deer—there's no natural predators here, and they eat everything that grows. So, you have to cull them every year. But grazing by horses and wild cattle will fertilize the ground, so more varieties can grow, and other kinds of animals can come back."

"So you have to do something artificial to get back to nature."

"Yeah, that's about it. But with the least imprint. No heavy machinery, see."

"I see."

I notice him again, in other places: later, that afternoon, down in the valley beside the tall pine woods, near where the Roman villa was excavated, then far out on the moor towards the deserted farms where the wild cattle and deer graze. His van, his stout little horses, his home-made machine. We wave to each other, and I walk on. But not before I've seen the three young men, boys really, crouched in the hedge beside him, spreading tobacco on Rizla papers on their knees to roll their little tubes, then one leaning to light the other's skinny cigarette. The bracken-clearing man is talking to them, across the horses' backs, but I can't hear what any of them says. The boys are black-haired, dark-complexioned, and wear jeans and T-shirts like boys everywhere. My wave includes all of them, but the boys don't look up but rather seem to shrink back into the hedge, as if to hide from view. I catch a glimpse of scared, defensive young faces. Who are they? Romani, or Gypsies—no, they are too fashionably dressed. Tourists? I don't think so. Italian or Greek, maybe, with that coloring. My reddleman waves back, gestures to me to come over, but I shake my head, walk on. The way those boys shrank back from my gaze tells me that they don't want to be seen, by me or anyone.

LATER THAT EVENING, BEFORE SUNSET when the shadows are long, I go back to the place and find my reddleman boiling a kettle on the stove inside his van. The boys who were here earlier are gone.

"Sit down," he says. "Could you do with a cup of tea? It's thirsty weather out there."

"Just water would be fine."

"I saw you earlier." He hands me a tin cup of cold water and I sit perched on an upended log, as he does. They make useful stools, but are hard on the behind. I tuck my legs up and sip the cold water that tastes tinny but clean.

"I saw those boys, smoking. Friends of yours?"

"Ah, them. Well, if you don't mind, don't tell anyone. Okay? It's better than nobody saw them, if you get my meaning."

I say, "Okay, fine. I didn't see them. So what else is new?" If I want information, I have to talk to people, locals, anyone who may know. "You heard about those bones they found? Talking of things that nobody has seen, or at least not for a long time."

He answers slowly, after a puff at his skinny cigarette. "Turns out she may have been hit on the head, maybe by a rock, more likely by an instrument of some kind. They didn't think she was murdered, not first off, but now they aren't sure. I hear things, see. I heard the cops talking, down by the station, in Wareham when I was coming here. I have to come round by the road, see, can't take this van on the ferry with all my gear. Turns out it wasn't recent, dated from back in the last century—but it wasn't, like, historical, either."

"Who was she, do you know?"

"Foreigner, I heard. Not from here. They can tell from dental records. Eastern European, they said."

"Thanks for telling me."

"Why are you interested?"

His question shocks me and I want to back off, claim no more than a normal interest in a body being found locally. "No particular reason. It's just weird—you know, her being there it seems for a long time, and only just found now."

"I s'pose. Things happen when they happen. Like, you know, with archeology. Sometimes it takes centuries."

"She was a person." I flounder on, wanting to make him understand, this person I don't know from Adam. "A woman. I feel bad that nobody knew her name, that's all. We shouldn't have to die without anyone knowing our name. Everybody has a right to be known, don't you think?"

"Guess so," he says, and stares into the distance for a moment. The ponies graze, tearing at the short turf, a regular cropping sound. "Mine's Jared, by the way."

"I'm Nessa."

"Pleased to meet you. I've gotta get on my way now, I have a job over at Arne tomorrow, got to get these fellows inside, get my van on the road."

I watch him lead his ponies one by one up the ramp, and shut them in. An eye looks out, the rolling white of a chewing pony. The smell is of dung and hay and kerosene from the stove.

"See you," he says, and gets into the driving seat.

"Goodbye." I wonder if I will. It seems absurd to thank someone for a cup of water and a scrap of information, so I just lift my hand to wave goodbye. Where they have been, the grass is flattened, scattered with wisps of hay, and the warm horse smell hangs in the air.

ON THESE LONG SUMMER EVENINGS, deer come out late from the relative cool of the woods to graze on the dried grass of the field near the house where the young man's van was. I meet them when I stroll out after dinner in the sudden shift of the air temperature at

twilight, and we stare at each other, stock still and silent for minutes at a time, and then I make the slightest move and they leap
away, three young hinds flashing their white tails between stripling
oak and birch trees and deep bracken at the edge of the moor. The
stag comes out and raises his head to sniff the air, his antlers, ten-
point, carried like a weighty crown. Then he too plunges on. I hear
his bark, sharp as a hurt dog.

At the far edge of the peninsula, down by Poole Harbour, the
fields are reverting to moorland, as Jared said. Sometimes the
wild ponies come closer to the village and I see the small prints
of unshod hoofs in the soft soil of the moor. The cattle that graze
freely are red and solid-looking, the ponies New Forest bays
or darker Exmoor with mealy muzzles. The place is alive with
animals and I feel them moving around me, as the birds do: the
blue-tits acrobatic in the hedge beside the house, the chaffinch,
the territorial robin and his mate. The squirrels that run along
the telephone wires and startle as I open a window, take a leap
into the oak tree and disappear. A fox pauses in his tracks, right
opposite the house, his brush carried low and shining red in the
setting sun. When I was a child, there were no deer here, no wild
ponies, no cattle left loose to roam. The land was essentially the
relic of a battlefield. Sixty-five years on, there is change. The moor
and the fields and woods around here are restoring themselves
to a former liveliness. Foresters are coppicing the hazel woods,
using the branches twisted sideways and threaded together to
make fences. Fields that used to be fenced are turning back to
open moorland. I stand under spreading oaks that used to be
smaller trees and see thick branches against the sky like endless
forking puzzles set for the birds and squirrels that live there, and
for any hardy climbing child who might try them. The land is
recovering at last from its wartime scarring and from years of
over-control and agriculture based in chemicals. In a world that
is shrinking and diminishing in its natural abundance, this small
corner of England is at least growing more diverse. You could say

that this is artificial, but where destruction has been deliberate, perhaps revival has to be deliberate too. I walk home feeling the unripe berries on the hedges—the blackberries will be early this year with all this sun, but will be small. Rose-hips are hard as little bullets, but rosy red. I am sinking back into a landscape that feeds me with its details—a grass snake on my path yesterday, a hawk hovering, an owl call at twilight—the way its darkness and silence feed my sleep at night.

I think of Jared and his horses, and of Joe the plumber—divorced, evidently, and sharing custody—and of Thomas Hardy and the way he gives a voice to Egdon Heath, on which his characters are simply tiny figures, struggling with their fate.

WHEN BRUNO CALLS ME, I'm on my way to bed. I imagine California, that sheer Pacific edge.

"Nessa? Sweetheart, how are you?"

"It's been quite a day. The plumber came, and he brought his kid with him and I met a man who clears bracken using horses and a contraption he made himself. I've just been out to look at the sunset and saw a whole lot of deer, rushing about in the dark." To tell him about the teenagers I saw seems just too complicated and perhaps pointless.

I hear the surprise in his silence, so I ask him, "When are you going home?"

"Tuesday. I'll call you when I'm back. I'll be a whole three hours closer then. So, you're seeing a lot of locals, and animals? Are you lonely?"

"I miss you." What I miss is the sanity of daily life with him, the details we pay attention to, the lack of drama.

"I miss you too."

"I'm glad you're coming over soon." I've been wondering if my worrying about the bones has been on account of being too much on my own. But before he gets here, there are things I have to find out—and find out alone.

"Only a couple of weeks now. Any news about those bones you told me about?"

"Everybody here is talking about them but nobody knows much. They're still in the forensics lab in Southampton. Some people are saying it could have been a murder. She was hit on the head with a rock, or some weapon, it seems." She. As I tell him, I feel that I'm giving out private information about somebody known only to me. Bruno belongs in a world that does not contain this woman. That is, perhaps, why I am married to him and why I want him—yes, I do—to cross the ocean and come to find me, and put everything back in its place.

"Maybe you could find out something from the forensics lab?" he says. "If you really want to know more."

"Oh. Good idea. I might do that." Bruno will always go for the science, I think. For him, it organizes the world.

"I love you, Nessa," he says. These days, it's a reassurance, not a surprise.

THE FOLLOWING DAY ONLY A FEW DROPPINGS are left from the horses, the wisps of hay are scattered, the two upended logs where we sat, the hard trodden earth leave no trace. The bracken is cut back where Jared and his cart went, and a clean edge separates cleared ground from the green depths of stalks to its side. The earth where the horses and cart passed is still smeared with green, juice bled from the cut stalks. A highway has been cleared through the valley, so that the slow heather can grow back.

I sit on one of the logs, my arms around my knees, and look out. I feel ageless, sitting here like a vague girl, not counting time as it passes. I could be ten, or twenty, or any age at all. People come and go here, they have done so over centuries. They pass through, and on. Stories are told, and then forgotten. I was here, and am here now, and one day I will not be here again. As I get up to go, I notice a small spot of white on the rubbed grass a yard away and bend to pick it up. A clipped bus ticket, torn in half, with a price on it in euros. I put in my pocket—evidence of what?

MY SUNDAY MORNING WALK TAKES ME along the shoreline at low tide. I try to remember how it used to be—surely the beach was shorter, the undercliff less accessible? When the tide is out like this, I can walk right along the beach towards the headland called Handfast Point till I'm standing in the shadow of the cliff that runs out towards the Old Harry rocks. So much erosion has occurred here that whole trees lie propped on their branches across the high-water mark: mature oaks, chestnuts, sycamores. They still wear their leaves, and only the low branches have been eaten clean by the tides. The cliff has collapsed in several places, rubble spreading along the soft sand, enough to bury a house.

There are few people about: just a few kayakers out at sea, an elderly couple sitting on their towels with their dog beside them, two teenagers kissing under an orange umbrella who break apart and grin as I pass. None of these people seem to be worrying about cliff falls. I think that most of us assume it's not going to happen to us—the sudden lurch, the collapse of the earth on top of us. Most of us don't think of being buried until we are dead, if then—the airy lightness of cremated ash may hold more appeal—and certainly not when we are alive. We don't imagine earthquakes, or even sudden storms, until they are upon us. It seems that humans are gifted only with the amnesiac present, just as it is—until it is no more.

But under the cliff, where I walk, there is the sign posted *Beware: Rock Falls* and a picture of a person falling backwards into the sea, a rock coming down on him. The cliff where it has moved still looks fluid, its layers drawn in parallel waves. I go on to the end of the beach, where it curves round under the cliff and the sandstone turns to chalk, in the astonishing geological patterns of this part of the coast.

There's a small cave in the cliff, its entrance narrow and dark, like an open door. A child could hide there. Or a small adult. The sea has retreated from the holes it made, this cave and further ones, where there is no beach to walk on, only slimy rocks. I wade through cold and slippery seaweed and bend to peer into the cave. There is something on a rock, a way in from the entrance. I go in, bent double to have a closer look. It's a blue cloth, stained and wet. And an empty can, obviously opened with a knife, with *haricots blancs* written on its torn label, that has the logo of a French super-market. White beans, in French? I poke the cloth with a stick from the beach and it comes up limp and wet and not very large, a torn blue T-shirt. Hmm. Somebody came here and left a wet shirt behind and ate a can of French white beans? The cave is too low-ceilinged for comfort and the water is already lapping closer to its edge. I've never liked caves, and the interior, chalk with green stains, is not where I want to be. I take a quick look, but find nothing more. So, I place the tin back on the rock and leave the T-shirt where it is in case anyone comes back for it. I go out quickly, the cave mouth behind me, my feet deep in weed, and breathe the outside air with relief. Who could have left a shirt and an empty bean can in a cave? It can't have been long ago, or the tin would have rusted and the label disappeared. What remains never tells you the whole story. We live with partial information, always. I've heard that when you dig bones up, even a whole skeleton, they are often infected, not clean at all. I think of what we are all made of—frangible stuff, flesh and bones, given to decay. Dust to dust—yes. The cliffs are collapsing more regularly now, more trees are falling on to the beach; will more buried bones be discovered? Once, I remember, the only notices were to warn us about unexploded missiles. Different era, different fears. The human body just as vulnerable, flesh just as weak.

I WALK BACK ALONG THE BEACH AND up the well-trodden path under the leaning trees, and see that the yellow tape and the barrier have gone now. No trace left except for the slashed branches, their breaks showing white, where the hasty machinery passed.

The path goes past the church where as children we used to sit every Sunday evening for Evensong, scrubbed clean in our white sweaters and brown sandals, fidgeting through the sermon, studying the inscriptions on the wall until the vicar stopped talking, the choir sang, and the organ rumbled through us all like thunder. The same gravestones are here, with new ones added behind the church, newcomers slipping away down the hill. All of them named, dated: persons in their own right, even though now absent. I hear the falling cadence of the vicar's voice, the shuffle of feet as he finishes, the organ notes and the quavering then stronger voices rising in the last hymn.

People begin to file out of the ancient church now and huddle outside to chat, so I slip away between the yew trees, hoping to be unnoticed. I want to avoid more questions about why I'm here, and for how long, from people who might recognize me.

The three boys I saw with Jared are leaving the village shop as I walk up from the church. They cross the road to walk up the hill towards the bus stop. They are all wearing T-shirts and jeans and a young woman is with them—a girl, not more than fifteen I guess—has her hair knotted up on her head and a rather dirty red scarf around it. The young men are smoking again, all bending to catch their cigarettes alight from a single lighter as they go; they seem to have their pockets stuffed with chocolate and potato chips. One has his hand upon another's shoulders. They can't any of them be older than twenty. Probably younger. I glance at them, and they all look away—except one. Possibly the youngest, and the least guarded, a boy I remember from the last time, dark hair falling across his forehead, brown arms twig-thin in a threadbare white T-shirt, too young I'd thought then to be smoking and his glance less opaque than the others. He looks back at me, and then ducks away behind the taller boys, not before I've seen the look of sheer panic in his eyes. Who does he think I am? Does he remember me from the time with Jared? Does he think I will stop them, give them away? The snatch of talk I hear as they pass me, crossing the road in front of the shop, is not English, or any language that I recognize.

In the shop, I browse among shelves for my groceries, choosing vine-ripened tomatoes, hoping they may taste of something, unlike the ones I buy in the US, pausing to feel the softness of a local goat cheese. Eric and his wife Suzanne are talking behind the counter as they sort the bread and meat delivery. I lurk in my place around the corner, looking at headlines of the Sunday papers.

Suzanne says, "Should we say anything?" I knew her years ago as a young woman who worked at the local riding school, before she married Eric. Now, she is pregnant, visibly so.

"I reckon it's not really our business."

"If anyone comes asking questions?"

"Then I'll tell them. Reckon it's right to give them a fair chance, after what they've been through, most likely."

"So what would we say?"

"Wait till we're asked."

"Hmm. But there's gossip. People talk. You know, not everyone would agree."

"Take that chance when it comes to it. I'm not going to refuse a few bars of chocolate to a bunch of kids, whoever they are and wherever they come from."

"You," Suzanne sighs, "you know they stuffed their pockets before they paid for those chocolate bars? Your soft heart will get you into trouble."

I come out from behind the shelves and pretend I haven't heard them. I put down my basket on the counter. "Can you add in last week's paper? I didn't have the cash. How's business?"

"Picking up well, thanks. The weather brings the tourists, should be a good season."

We smile at each other in the way of people who know each other from way back but always in the same context, and I pick up my bags to be on my way. Something is going on here that everybody knows about and nobody will explain—because to bring it out into the open would implicate them all? I have been trusted, though with what, Eric hasn't said outright. I'm in on it—whatever "it" may be. I feel the outline of the torn bus ticket in my pocket and put it together in my mind with the bean tin, and the shirt on the rock, and the teenagers walking up the street. You can add two and two and still wonder if it makes four, or five, or even six.

THE POLICE COME BACK, THE FOLLOWING DAY. I see the yellow-striped cars, two of them, parked up by the church. On the beach, a man in jeans and a sweatshirt. He bends once again to search with what looks like a metal detector the place where the bones were discovered. Once again, it is cordoned off—a square of yellow tape. I think of what Jared told me—the dead woman may have been hit over the head by something, a rock or a sharp-ended instrument. That is, by the cliff itself, or by a person. If she had jumped, deliberately, or been pushed over the edge, her bones would have been broken differently, surely, from the way they would have been if the cliff had fallen on her. The shock of impact, rushing up through the body, condensing it; not the downward falling weight of earth and stone. I walk along the shoreline, wishing for a moment that I had a dog to walk, to give me an easy alibi. Especially with the question I have to ask.

The man in jeans and sweatshirt stands up, and the policeman in uniform at his side talks into his phone. The plain clothes man has a blunt, rather brutal face that improves when he raises a hand to me and smiles. Nice blue eyes, a boxer's flattened nose. "Want to know what we're up to, hey?"

"I was just passing."

"Yeah, and everyone in this place is just as curious as you. There's nothing to hide. We're just trying to rule out foul play. But the fact is, she's been dead so long that nobody will ever know, most likely, and anyone who wished her harm is probably dead too."

Foul play, although I know it's a technical term, always makes me think of something dirty and degrading—a disgusting game. "Do you know who she was?"

"Who? You mean, a name?"

"Well, yes."

"No way to know that now, is there. We know she's from Eastern Europe, was around thirty when she died. The lab has told us that much. Why she died, and how, that's another matter. That's going to remain a mystery. Unless anyone comes forward with some new information. Most likely the case will just be closed."

"Are you a detective?"

"Plain-clothes CID."

"It seems so odd that the bones were found just now."

"Odd? Well, they dug up the cliff, cleared the trees away, didn't they? That's how you find things. You change the set-up. You alter the environment. Not me, actual digging's not my job, even though I'm out here today. We thought we might have missed something. A bit of clothing, a tooth, a zip fastener, you never know."

"Have you found anything? Or maybe you're not supposed to tell me."

He straightens, delves into a small plastic bag and shows me the eye of a shoe, where a lace would go through. It lies in his palm like a grain, a tiny round fragment of the man-made world. "That's it. From a sneaker, I think. An old-fashioned tennis shoe or plimsoll, as they used to call them. There must be more of these in the sand, somewhere."

"Hers." I look up at the cliff, where it has slipped and fallen. The tangle of trees at its summit. Yes, this is the place, where I stand now.

"Yeah, probably. Though it could be anybody's. We'll find out."

"How?" I stare at his open palm, notice a wedding ring, callouses, lifelines.

"Date what it's made of. These things change all the time. It's metal, see. Nobody has metal eyes to their sneakers these days."

"If you do find out who she was," I say, "would you let people know?"

"It's hard to stop journalists putting out what they want to. So, in an indirect way, yes. And there'll be a police report, however sketchy."

"Thanks," I say. He puts the tiny eye away in the plastic bag, places it in a black canvas back-pack, turns to go on working.

Then he looks up and says, "Why are you interested? If you don't mind my asking."

Again, that question. Why wouldn't I be interested? Why wouldn't anybody be interested? I feel all at once defensive, and want to cover my tracks. "Well. I've been coming here for years, my family has a house here, and so—we'd no idea that she was here, buried, all that time."

"Well, nobody had any idea, so you're not alone. Unless somebody knows who put her here, that is."

"Of course."

"This whole world's a mass of bones, when you think about it," he says. "All the people who die and are buried, all stacked on top of each other. We can't know how most of them died. We have to investigate, up to a point. After that, we just have to let go."

"Yes, I suppose so." All at once, I don't want to know more. The tiny clue, the metal eye of an old-fashioned sneaker, is too much to take in. I know exactly what those shoes were like, the thin-soled gym shoes or plimsolls we all had, the way they had to be whitened with paste from a tube, that dried to a powder. Blanco, it was called. How can the metal eye from an old gym shoe survive when so much does not? He seems to sense my withdrawal, and stands up to face me.

"One more thing, before you go. You haven't seen anyone landing here these last few days?" His voice has slipped from casual friendliness into the flat register of interrogation: don't let the prisoner know why you're asking.

"Landing? You mean from a boat? No. No, I haven't."

I feel his gaze following me down the beach, until I turn and walk back up the path between the trees, my heart thudding in my chest.

THAT EVENING, AS I SIT IN GROWING DARKNESS with my glass of wine and watch the light fade over the moor and the first stars appear, it comes clear to me. The seed, the first thing: the tiny metal eye of the shoe, made for a shoelace to go through; the shoe itself, white and thin-soled, for clambering across slippery rocks; the shoe kicked aside, with its partner, so that feet with painted toe-nails can emerge, and pale legs that open wide beneath a rucked-up skirt. Bright hair thrown back. A fast movement of limbs. Images rush past me like deer leaping in the dark. I do not want to remember, but I do.

THE TIMING IS TOO STRIKING TO IGNORE. Just a few days before I arrived here, they found the bones. So, what does this mean for me? I think about this as I go around the house, noticing what needs to be mended or replaced, as I sit with my glass of wine at the window in the evenings, as I lie awake in bed and listen to the silence around me. I was ten when it happened, and now I am old. Fifty, no sixty years in between. Years in which I hardly thought about this place, or those people, years in which I was getting on with my life, as I thought of it, as if life had to be urged into action, made to progress, all doubts pushed to one side. I'm sure now that the bones are what remains of the woman I once met, whose name I once knew. But what I can, or should do with this knowledge, I'm not sure.

What strikes me now as having altered the course of my young life is how Anabel convinced me of her version. Her verdict, not guilty. Not guilty, because not even there. We were careless, excited, full of notions about spying on people, children of our time, when our country was only beginning to get over the effects of a six-year-long war, when nobody was there to tell us, or explain to us—when we were unable to gauge the effects of our actions. We were kids, for God's sake. I tell myself this, late at night, as the long darkening twilight creeps over the moor. Midnight, and the sky is still pale at its edges, the last glow of sunset a faint pink stain.

What is the message of today? I've read Jung, and been impressed by his theory of synchronicity. I can't dismiss the finding of the bones as a coincidence, nothing to do with me—sheer random chance—as many of my colleagues would. The meaning, the message of these bones—well, it's far from clear to me, but I know it's important. I felt it standing there on the spot where they were found, the plainclothes man sifting through sand at my feet. Look back at your life, it seems to say. See where the falsehood began, see where you lied, or prevaricated, map where you took that turn towards the convenient rather than the true. Is there a place? Can you find it? See where the connections are, the necessary links. The small bones that create the chain of life.

I'm approaching the last part of my own life, that is obvious—but I still have time to grasp something, understand something, even make amends. To whom, and to what, though? Perhaps, to start with, to the child I was before it all began. Young Nessa. The child in the old photograph, gazing out from under a mop of hair, feet planted, refusing or unable to look away. That steadfast stare, as if someone dared me to flinch. There's only so much you can glean from a photograph, especially a small, old, bent one stuck in an album, but I know that it was taken before we ever started on our quest, that summer, before Anabel had co-opted me, before I had let anybody down by choosing the easy lie. I gave in to Anabel, my cousin, because she scared me. She was older, more sophisticated; I needed her approval. It happens, when you are young. I can't say that I completely believed her, but I did need to agree, and be silent about what I knew deep down, where the truth hides out, when you are too young to know what to do with it.

PART II
PASSWORD: FOUGASSE

FIVE

IT WAS 1952, JUST SEVEN YEARS after the end of the war that convulsed the world. I—Vanessa, called Nessa—was ten, Patrick—Paddy—was eight, and Charlie was the newest baby. The war was over, we were told, so we could go to the seaside and nobody was going to come at night to bomb our houses ever again. Our maternal grandmother, Lucy Barclay, bought a house by the sea in Dorset, because it was going cheap, and we all needed to have seaside holidays, we children in particular. Yes, the war was well and officially over. Nobody said that in Europe it might still be going on. We had our ration books still, our points, sweets were rationed for another year or two, so there was no chance that we would rot our teeth. We had free orange juice, and cod-liver oil against rickets—thanks to the recently formed Welfare State—and sometimes we even had those unknown fruit, bananas. I did not see my first banana until I was seven years old. Everybody was relieved, even though still hungry, still bombed-out, still trying to put a country together that had been ripped apart. My father, James Halloran, was involved as an engineer in rebuilding bridges and roads still. The country needed infra-structure, he said—you know, Nessa, like its skeleton, you have to have it to make everything work.

The most important thing for us children, everyone said, was to be able to go to the sea. That was what childhood was, on an island not at war. Beaches, cliffs, the long clean stretches of sand underfoot, the ripple of waves. Unmarked days: childhood, as it had once been.

The beaches of the Dorset coast still had mines buried under sand, so you had not to touch anything, you had to be careful, you had to wear closed shoes and stay on the path, they told us, and walk with a stick in case of snakes. Inland, there were metal spikes and the remains of trenches dug in the soft peaty soil, and on the cliffs, concrete look-out posts with gun-slits for soldiers to watch in case Germans came ashore. The Germans were gone, back to their own miserably depleted country, but the stories lived on, the myths, the remnants, the half-buried things. A shell my brother Paddy found. Bullets, some of them still live. A mine shaped like a diving bell that was dragged up one day out of the sea.

THE WHOLE OF THIS EXPANSE OF DORSET moorland had been used for tank practice during the war. Decoys had been set up here, at the isolated farms and villages, to lure the enemy away from Southampton Water. Targets had been set here—false targets, to lead German bombers astray. There had been a munitions factory hidden on the arid stretch of the heath inland. Hideouts in the villages whose jetties, built for exporting clay, reached out into the harbor. Soldiers had crawled and crouched in the clefts and hollows of this wild country, waiting to attack if the Germans invaded, biding their time. There were the rounded craters where bombs had fallen, sparsely covered by bracken and young heather. A path led up from the end of our unmade road, winding up the hill between gorse bushes and stands of bracken. We ran up it in single file to the top, from where you could see the whole wide stretch of the moor, its marshes in low places, its hilltops and places where sudden ponds appeared in the hollows left by exploding bombs. At the far edge of the moor was the Goathorn peninsula with its lonely farms, then the islands of Poole Harbour, Brownsea, Long Island, Furzey Island, all of them out of bounds still. To the east, the village of Arne that had been used to decoy German bombers into destroying it rather than Southampton, a ghost village where roofless houses stood among rosebay willow-herb and nettles. It was a map of destruction; or, of nature beginning to grow back over destruction. Seven years after the end of the war, you could see that history could fade slowly back into geography, the raw marks of warfare gradually soften into landscape again.

This was the background to that summer of 1952, when we stayed in the house our grandmother had bought, and our aunt and cousins rented the one next door; when I learned the meaning of secrecy and betrayal. Living in the aftermath, in our childish recreation of it all, handling its debris, spending our days in its dug-outs and trenches, learning what nobody had wanted us, post-war children, innocents, to learn.

OUR MEMORY, WHEN WE ARE YOUNG, takes everything in. We are addicts of detail, gleaning information, we are already detectives, easily picking up every detail of others' lives. Whole swathes of later life can go by and be forgotten, or vaguely remembered. But during those early times, nothing escapes us. We soak it all up, process it, without even knowing what we are doing.

I remember our arrival, that first time. The house itself was square and solid, and its walls looked as if someone had hurled small stones at them until they stuck. It had a slate roof and two chimneys, symmetrical like those in a five-year-old's drawing. There was a wooden verandah, with French windows that would open on to it. It all looked very empty and bare, and the *For Sale* board still stood there propped against the wall, even though Gran had bought the house months ago.

Paddy had the key and unlocked the door, and he and I ran in and up the stairs, shouting our finds. We ran through the house claiming our spaces: his and mine in the front bedroom, where we threw our bags down on narrow beds and I, faster, older, got the one by the window. Later, Jean-Ann, my friend from school, would move in with me, and Paddy be sent to the back bedroom, to share with little Charlie. A visiting girl could not be made to share with a boy, everyone knew that. But now, we had the room we wanted, a view over the moor and the sea, all the way to the harbor and the lights of the mainland, far away across the water. We were on an island; our father corrected us, a peninsula, *pen-insula*, an almost-island. But islands were in our minds and our imaginations, the sites of treasure and adventure, tidal seas washing all around them—so an island it would be.

Darkness came in late; it was still high summer. The long twilight drew shadows across the road and down the sloping garden at the back of the house. Out at sea, as the light faded, a flashing light came on and off. We sat on my bed to watch. I nudged Paddy and pointed and he looked out and tightened his lips in a conspirator's grin and nodded. He got it, he knew what I meant. Signals, spies, flashing lights, undercover activities were in both our minds. It was a sign, we knew—but of what?

MY FAMILY EXISTED AROUND ME THEN like furniture, or vegetation, so much a part of my life that I hardly needed to notice them. Paddy was almost an extension to myself—a brother, an ally, an irritation, a challenge. When the others began to arrive, we had to study them, relative strangers with odd habits and sayings, an alien tribe. We observed them from the vantage point of our little family, and gossiped among ourselves.

Anabel, our cousin, arrived the following day with her mother, Aunt Laura, who was my mother's sister, her elder sister Liz, baby sister Susie, and our grandmother, Lucy Barclay. They came in a taxi from the station where the London train stopped. Our family never took taxis, so we watched with interest the family that did. I knew that my father thought that they wasted money on the wrong things—though why a taxi was wrong if you wanted to go somewhere, I couldn't think.

Anabel was twelve, nearly thirteen, a couple of years older than I was. I watched her get out of the taxi and stand in the road, staring at the house, and at us. She wore a neat blouse and a divided skirt, not shorts and a T-shirt as I did. Her white ankle socks were turned down and her shoes were polished brown loafers. Her hair was pinned back with a tortoiseshell slide and cut in a blunt shape at the back of her neck. We had met before, of course, at various family parties, but here was a new version of her, a near-teenager, while I was still a child. I watched like a cat from the safety of our house, until my mother told me sharply to go out and say hello.

"Oh, hello, Nessa."

Were we supposed to kiss, shake hands? I scuffed my sandshoes in the dirt of the road. The taxi went up the road and turned to come back. Suitcases and bags lay stacked in the road, as if none of these people could pick one up. Paddy ran up and seized two of them, showing that he could, as the resident male, and dragged them towards the house next door, that Aunt Laura had rented. My mother took one bag, and I another. Aunt Laura carried the baby, Susie, who wore a cotton sunbonnet but had a very pink face and looked about to explode.

My grandmother folded me in her arms. She smelled of perfume and powder, and her skin was very soft and loose. "Nessa," she said, and I was absolved of everything.

"Did you have a ghastly journey?" my mother asked. According to her and her sister, all journeys were potential nightmares. They always exaggerated when they were together, and laughed at themselves as they did so. I could imagine my father—who had been dropped off at the station early that morning to get the train back to London—raising his eyebrows behind their backs.

My aunt sighed and said, "Oh, it was pretty ghastly, the train was so crowded, there wasn't a spare seat anywhere. Mama must be exhausted. We had to wait ages for a taxi. And it's so hot. Susie's been *fearfully* good, but I'm afraid she needs changing. Lizzie, would you mind taking her please?"

Liz, who wore navy slacks, a white blouse with a red belt, high-heeled sandals and red lipstick, took her baby sister with little enthusiasm, and held her like a parcel at arm's length away from her clean blouse. "Mum, she smells *awful.*"

My mother said, "You should have let us know."

"I wasn't sure which train we'd get."

"The one you were on was the only one there is, in the afternoon."

I thought that my mother and her sister wasted just as much time arguing as ever Paddy and I did.

My aunt said, "Lizzie, be an angel, take her in and change her, and I'll see to the luggage. Nessa, darling, that must be too heavy for you."

"No, no," I shrieked, joining in with the general mood of exaggeration, "No, it's absolutely *fine.* Honestly. Where shall I put it, in the hall?" Paddy, guardian of the keys, had dramatically opened the door of the house next door, where there was a narrow corridor that led to the kitchen, and wooden stairs with no carpet. He held it open like a conjurer.

"Where's your father? Di, isn't Jim here?"

"He had to go back up to London this morning, for work."

"Oh, so we will be *entre nous.* What fun. All girls together." Aunt Laura lit a cigarette, stuck it out of the side of her mouth. My mother shook her head, no thanks. She only smoked sitting down with a drink, while Aunt Laura did it all the time, puffing sideways, her lips braced taut to hold the cigarette, like a gangster in a film.

"Hey, I'm here, I'm not a girl," Paddy said, dumping the last suitcase in through the door.

"Oh, of course. The man of the house. Houses. Well, you'll have to keep us all in order."

Anabel had given in to carrying at least one of the bags. "Why do we always have to travel with all this stuff?" She heaved it up the wooden stairs.

"When you have a family, darling, you'll know. At last half this stuff, as you call it, is for Susie. Babies need a lot of looking after."

"Well, it seems to me that most of it's Liz's clothes."

Liz herself said, "One does want to look half-way decent, even if one is on holiday with one's family."

Anabel said, "She's hoping to pick up some fellow on the beach."

My grandmother seized my hand then, held it high, close to her side, and steered me into our house—as if we were the only sane people there.

I OBSERVED ANABEL LIKE AN ANTHROPOLOGIST, gathering details. She was left-handed and wrote in a tiny crabby scrawl, holding her pen between the second and third joints of her damaged fingers. She had eczema on her hands and behind her knees. She read spy stories and Conan Doyle and *The Scarlet Pimpernel* and was often taken to the theatre. Living in London, she had London clothes and London habits, as well as an older sister, Liz, who was going to be a debutante.

She knew more than us, had listened at more adult dinner tables, heard her father's friends talking, even read newspapers; but above all, she had read everything she could find about spies, the black market, enemy aliens dressed as nuns, the whole subterfuge and secrecy of the world she had been born into—1940, a couple of years before I came into it.

When she arrived with her family, she seemed fascinatingly separate from them. She stood apart as if to make it clear that they were nothing to do with her. How could this be done, when family was all you really had? I wanted both to keep out of her way and impress her. But this was before I heard the ideas she had, the facts she knew, and before we began to feel our way into a cautious friendship. She could also be suddenly charming, just when I was thinking how I hated her. She came and knocked on our door that first day, after we had seen them into their house, and told our mother, "Mum's next door, Aunt Di, she'd love to see you, do go through, she's feeding Susie." To me she said, in adult tones, "Nessa! How lovely to see you." I felt reprieved, included. She had me, from then on, and I no longer thought her clothes too grand and her accent affected. She wanted me. She was pleased to see me. It could have been just put-on London politeness, but I felt it was more than that. How did she know who I was? Then the whole cycle—admiration, dislike, charm, acceptance—began again.

Her mother and mine had both had late post-war babies. So their attention was mostly elsewhere, fussing over these children who had arrived—*Surprise! You have another little brother!*—to add to their existing and perfectly-sized families. I loved my baby brother and Anabel loved her baby sister—you had to love babies— but it was soon agreed between us, with a certain look, a rolling of eyes, that our mothers had made foolish mistakes. The mistakes, though, left us free to lead our own lives, so we ducked easily out of sight, out of range and knew our mothers could not follow us. Liz, Anabel's older sister, nearly eighteen that year, was preparing to become a "deb" and "do the season," whatever that might mean. She left glossy magazines lying around, worked on her tan at the beach, sighed when a cloud passed over her, and owned an incredible number of little bottles of face and body cream. So, she too was occupied, though possibly bored with it all and waiting for her real London life to begin. She did not want to waste her time with her younger sister and cousins. Our fathers were mostly at work, although mine sometimes came down for weekends. We rarely saw Anabel's father, who spent his weekends playing golf after his weeks working in the City. Later, Anabel told me that he had a girlfriend who also played golf, and that they drank G-and-Ts together at the Club House, but I was not to say that I knew. I had never thought of fathers having girlfriends, but there it was; Anabel said it quite airily, as if it were normal.

ALL THIS WAS WHY WE HAD SO MUCH FREE TIME, so little supervision; why we were free to invent our lives, our only obligation being to appear for meal-times and be in bed by nine. Our mothers were busy, our fathers absent, and our grandmother just watched what went on, mostly without comment, and seemed to have given up any idea of exertion. Everyone just accepted her as she was, now that she was old. She had bought the house, she had set all this in train, and now she could just sit in her favorite chair and look out on the moor, think her own thoughts, and wait for someone to bring her a glass of whisky at six. I did wonder what it would be like to be at that stage of life, and give up all the fuss. Sometimes she pulled me towards her, or linked my arm with hers, or looked into my eyes, saying "Nessa?" as if searching for something only I might contain—but what, I had no idea.

JEAN-ANN, MY SCHOOL FRIEND, had to be picked up next from the Swanage train. She came down the platform with her lost look and her hair falling out of its plastic slide, carrying a suitcase that she set down every few yards. As soon as I saw her looking lost, I wished I had not asked her to come. If she was my friend, Anabel would look down on both of us. With Jean-Ann here, I hadn't a chance of impressing my cousin. Then I saw that Jean-Ann was pink in the face and close to tears, and I hurried forward to meet her. I was the hostess, after all. It was complicated, and this annoyed me.

"Here! We're over here! Dad's outside in the car."

"Hello, Nessa." She was not going to tell me how close she had come to panic, getting off the train at a strange place, seeing nobody she knew. I took her suitcase. "How was your journey?" I knew you had to ask a visitor this, be polite, give her a chance to complain.

"Oh, all right."

"Have you had lunch? Are you hungry?"

"Mum gave me sandwiches for the train." She was not going to demand much of us, I saw. She had been trained not to be a nuisance. I imagined her mother saying, "Now, Jean-Ann, you're to behave yourself, don't be a nuisance, all right?"

Paddy ran to meet us, jumping up and down, "Hello, did you bring stones in your bag, Jean-Ann? It weighs a ton. Can you swim? I can swim miles now. Do you know Morse code?"

Jean-Ann said, "Yes, we're learning it at Guides. And Semaphore." Perhaps she was going to be useful, after all.

She wore her brother's cast-off shorts, and when we went to the beach, a boy's trunks to swim. She still wore water-wings. She had what we called "an accent." I saw Anabel's swift glance of scorn at her boy's trunks, and then no comment. I saw Paddy's amazement. Still, she said she knew Morse and Semaphore. We were all picking up signals as if we lived in code: class, money, age, family situation all came into it. Of course they did: the country may have had a socialist government for years after the war, but English attitudes are hard to change.

"DON'T YOU CHILDREN WANT TO COME TO THE BEACH? It's such a lovely day." My mother pleaded. The beach had been the aim, the destination—that flawless rim around England that had been forbidden to its inhabitants for so long. But we were on to something else, we wanted the freedom of the moor, and its sinister history of wartime secrecy, its dour enchantment.

"No, we're going up on the moor! We'll be fine, we'll be back for lunch!"

"Well, don't pick anything up out there. Don't touch anything that looks funny. And look out for snakes. Take a stick. Do what Anabel tells you, she's the eldest. And take care!"

With the voice of caution ringing after us, we ran out of our houses after breakfast, up to the end of the rough unmade road and in single file up the path on to the moor. It was sand and peat, marked by rabbit droppings, and it zigzagged to the top of the first hill, where bell heather bloomed and rasped at our ankles, and gorse grew in sharp little clumps, flowering yellow, fierce as needles. Bracken uncurled pale green fronds and sometimes tripped us as we ran. We came out on the hill-top, facing out towards the harbor and the islands, drunk with the possibility of all this space.

Clouds swept down over the bare hills, and away inland. For children reared in towns and suburbs, it was intoxicating to run here, bellow into the wind, watch the cloud shadow race across the purple undulations of the hills, know that it was ours. Few people ever came up here, it seemed. We roamed and stared and threw ourselves down on the springy clumps of heather, ventured into bogs and soaked our shoes that turned rusty brown with bog water. We learned that the white flowers of bog cotton marked the marshy places, that gentians grew in the bogs, that green moss meant treacherous footholds, and dry heather the safe places to tread. We watched the paths, for intruders; we followed walkers, but there were few. We listened with the close rustle of the heather in our ears, for the step on the path, the distant voice, that would tell us of a stranger's approach.

On the far side of the hill, on one of these mornings, Paddy fell out of sight as if the earth had opened up beneath him.

"Help! I've fallen down a hole!" His head poked out from between clumps of heather at last. Then, "Hey. There are tunnels down here! Come and look."

Like this we discovered the linked underground trenches in which warfare had been so recently practiced. We lowered ourselves through the tangle of plants that roofed them, and squatted close to each other on white sand. Under the heather that sprang tough and wiry, ling and bell, above our heads, we discovered the extent of the passage-way, and the trenches cut in the peaty earth that led from it. We stuck our heads up through the heather to talk and point. It was an ideal look-out point on the side of the hill. From here you could watch the double track path that the tanks had made and see who came up it. You could watch, and yet be invisible. Roots twined above our heads when we ducked down, the heather growing back as if nobody had touched it. We heard the rustle of wind in the dry pods above us. We stayed tucked in, waiting, in our womb of peat and sand.

Out here on the moor, we gradually shifted from being the people we were with our families. Anabel became the leader, being the eldest, but she did not patronize us. It was as if some layer of falseness had been lifted from her. She was being her real self, perhaps, not the London sophisticate who had to keep up with her elder sister and the girls at her posh school. I noticed her dreaming, her eyes on the horizon, as if she had forgotten for a moment that we were there and that she was supposed to control us. Paddy was quieter too and plodded ahead, striking the tops off bracken plants with the slash of a stick, making himself the advance guard, the stout stick carried in case of snakes, his sharp eyes alert to warn us. He was proud of having found the "holes" as we called them, in the first place, even if he had done it by falling into one. I followed Anabel, and Jean-Ann followed me, single file up the narrow paths, dodging between gorse bushes, scuffing up sand.

I was no longer quite sure who I was, this summer. Everything began to shift and change around me. I still wished from time to time that I had not insisted that Jean-Ann, my friend from school, should come to stay, as now I felt responsible for her. Up here on the moor, and keeping my lonely look-outs from the bedroom late at night, I wanted the pride and silence of my solitude: not to be known, not to be guessed at, not to have anyone know what I felt or thought. I walked, and said little, but kept my eyes open. If Anabel was the leader and Paddy the scout and Jean-Ann the fellow traveler of the company, I would be the master spy.

Six

On the north-east side of the peninsula, the sandstone rock called the Agglestone jutted up on its shallow bracken-covered hill, anvil-shaped, red and yellow and tawny brown. It was at least twenty feet high when we first saw it. Some people said that the devil threw it at the Isle of Wight—others, at Corfe Castle. Either way, he missed his target by a long way. It's the result of erosion, in fact, and its soft stone is eroding still, until one day it will not exist anymore. Its flat platform-like top has tilted, it has listed and sunk down into the soft sandy earth around it so that it no longer resembles an anvil. But in our childhood it was still solidly at the center of the moor, upright on its hill, its flat table-top with its hand-hold crevices on the way up a temptation to climbers.

We had never before climbed rocks without our father's help, a long arm and strong hand to haul us up the last difficult part, dangle us till we found a foothold.

"You go first, Nessa."

"No, you."

Anabel said, "It's better that Nessa goes first, then Patrick, then me." So that is what we did.

I scrabbled my way up the rock face, feeling for crevices in the sandstone, my fingers blindly ahead of me, my feet in gym-shoes stretching for ledges, my body plastered against the body of the rock, wind in my hair, sand scattering around me, ahead of me the lump that jutted before I could reach the edge. I hauled myself up over it, avoiding tufts of grass that would come away, as my father had taught me, and at last pushed myself over the edge of the platform, scratching my stomach on the sharpness as my T-shirt rode up, and lay panting flat on my belly on the top. I called down to the others, "It's easy! Come on up!"

I saw the top of Paddy's head as he began to climb. His shorter legs and arms made it harder for him than even it had been for me. I leaned over, shouting encouragement. He arrived, scarlet in the face and fighting off tears, but grinned at me as he pulled his whole body over the edge and arrived beside me. We lay flat together, pleased with ourselves. Getting down would be another matter, but for now, we were here. Anabel came after us, her feet scrabbling against the rock surface, her hands unsure. We leaned, called to her: "That ledge there! That handhold! Reach around, it's only an inch away. You have to have three firm holds before you move!"

Paddy and I were pleased that there was something we could do better than she could. Jean-Ann, scared, shook her head—no, no— and stood at the bottom, watching us. Then I realized that someone else was already up here, behind us. I turned my head, feeling a presence, hearing a voice in the wind. Two boys stared down at me from their crouched positions. The wind tore at my hair and my fingers still scrabbled against rock. I saw blood trickle down my leg from a scratch on my knee and I licked my hand and rubbed it away. I could hardly believe I had done it, and was here, dangerously, triumphantly on top of the world. But like Scott at the South Pole coming across all those miles of ice only to find Amundsen's camp, it was only to discover that someone had got there first.

"What are you doing here?" the taller one demanded.

"Just climbing up. What are you doing?"

"It's our place."

"No, it's not. It's everybody's."

"It's our place. You can't come up here."

"Well, I'm here, and so is my brother," as Paddy, still red in the face and speechless, stared up at them, big boys, much bigger than him. "And it's ours as much as yours."

"No, it's not, I'm telling you. We have meetings up here."

"What for?"

"To make plans. To decide what to do."

"About what?"

"Spies. Strangers. People from outside." As he spoke, I saw Anabel's face appearing at the rock edge, and her hands and elbows as she hauled herself up to join us. If she had been there minutes earlier, I would probably have left the talking to her. But I was first up here, and they had seen me pull myself up, a girl younger than they were.

I said, "Well, if you can do that, so can we. We have a secret place too, only you'll never know where it is."

The boy looked down at me, the taller skinny one with the wild brown hair blowing and dirty knees. "You can come up here if you'll show us your place."

Paddy, breathing hard, said, "Who are you, anyway?"

"I'm Ted. This is Roger."

I said, "Well, I'm called Nessa and this is Patrick—Paddy. And this is Anabel, our cousin. We have another friend down there, Jean-Ann, only she doesn't know how to climb."

Anabel surveyed the group of us, crouched there on the anvil-top of the massive rock where she had arrived. "Okay," she said at last. "You can follow us, when we go down. We'll show you. Only we'll have to swear you to secrecy. Our place is secret. Nobody else knows where it is."

The boy called Ted stood up, his thin shirt and shorts billowing full of wind, and pointed across the moor towards the sea. I noticed the muscles in his skinny arms, and his narrowed eyes as he stared. I already knew that I wanted to impress him, even more than I wanted to impress my cousin. Very soon, probably even later that day, I simply wanted to be him—a state of being that I think now precedes being in love when you are too young to know what that is. In the Blyton books I read, the heroine, called George, wants to be a boy. I did not want to be a boy, although I admired her tomboyish attitudes. I wanted to be Ted—or his equal.

"Look, you see the wreck?" There was the wreck of a schooner, its masts slanting, its hull underwater, between here and the Old Harry Rocks. He said, "Wreckers, see? A lot goes on here, has done since the war. Okay, so, you can come up here, but you have to show us your place first. Right?"

We climbed down, a feat harder than going up as you had to lower yourself backwards and blindly over the edge, negotiate the bulge in the rock, and let your feet scrabble for the footholds, as your legs spread and you hung like a spider, moving one limb at a time. Ted and Roger came last and sprang easily from the last rock foothold to the sandy ground. Jean-Ann stood at the bottom, looking up, worried for us, frowning the way her mother did when she was late home. I watched the two boys jump down in an easy motion from the last rock like gymnasts, and wished that I had known how to do the same.

When we reached the house, we knew not to say anything about our rock-climbing or our meeting with Ted and Roger. Nobody had to be sworn to secrecy—it was understood. I myself knew already that what I felt about Ted had to be protected from everyone, if I was ever going to matter in his life.

Seven

"Hey, you two, something to report." He told us standing up there on the hilltop, his hair on end, shorts held up by a snake belt. "I just heard two people talking foreign. They were down by the farm. They were definitely suspicious."

Jean-Ann was with me to keep watch on the hill, always a little anxious, her bony legs drawn up under her. She listened to Ted but said nothing. I thought, she too knows that you can't just "talk foreign"—it has to be an actual language. Anabel, a blue speck of shirt, a waving arm on the moor path, was coming up to meet us.

I asked Ted, "Who were they? How do you know?" Always ask, always check for proof, my father had told me.

"I think it was German." As if he had recognized his mistake, or could instantly recognize German, or anything else. "After they finished talking, he gave her something she put in her pocket; then they went separate ways." He told us his news before Anabel arrived. He opened his pocket-knife and stuck it in the ground and pulled it out clean. Then he glanced at me, not Jean Ann. Who did he want at his side?

"So," I said, glad I was getting the news before Anabel, "It was a man and a woman? What did they do?" I tried for Anabel's serious tone.

"I followed the man. He walked down towards the little beach and sat on an upside-down boat, looking out to sea. I tell you, they looked suspicious. Rog followed the woman, right, Rog? But she got on the bus and he didn't follow her. She waved to him from the bus. I wrote down a description."

He pulled out his notebook—Ted's pockets were always full—and pointed to what he had written. "Man. Not old, not young. White shirt, grey trousers. Dark hair. Went to beach, looked out to sea. Woman. Younger. Blue skirt, white blouse, blond hair. Def. foreign. Took something from him—paper?—put it in pocket in skirt. 15.00 hours, Monday, village cross, seen by T. S." He flipped the notebook shut and grinned. "You lot seen anything suspicious? If you see something, write it down."

We all knew the poster that said, "If You See Suspicious Behavior, Notify Authorities." It was left from the war, but still stuck on hoardings and outside shops and the post office and on fences everywhere. In some places it was ripped and illegible, in others faded to blandness by weather. We all longed to find suspicious behavior, to become the child heroes of our time.

Anabel said, "We should definitely take this seriously. We should follow these people up. There are foreigners coming to this country, I know it for a fact. They want to take revenge on England for winning the war. To assassinate people, even, to get their own back."

Anabel and Ted both had a quality that people call leadership—as if they were born to it, a look in their eyes, a way of directing others—or of making others want to follow them. When I was young, it seemed to be mostly about their being older. Later, I recognized this quality as a certainty—often against the odds, other people's opinions or even common sense—of being right, as well as an ability to make others believe it too. I wanted to believe them: to be their willing lieutenant. Jean-Ann kept quiet, followed along. I wondered what she really thought, and if for her it was simply too risky to disagree. I saw her fold her lips and listen politely. I wondered if she was a traitor in our midst—someone who would give way under questioning.

"Assassinate?" Ted said, "You mean, like murder people?"

"Yes, only it's more political. They don't just kill anyone. They have targets."

"How do you know?"

"I read it. It's to make up for us winning the war. They have lists of people to kill."

"Blimey," said Roger.

He was a boy who injured himself just slightly all the time, and bore the marks of his hectic passage through life. He scrambled, he darted, he bumped into things, he fell. I looked at him picking one of the scabs on his knee.

"And that's not all," Ted said. "Rog, tell about what else we saw. About what you found."

Roger screwed up his eyes and rubbed a hand across his face. "You mean, the gun place and that?"

"Yeah."

"Okay. If they won't tell."

Anabel said, "I've just told you what I know. So get on with it."

"Follow us. Single file. And no talking when we get there."

We came down the side of the hill and headed towards the dark mosquito-breeding pool under the trees, the stony path that led to the road, and single file along the road till we came to the back gate of the hotel where Roger's father worked. It was a rambling stone building with many turrets and small paned windows, and a roof made of heavy Purbeck stone tiles. It was like a fairy-tale castle in which everyone had fallen asleep for a hundred years. The gardens had been vegetable gardens and lawns before the war. Bindweed and sticky willy, brambles and old man's beard grew everywhere, right up to the windows. I couldn't imagine anyone choosing to spend their holidays there. The man who owned it was a Major St. John, pronounced *Sinjun*.

My father said that nobody deserved to be both a major and a saint, it was probably a made-up name, and anyway it was a robber's den and the man looked like a spiv. Roger's father was only the manager, not the owner. So we had to creep in and not be seen, or the Major would come and throw us out. We walked in, careful and silent, past the bar that smelled of old tobacco and the sharp whiff of spirits. The whole place reeked of dead fires, and there were cobwebs in all the corners. At the bottom of the stairs we paused, as we heard someone creaking overhead who might be coming down.

"Come on," said Roger, "Follow me." Even from his back view, I could see how Roger felt proud of his discovery. He marched, his head set high. He led us past the kitchens and scullery and out into a small back yard where there was a green door, with a latch. It was open, and we all went through. The grounds of the hotel, on the beach side, had gone to seed and were more like a hayfield, with long grass dried in the sun and big trees all around the edge. I guessed it might once have been a croquet lawn, or even a tennis court. The blue of the bay was beyond it, and there was a narrow, partly overgrown path down towards the beach, private, as Roger said, and this was the only way down. Halfway down, thick vegetation began, hazel and oak, holly and elder, a tangle of bushes that were sprouting into trees. The path dwindled, and disappeared. The soil underfoot was soft and sandy, orange-colored. Banks of nettles made us hop and jump. Roger turned towards the cliff, following a faint track that maybe rabbits or foxes had made. I saw now why he had so many scratches and scabs on his legs. I licked my hand and swabbed saliva at my own, nettle rash stinging my calves. Roger turned and faced us, his hand against a gray concrete wall: this was his moment of triumph, and even Ted could not upstage him.

"I came down here the other day, just exploring. I found this place. Look." He led us along the wall to a narrow entrance. The floor was dark and slimy.

Jean-Ann said, "I don't want to go in there. Do we have to?"

Anabel said, "Come on." So she followed us in. Paddy came last. He said, "Watch out, Jean-Ann, there's ghoulies and ghosties in there." He was close behind me, not wanting to be far apart. I put my hand against the wall and felt its rough cold surface in the dark. I smelled earth. It was like being in a tomb.

"But look," Roger pushed some creeper away from a long slit of a window in the wall. "See? It's where they looked out to sea. The army built it. I don't think anybody else knows it's here."

"They must do," Ted said. "It must've been here for ages. Since the war."

"But nobody comes here. They can't, unless they come the way we came, through the hotel. The cliff's blocked off, there's no path."

"So now, only we know." Anabel said. "So the thing is, we can keep watch from here, and nobody can see us from the outside."

"Right," Ted said.

"Bingo," said Roger.

I wanted to ask somebody what exactly we were watching for. All the nights we had spent sitting up watching a flashing light out at sea, trying to decipher its code; all the vigils on the moor, as we waited for suspicious characters to come past so we could follow them. What was it all for? After several weeks, I did wonder. But to have said anything would have changed something I did not want changed: the charged, excited feeling between us all, as we stood close together in the clammy darkness of the gun emplacement on the cliff. It was like knowing something was going to happen, and dreading it and longing for it all at once.

Ted said, "But this isn't all. Look, over here."

We followed him to a far corner of the building, watched as he scraped dirt and leaves away with his shoe. "We covered it up again so nobody else finds it, see."

There was a trapdoor set in the floor, with an iron ring in it. Roger and Ted tugged on the ring and heaved it up. We all peered down into darkness.

Ted said, "A tunnel. We reckon it goes back to the hotel, or up on the road maybe, so whoever was here could get away if the Germans came. They could just pull down the lid over themselves, see, and nobody would know there was anyone here."

Ted and Roger sat back on their heels. Paddy said, "Did you go down it?" His admiration for the older boys showed as clearly as Anabel's quiet excitement. In the books we read, there was always a secret passage or tunnel—but I had never expected to find one in real life. I could see that Jean-Ann was truly scared, now that she was presented with actual evidence, so I had to pretend that I was not. This concrete bunker, this dark hole beneath a trap door was real. Ted rolled the cover back into place. Roger said, "No, we thought we'd better wait till you saw it. We need torches, anyway, if we're to see anything." I knew then that he too was alarmed by his find. What had we uncovered? A world of hidden things, a place in which maybe men had died, and we might just die too, stuck with no possibility of rescue.

"So, who do you think the tunnel was for?"

"Like I said, for people to be able to escape. All the top brass was here," Ted said, "So they had to find a way of getting them to safety, didn't they? That's why I think it goes to the hotel. My dad told me this whole place is full of old quarries and tunnels. Maybe they just used an old one. The smugglers used to use them, ages ago, after the quarries by the sea got used up and they moved them inland. He said the place was like a honeycomb, he got it from talking to the old blokes in the pub, people who've lived here all their lives. There's passages and tunnels all over. You have to talk to the old'uns, he said to me—and that's what he does when he goes for a pint."

"I asked my granddad," Roger said. "He's old now, but he remembers it all. When Churchill and Monty and all came here, and they had to have lunch, oh, he said they even brought their own whisky. That was at the beginning of the war, when they all thought the invasion was going to be here. They started putting up pill-boxes and stuff. There's a pill-box down on the beach, and one out on Old Harry. They had a man in each one, they had a Lewis gun. Then, there was Dragon's teeth, anti-tank stuff later." He breathed fast with excitement, at being able to tell us. "They set fire to the water, like I said, poured a load of petrol on it. It was called Project Fougasse."

"What's that mean?" Paddy asked.

"I dunno. It's just what it was called. Then after the Battle of Britain, I think it was, they started pretending this was France, so they could practice for D-Day, you know, when all them little boats went across."

"No," Ted said, "That was Dunkirk. D-Day was the invasion of Europe. Later on."

"Oh, yeah, sorry. D-Day. Then it was called Operation Smash. They practiced it all here, millions of soldiers from all sorts of countries came, and they all pretended this was France and they were invading it. So, that was the next time, and the King came again then as well as Mr. Churchill, and General Eisenhower and even Mr. Roosevelt, I think. And they all had to have lunch again. They watched it from the back of the hotel, where we were just now. My granddad said it was a sight for sore eyes."

We were out of the dank underground place now, with the gun emplacement just behind it, and we all collapsed on the grass at the very edge of the overgrown meadow that had been the lawn of the hotel, behind a bramble bush where nobody would see us before we made our final dash out into the open.

"Well, crikey, Rog," Ted said, and clapped him on the back, "Your family have been in history, then. Right slap-bang in the middle of it all."

"Yeah," Roger said, "And there's another thing. They had tanks you could drive in the water."

"Amphibious," said Anabel.

"Yeah, that was it. They had sort of skirts. They were called Valentine tanks. DD tanks too. That stands for Duplex Drive. But they didn't work all that well."

Ted said, "Just imagine them, coming ashore, right down there."

Roger said, "But one went down off Old Harry Rocks, because the sea was too rough. My dad knew one of the men who drowned. So they didn't actually come ashore here, I don't think."

"But the men did."

"The men did, yeah. The ones that didn't drown."

Ted said, "My dad told me they shelled the moor with live ammo that time. It was the biggest exercise of all the war. And there were scientists came here, they worked up at Worth Matravers on radar, it was all top secret but he had to deliver some stuff for them, building materials I s'pose for making bunkers. They had to have these underground bunkers. And," he paused for effect, "did you know that nobody was allowed out, nobody was even allowed to look out to sea? You could be arrested for just looking. They all had to stay in their houses. Except my dad; he had to take the stuff up to Worth, so he was allowed out."

"Yeah, and there was that plane that came down, in the field in front of the cottage next to the pub, Ted, remember?"

"It was a Messerschmitt," Ted said, "It crashed, just over there, front of Mrs. Day's house, that was. Brrr-zoom!" He moved his hand sharply through the air, crashed it and made it explode on contact. "They went out from the farm to capture the pilot, but he was a goner. If she'd been in her house, she'd have seen the whole thing, or she might even have been killed, but she was out the back. All you could see, all over the village, was thick clouds of smoke."

Ted and Roger had us now; they were in charge, and they knew it. They might not know how to spell or recognize foreign languages, but they knew far more about what had happened here than we did, and they brought out the details as if to stun us into being fascinated by them—which we were. There was so much to know about the mysterious time of the War. Roger knew about Operation Fougasse, and the men drowning off Old Harry; Ted knew about scientists doing radar and crashed German planes. I wanted to know how such a thing as war could happen, making the whole world different from how it had been before.

"So you mean, nobody could come in to the village or leave it?"

"Nope. My dad stayed, my mum went to her mum, over in Dorchester. That was where she had me. There was curfew, every night. And like I said, nobody could go to the beach, nobody could fish, it was all barbed wire and mines, in case the Nazis came, and you weren't even allowed to look out to sea."

"It sounds awful," Jean-Ann said. "But then the whole war was awful."

I looked out at the blue line of the horizon—how could anybody live here and not look out to sea? It was as if the sea drew your eye towards it, so you wouldn't be able to help looking. And how would anybody know, if you just gave it a quick look, now and again?

"They cleared everybody out of Tyneham, you know where that is? On the other side, where the army ranges still are. They told them they could come back after the war but their country needed them to give up their houses, so they did. And you know what, nobody's been allowed to go back to live there; the Army still have it, and it's full of ordnance. The whole village was bombed, just for practice. So we were better off here, at least."

"My uncle was killed in the war," Jean-Ann said. "In the RAF."

She had said what she had to say, and it silenced us all. None of us had lost a family member in the war. Our dad had come back to us from the army, whole but exhausted, and Anabel's father had been in a reserved occupation, which meant he mostly stayed at home reading the papers, when he was not seeing his girlfriend, Anabel said.

We sat on the grass, hugging our knees, staring out to sea. But I knew somebody had to say something, so I said, "Oh, that's awful. Poor you."

Ted said, "The RAF was really dangerous. He must have been a brave man."

Anabel said, "Well, a lot of people did get killed, after all." She did not sound quite sympathetic enough.

Ted said, after a silence in which we all tried to think what else to say to console Jean-Ann for her uncle, "Hey, we could have this place for our O.B."

"What's an O.B.?" Paddy asked.

"Operational Base. It was what the Home Guard had to have. My uncle, my mum's brother was in it, they had to sign the Official Secrets Act, and you know once you've done that you can't tell anyone what you've done for thirty years, or they will come and kill you."

"So, what's an O.B. for?"

"They were underground, like sort of pre-fab huts at first, then they had to be made of concrete. They had turf over the top of them so you couldn't see them at all. They had everything they needed there, cooking stoves, bedding, stores of food and explosives. Then these blokes, the Purbeck men, had to stay put if there was an invasion, let the Germans go over their heads, then pop up and attack them in hand-to-hand combat. There were men hiding underground all around the coast of Britain. They got super-good training, because they were the only hope, if the enemy got here. My uncle Bob had a special knife for doing that. It was called a Fairbairn-Sykes. He showed me a picture. With a really long thin blade, super-sharp. They had to learn how to kill people quickly and silently. Cut their throats, schhhtt," and he drew a sharp finger across his own. "Only of course the Germans never landed, so they didn't have to."

Anabel said, "So did your uncle Bob get killed for telling you all this?"

Ted opened and shut his knife, as if he wanted to use it for that purpose. "No, because after the war he reckoned it was safe to tell, if we kept it in the family."

"And now you've told us. It isn't thirty years, yet, it's not even ten."

"Well, you have to swear not to tell."

"We swear," Paddy said, his eyes wide open. We all swore, so that Ted's uncle Bob would not get killed—by whom?

"MI6 I should think," Ted said. He put his knife away in his shorts pocket. We were silent, impressed.

EIGHT

MY MOTHER CAPTURED ME AFTER BREAKFAST, as Paddy and I waited for Anabel to emerge from the house next door so that we could all run up the path to the moor and meet our allies. She tipped up my chin and inspected my face. "You have black rings under your eyes, Nessa. You look awful. What are you and Jean-Ann getting up to at night? I'll have to separate you if this goes on."

"Nothing," I said.

In the books we read, parents were either dead, having been killed instantly in a car or plane crash, in India running the Raj and dying of cholera, or otherwise absent, leaving children to be looked after by vague aunts who were writers or uncles who were mad scientists. Nothing could happen otherwise, obviously. So the children were only slightly sad, never very confused or disturbed by these sudden disasters, but set off instantly, free of supervision, to have adventures. I hardly noticed my own parents' existence during this time, but took for granted that there would be meals, clothes for us to wear, and bedtimes. We hardly needed them to be killed or in some foreign country. They were there, but well in the background.

My mother and Aunt Laura wheeled the babies down to the beach in their push-chairs, accompanying our grandmother to the beach hut we had, where they set out their chairs on the sand, brewed tea over a lamp of methylated spirits, changed into discreet bathing costumes and toweling jackets and sat chatting and smoking cigarettes while the babies scuffed about in the sand. Our father went down on these expeditions when he was here at the weekend, and swam energetically out to sea, pounded down the beach to get dry, then set off for one of his long walks across the hills. They were free of us all, except at mealtimes, where we made brief appearances, and before bed when we had to be reminded to have baths in the tub that held brown peaty water off the moor, that was supposed to be full of iron, and therefore good for us.

JEAN-ANN AND I SAT ON MY bed, nearest to the window, keeping watch.

"Nessa?"

"What?"

"Is it real, or is it a game?"

Outside, the twilight deepened: the days were long still after midsummer. The light beam we were watching flashed out in the dark sea. "You mean, what we're doing?"

"Following people around and stuff."

I didn't want to be asked this, as I was not sure myself. When did something become real? When you actually saw it in front of your eyes—like the tunnel under the observation post? When enough people believed in it? "Of course it's real."

"Oh. Okay. You mean, they really are spies? Then shouldn't we tell the police?"

"Well," I improvised, "We probably will tell the police, but first we have to be sure; that's why we're finding out as much as we can. We don't want to bother them with false alarms. Only, quite a lot of people are spies, they're still around, so we can't relax our guard, can we? We need cast-iron evidence." I liked the phrase. "When we've got that, we'll tell the police."

"I see." It sounded as if she didn't. "We have to be patient, it may take time."

Jean-Ann said nothing for a long moment, but I could feel her worrying beside me. It was like being with a dog that has its jaws locked on a bone and gnaws it in silence. Then she said, "Only, I don't think we should be doing anything dangerous, do you?"

"No," I said. "Of course not. Or not very dangerous, anyway."

Her question—is this real?—bothered me. It was like walking along a path making sure you didn't tread on any sticks that would crack and give you away. I got out my notebook and devoted my attention to the dot-dash flashing out there and what it might mean in Morse code, and she sat silently, the question still unanswered between us.

WHEN WE WENT BACK TO THE look-out place that Ted had named our O.B., we took the small flashlight that Anabel had found in the cupboard in the hall, put there in case of black-outs. Ted had brought one too, so when ours flickered and went out, its battery predictably dying after being in the hall cupboard for so long, he switched his on to peer down into the darkness of the underground passage.

"There could be water down there. Somebody get a stone; we'll drop it and see."

The pebble Roger passed went down, but none of us could hear a splash. Was it deep or shallow? It was really close to the sea, and could go down into a cave. How far did it go? No clue.

"Well, I can't see much. Looks like there might be footholds further down."

"No steps?"

"Nope. Not that I can see. I think I can see something sticking out from the wall. Like they have at docks, you know, sort of cleats so you can go down to boats at low tide."

Jean-Ann said, "You're not going down there, are you? It looks dangerous."

"Yeah, it's dangerous all right. Bit slimy too." Ted sounded as though neither of these things was enough to put him off. But none of us really wanted to go any further with our investigations. The black hole open in front of us, into which a man might slip if someone were coming to kill him quickly and silently or any other way, was too much for all of us.

"Okay, shall I close it up for now?"

Anabel said, "Yes, probably."

We sat back on our heels around the trap-door in the concrete floor. I felt the dizziness again that was happening too often for comfort; as if the whole world had begun to whirl around me, and it was impossible to know if I was looking down or up. I blinked, shook my head, watched an ant crawl up part of the concrete wall in front of me. Ted levered the cover back on to the hole and sat back. I saw him glance at me. "Nessa, are you all right?"

"Yes. Just got a bit dizzy."

"Okay, let's get out of here."

Were boys of his age ever scared of things the way I was, the way Jean-Ann was, the way we tried so hard not to let others see? I had heard boys sneer at each other, "Don't be such a girl!" I would do anything not to let Ted or Roger see that I was afraid—girly, wet, scaredy-cat, sissy, all those words of insult—and yet at that moment I saw a possibility that they too had unearthed more than they had wanted to find.

IF SOMEBODY HAD WATCHED US, INVISIBLY present like Hardy's reddleman, would they have reported us, our movements, would they have remembered, later, when the questions were asked, what they had seen? I don't think so. The movements of a gang of children go unremarked, unless their parents are looking for them. We moved about as invisibly as animals, leaving little trace—a dropped coin, a shell, sand leaking from a pocket, a sneakered footprint, grass only just beaten down. Nothing to report. We were playing, weren't we? We were innocent bystanders, if we were there at all.

BY NOW, WE WERE ITCHING FOR something to happen. We wanted information, action. It was a time for wanting to be sure of what you saw, even when you were not. Things blurred at their edges. We were actors in roles, hamming for an invisible camera, for each other. At the perimeter of objects, of people, a vague shifting, an unsettlement. I sometimes wondered where the truth was, and if it mattered. I felt uneasy, wondering what was real and what was not. At such times the world seemed to reel around me, stunning me with its presence, and I wondered if I was sickening with something, or simply growing up.

Ted and Roger were already waiting up on the hill on the moor as we trudged up to meet them. Ted was twirling the stick he always carried; Roger had his arms crossed over his chest. Nobody had mentioned it, but we had all gone up on the moor instead of meeting at the gun emplacement on the cliff.

"What's the password?"

"Mystery."

"We should change the password in case it gets known. Anyway, that one's a dud, it's too obvious."

"Okay. What?"

"Fougasse," said Ted. "Rog thought of it."

"Right. Fougasse."

"Fougasse," we all murmured, and clapped our right hands against each other's in our salute.

Anabel called a meeting. We sank down into the heather around the trenches, our legs crossed, sitting in a semi-circle.

"I've seen them. The couple Ted was talking about. They're definitely up to something."

"Where were they? What did you see?"

"I saw them outside the Higgins' shop, coming down the road. I had to go down to get stuff for dinner tonight. Mum wanted lettuce, and there wasn't any. Anyway, as I was coming out, just as I was coming down the steps out of the shop"—she spun it out, enjoying our attention—"there they were, walking along one behind the other. So I followed them down as far as the crossroads and they went down towards the beach, but I had to come back because Mum was waiting."

Ted said, "Let's have it. We don't want to know about your mum, and lettuce." He got out his knife and began to peel his stick.

Anabel said, "Shut up. I'm telling you. I won't tell you if you interrupt."

"How did you know," I asked, "that they were up to something?"

"Well, they were whispering to each other, and they're definitely foreign, or she is. So anyway, let's make a plan."

Ted said, "Did you actually hear anything? I mean, actual words?"

"Well, no, I was too far off. But I could hear she had an accent, I'm sure of that."

If I felt again a certain hollowness at the heart of this adventure, I didn't say so. I was glad that Jean-Ann was not with us, as she had twisted her ankle the day before; she who had what I guessed later was a conscience but that at the time I felt only as discomfort, like a blister rubbed by a shoe. We were supposed to be looking out for suspicious characters and these people seemed to fit that description, although I had not yet seen them myself, only relied on Ted's and Anabel's reports. You see what you want to, in the end. Our eager search for suspicious characters was bound to produce some, before long. We had not exactly invented them, but we had perhaps drawn them into our orbit by our waiting—as the soldiers at the gun emplacement may have done when they were waiting for enemy ships to appear.

MY FATHER HAD TOLD ME, NEVER BELIEVE what anyone tells you until you have verified it for yourself. Seeing is believing. I needed to see these people. The rest of us followed Anabel along the double track left by tanks that led round the next hill, came up the stony path and the road, and arrived in the village without having to pass the houses where our parents might catch us

and make us go with them. We hopped over trailing brambles
and heather roots, pushed through knee-deep bracken on the
way. There was a stream you had to jump across, to arrive at the
stony part. We came up out of the deep tree-covered way that
was the old road to the village, before the new road to the ferry
had been built. At the cross-roads we turned down towards the
beach beneath the sandy outcrops of cliffs where the concrete
bunkers were. The tide was out, and you could clamber around
the end of the point, but not reach the gun emplacement, not
unless you went through the hotel gardens as we had yesterday.
There was a ruined cottage, roofless, its walls usually deep in
water, but visible at low tide. Beside it, a defunct jetty, ending in
rusting iron where its boards had dropped away. Ted said that
boats used to come in here but it had been abandoned since the
war. If you swam beneath it, in the shadow of its overhang, you
could hold on to its iron props and hang there among fish that
swarmed around you, as if they did not see you, or care. You
could feel them in the passage of water around your body. Bright
green weeds streamed from its rusty structure like hair. It was at
once alarming and enchanting, a shadowy darkened world. But
now we were not here to swim.

"Look, there," said Anabel, ahead of us in her divided skirt and
blue aertex shirt. I saw the backs of her knees, the hidden H of the
tendons that we all have, her smooth calves above socks and tennis
shoes. Anabel, our leader.

I looked where she pointed. They, the couple, were picking
their way around the point, just below the place where we had
been, under the hidden concrete look-out. The woman was barefoot, held her shoes in one hand, had hiked her skirt up. The man
had rolled up trousers and bare feet too, and wore a shirt with
sleeves that flapped. They tottered a little, clutched each other; the
rock must be slippery underfoot. Their clutching looked deliberate, though, as if they really wanted to hold on to each other and
not let go. The tide was coming in, beginning to fill the rock pools

and lift the green salad-like seaweed, and some of the rocks were smooth and wet already.

Ted got out his notebook and licked his stump of pencil. Ted, Anabel, Roger, Paddy, and I crouched in the shadow of a rock and watched our suspects come towards us. Ted moved his lips as he wrote, shoving his blunt pencil hard along the lines of his notebook. I liked that he always had that little notebook, and took things seriously. I also noticed and felt embarrassed for him that his writing was in capitals and often had spelling mistakes. The couple came slowly down the beach, careful over the rocks, sometimes up to their ankles in shallow water. The paddle-steamer that crossed the bay daily passed, far out. The beach huts were locked, further down the beach; nobody had come down for a swim or a picnic. Perhaps it was too early, or not yet warm enough. It could rain, as the clouds were moving in from the west, looming over the hill sideways like smoke from an invisible fire.

I watched the couple as they walked, he a little ahead of her, she trailing her feet in water. They looked ordinary enough. I began once again to doubt, which I discovered much later is the first sign of either losing or firming up belief. They were too far away for us to hear what they said. But since there was no way up from the end of the beach, they would have to come past us to find the path. As they turned, and came back towards us, Ted said, "Look normal!" We followed him out from behind our sandstone rock as if we'd just been out for a walk all along.

"Hello," said the man, as he passed. Foreign or not foreign? Hard to tell.

"Hello," some of us said.

The woman smiled at us. Anabel said boldly, "Nice morning," and the woman replied, "Yes, isn't it?"

An accent. Very definitely an accent, and not Scottish or Irish either. *Eessent it.*

They went ahead of us, towards the only path that led up to the village, if you didn't want to go paddling round the point again.

The tide had come in—I heard it in its altered whisper, as if a person had cleared her throat—and was slowly covering the rocks and filling the pools. The shining flats of sand were covered, the ruined cottage sank back underwater, the underside of the pier with its hanging green curtains was no longer visible. Everything changed here with the tide—perspectives, distances. As we came up the path behind the couple, keeping far enough behind them while straining to hear, small rain started pattering on the leaves above us.

We found it hard to hear the actual words they spoke and impossible to be sure enough of them to write them down in Ted's notebook. Ted said that they were speaking German—but how did he know? All we knew was from spy films, war films, people shouting *Achtung!* or calling each other *Schweinhund*.

The couple moved out of earshot soon enough and walked on down the beach and up the narrow damp path back to the village. They walked close, not exactly hand in hand but touching hands occasionally. When they spoke, they leaned in close as if towards a common space that neither quite inhabited. I noted their clothes, as that was easy to do. She: a full flowered skirt, white on blue, a white blouse, sleeves pushed up, a blue necklace, a shoulder bag made of woven material. She'd leaned for a moment to put on her shoes, one after the other, using a tree to prop herself rather than his shoulder. One tennis shoe, a rather dirty white, then the next. He: a light gray shirt with rolled sleeves, gray flannel trousers also rolled up, a belt, and brown shoes that looked a bit foreign to me. No socks. No bag. Nothing in which anything might be hidden. His hair waved back from his forehead, dark brown. He had a small bald spot. Hers was fair, and in little wisps around her head, curling on to her cheeks. She brushed it back from time to time as if she were too hot. It was a sultry morning in August, and we were all damp with sweat after scrabbling through bushes and then striding, half-running, bent so as not to be seen, to keep up with them. The rain began in small spatters, as if the clouds were leaking. They went into the shop nearest to the beach, where rubber balls and buckets and spades were hung outside, with bent postcards on a rack. They must have bought cigarettes, as he came out smoking, and she shook her head, no thanks. Then they walked quickly towards Roger's dad's hotel, he with a newspaper held over his head.

They strode in through the open front door under the witchy gable, as if they were expected. An inner door closed behind them. We had run up the street behind them, silent in our rubber soles, and dodged behind the hedge to watch them go in.

"They must be staying there!" Ted said. "Bingo! We'll be able to set Rog on them; there'll be super spying opportunities."

I said, "My dad says it's a robber's den."

"What's that mean? People actually get robbed?"

"No," Anabel said with her superior look, "she means that it's expensive for what it is. Apparently the food is terrible and if you ask for your points back they won't give them to you."

Paddy said, "Our dad went in to find out, once."

Roger said, "I don't think that's true about the ration books."

Anabel said, "It's normal to take people's ration books, but you're supposed to give them back if they ask. Anyway, it was ages ago, just after the end of the war, my uncle said."

"Dad said he was a spiv," Paddy said.

"What's that?"

"You know, the sort of people who were around after the war."

Anabel said, "Black marketeers. People who made a profit out of it."

"Oh. Right."

Roger was silent, but he looked uncomfortable. I nudged Anabel—his dad did work for the man, all the same.

I'd imagined the black market like a normal street market, only with the stalls draped in black. Anabel told me that it wasn't like that at all, an actual market, it was a way of getting hold of stuff that nobody else could. Spivs ran it—people in raincoats and slouch hats. Maybe Roger's dad was a spiv too, or the Major was. I pretended I'd known about them all along.

Ted didn't know about spivs, or ration books, it seemed, or points, or what you had to hand in to stay in a hotel. He'd told me that his family lived off food from the local farm, as most people in the village did. His father had a part share in his neighbor's cow, and there were always eggs and vegetables. It was different in the country.

"So," he said. I heard him trying to take back control from Anabel, "If they are staying there, what are they up to? It's a perfect place for signaling at night, anyone out at sea would be able to pick up a message. And there's the place Rog found, to hide stuff if need be. This is definitely suspicious." He put on his film-detective frown. Ted was always being either a detective or a commando. He read the Beano and Boys' Own Paper, I'd seen him with them. I don't know if he ever read books, but they had a TV in their cottage, I'd seen it flickering from outside, when he went in home. We did not, because we were on holiday, and even at home we only got it that year in time for the Coronation.

We went home, slowly dragging our feet up the road, not talking for once. Ted and Roger had gone back to their own houses, down in the village. After the excitement a sense of anti-climax was on us. What now?

I wasn't saying anything because the doubt I'd felt had not gone away. What if the couple were not up to anything? What if we were making the whole thing up? It would be impossible to say this out loud, especially to Anabel, who was walking with her head slightly bent, hair falling forward in a bell around her face, as if she were making complicated plans. I knew better than to interrupt her.

PADDY AND I WERE MADE TO GO TO THE BEACH that hot afternoon. We dug sandcastles for our baby brother to destroy with a smack of his fat hands, and then ran into the water to bathe, splashing each other and calling names. Our grandmother walked up and down at the edge of the sea with a big hat and a walking stick, making holes in sand and calling to us not to go too far out. Our mother lounged on a towel with the baby. We were a family again, not members of a gang. Aunt Laura and baby Susie sat on another towel and Susie gazed sadly at the sea and began to cry. Liz was stretched out on her own towel, surrounded by little bottles, a sunhat over her face, and her body looking sleek and white in a blue ruched swimsuit. When she went in to swim, she wore a white bathing cap with shell patterns on it, and I saw that she had red varnished toenails, as she tiptoed into the water. She seemed like an alien species to me. I could not imagine ever growing up to be like her. What happened to people like her? They became debs, then got married, had babies, had nice houses and husbands, I supposed. But what happened in between?

It was impossible to remain cross in the water, and Paddy and I came out panting and laughing, our swimsuits bagging around us, our feet thudding on the hard ribs of newly uncovered sand that drum up from your soles into your whole body. We flopped down on towels. It was a relief, to be there, to have adults watching us and giving us ginger biscuits and milky tea out of a thermos. It was like being let off, having free time after the dutiful stalking and note-taking and plotting you had to do to uncover a nest of spies.

Jean-Ann had left the day before, to join her family. I felt relieved, and a little ashamed. I had been worried that Anabel thought I had a sissy friend because she couldn't climb and cried when she was made to go and sit in the remote hole with old barbed wire in it that we called Solitary Confinement. There was something about Jean-Ann that had disturbed me. She was easy to tease but she had a sort of clarity about what mattered and what did not. I had felt— not exactly condemned by her inquiring gaze, but somehow found out. I had not stood up for her against Anabel, and I felt guilty, as she was my friend and I had invited her here, but there was also something tiring about having such a meek guest and having to look after her, and having to feel sorry for her and not say so.

Paddy said, when she left, "I know she's a bit wet, but she was really kind too."

I remembered that when he had fallen over and grazed his knee in the road while trying to keep up with us, Jean-Ann had stopped to comfort him and tie her handkerchief around the graze while I had simply hurried on to keep up with Anabel. He had noticed something I had tried to ignore. With Anabel, kindness seemed hardly to count.

NINE

I HAD SEEN TED BEFORE WE EVER MET ON THE MOOR, but I hadn't connected up my two visions of him. He sang in the church choir on Sunday evenings when we all went down to crowd into one pew for Evensong, our grandmother sitting right behind us, with Aunt Laura, Anabel's mother beside her singing too loudly in a sharp soprano that made me embarrassed for Anabel, our mother at the inside end of the pew, next to the wall, us children in a tight row. The procession always came in through the church door, the farm-yard behind them, and the door stayed open on warm evenings so that during the first hymn we could see the procession of cows coming in for milking, their sides splashed with mud or dung, the farm hand lazily switching them into a narrow throng to enter the farm-yard, their mooing pained voices in counterpoint to the high pitch of the choir. A church-warden led the way, carrying a long brass-topped mace and after him came the choirboys in order of size, the boy sopranos at the front—Ted, hair flattened, face clean above a white ruff, a blue gown reaching to his feet, which were still in the same grubby gym shoes he always wore. He kept his head up, as they all did, and looked straight ahead. His voice, blend-ing with the others, was pure and clear, not a note wrong. Beside him, another boy of his age, and behind them in ascending order, teenagers, young men, one woman, blonde above her ruff, her bosom puffing out her blue robe, and last of all, solemn and bald, hands folded, the vicar, following the church warden. The opening anthem came to an end, the organ wheezed a last note and the choir settled in to the ancient choir stalls beyond the chancel arch with its carved stone capitals, so that unless you went up for Communion, they were hidden from sight. So, there was another side to Ted, the boy who had scoffed at our hidden meeting place, the boy who knew everything and was permanently disheveled and scarred with scratches and insect bites and who seemed such a fearless leader. I watched him at the end of the service, the Sunday after we had met on the moor. Not a flicker, not a glance sideways. The procession moved back down the stone aisle of the twelfth-century church of Saint Nicholas, patron saint of sailors, the organ played the Nunc Dimittis, and the choir filed out after the churchwarden and were to be glimpsed dashing off to the vestry to change into their ordinary clothes. The vicar stood outside the church and shook hands with everyone, saying something to each of us. The organ reached its last notes inside the church. The cows were in their barn and their strong warm smell reached us as we followed our parents outside, to stand outside the milking sheds in our little groups before saying goodnight and taking one of the four paths away from the church, home. The long hill above the village darkened, insects buzzed, the church path was thick with holly and lavender and the trees curved overhead to make a tunnel.

I walked with Anabel. "Did you see?"

"Yes, can you believe it, he's a choirboy?"

"Well, I suppose anyone can sing. You don't have to be good to sing in a choir, do you?"

"Little angels," she said scornfully. "Well, at least now we have something to tease him with."

HIGH ON THE CHANCEL ARCH, INSIDE THE CHURCH, there is written *How beautiful are Thy dwellings, thou Lord of Hosts; my soul has*

a desire and longing to enter into the Courts of the Lord, my heart
and my flesh rejoice in the living God.

I was mesmerized by these words. They seemed to be the essence of a religion, a poetry that I longed to share in. The Dwelling was of course right here, in this church; the Courts of the Lord were our immediate surroundings, cow-sheds and barns included. My heart and my flesh were ready to rejoice in something, and maybe that something was the Living God. The green man who peered out between carved stone leaves, high under the eaves, with the other carved heads; a god of moorland and bracken, of undergrowth and trees; a god of the sea and the secret caves in cliffs; a god of the wind on the high hill that divided our village from the banal common-places of town on its other side. A god of secret places and quiet moments with nobody else there; a god I could imagine in the whisper of breeze in dry heather, as I waited, neck-deep in my trench, for whatever would happen next, and watched the slow progress of the ferry, back and forth across the harbor opening that separated us from the mainland. A Living God was somehow more accessible, less alarming than the God we were told about at school, always ready to disapprove and even punish, always on the look-out for bad behavior.

There were also the plaques and inscriptions about people—men—who had died in the War and the war before that. "Yours the anguish; his, oh his, the everlasting joy." Could you really feel everlasting joy when you had been blown up in a battle? And the women, not dead in wars, but with those long lists of dead children, some of whom had the same names, as if they had simply run out of both ideas and energy. *Oh, call him Theodore like the last one, that will do. He probably won't live.* I thought of them as I sat through the sermons, rose to sing the psalms and hymns, sank to my bare knees on the scratchy hassock embroidered by the Mothers' Union. Imagine spending your entire life having babies who died, one after the other. Being blown up in a war would almost be better. Either way, it was hard to imagine any everlasting joy.

Now that I knew that Ted was in the choir, I knew I would see him every Sunday evening, as the procession moved up the aisle and the singing choirboys, hymn-books in hand, took their seats. I would be able to watch him as he could not watch me. There was something satisfying about this that equaled things between us. In the week, whatever Anabel said, I would not mention his being a choirboy, as it would seem to break something open that should remain closed: a difference, perhaps, between private and public lives that everyone deserved to have.

I poked Anabel as we sat in the pew, when I saw him the next Sunday, walking past us in the procession. She said, "Butter wouldn't melt." It was something her mother said, when someone looked suspiciously good. I nodded.

The opening hymn ended. The choir sat in their choir stalls behind the chancel arch. I caught a quick flicker of a glance from Ted, looking up from his hymn book to catch my eye before he went out of sight into the choir stalls behind the stone chancel arch.

I WAS HARDLY EVER ALONE WITH HIM, because he always had Roger with him, and I was usually with the others. But there was a day—one of those nothing days, a Monday, gray and warm, when after the excitement of stalking the couple on the beach, for some unstated reason we had not met up for a while. We were outside the Village Hall. I was on my way to the shop for milk, and he— well, he was just hanging about.

"Psst, Nessa! *Fougasse!*"

"Hello. Oh, Fougasse. What are you doing?"

"Nothing much. You?"

"I'm going to the shop. What's up? Have you seen them?"

"Those people? No, not lately. My dad wanted me to help him, I was busy."

"Maybe we should try and find out more."

"Yeah. Hey, I've something I want to show you."

"What?"

"Come and see. Behind the hall, there's a place."

I followed him into the space behind the village hall, hidden by a tall bushy hedge from the house behind it, unseen from the street. The bushes were yew, thick and scratchy, like the trees in the churchyard.

Ted turned to face me. He looked urgent, a little flustered, and I wondered if he had found out something important that could not be talked about in the open. "You know what boys look like, Nessa?"

"Yes, of course." My naked brother, running up and down corridors; the baby, lying on his back to have his nappy changed, and his little tassel, as we called it, spouting up, making us laugh.

"Well, I've never seen a girl. So, you know, can I look?"

"You mean, with nothing on?"

"Well, if you just pull up your T-shirt, and let me look down your shorts, that would do."

He looked at me strangely, his eyes very focused. The yew bushes gave us shelter, and it was hot, and very quiet. I pulled up my T-shirt and saw him inspect my chest, nearly as flat as his own. Then I pulled my shorts down and saw him glance at my crack. Just for a minute, but it seemed like a long time. I pulled them up again, unsure of what I had just done. Paddy had seen me naked, of course, and so had my father, but I didn't think any other male person would. Then he pulled down his own shorts and after looking at his smooth brown stomach, concave under his ribs, I had a glimpse of something familiar, same shape as Paddy's, a little bigger, (but then he was older), and a wisp of dark hair. His intent gaze at me didn't waver.

"I know, I've seen my brothers. We have baths together, me and Paddy."

"Oh. Well, you see, I've never seen a girl before, but I suppose you're not grown, really, Nessa. Thanks, anyway." He leaned forward and gave me a quick kiss on the cheek, and then ducked away. I stood there, silenced.

I wondered if he would have preferred to look at Anabel, who was, as I was not, "grown." Nobody had ever kissed me who was not part of the family. I felt the spot on my cheek like a seal.

"It's okay." I said at last. "I better go, or they'll run out. At the shop. I said I'd be straight back."

"See you tomorrow. And, don't tell, eh?"

This. Something like this. Later, when I revisited this scene as a teenager, then as a young woman, I seemed to experience feeling something that possibly I did not feel at the time. There was nothing really sexual about it, as both he and I were innocent, I think, to a degree that few children are now. But I did revisit it in my mind— the first time anyone my age kissed me, the first time a boy looked at me, not exactly naked, but naked in the parts that mattered. I turned it over, every few years, to examine what it had meant—if anything. It seemed that events changed their weight and import as one grew older: important, even agonizing things lost their impact, while small events grew in size. I once told a therapist about it and was amazed at how interested she was, and how sure she was that it had affected my whole life.

In the end, there were just the facts: Ted and I, standing a little distance from each other. His request, my obedience to it. A lifted shirt, dropped shorts. A steady look, and then away. A silence, in which both of us I think were equally lost.

TEN

THE ADULTS—MY MOTHER, MY GRANDMOTHER, AUNT Laura—
were planning an expedition for the afternoon to Durlston
Head, to the caves there that were called Tilly Whim, after the
former quarry owner whose name had been Tilly. Whim was the
name of the kind of crane they used to lower slabs of stone down to
waiting boats—my father had told me this. Any other day, I would
have pretended to be excited about visiting the caves, just to sound
daring. I have never liked caves, or low ceilings that may fall on me.
Now, I thought, they are trying to get us away from what we are
doing—what we have to do. The beach hadn't worked; now they
would try the caves, and a picnic tea. Anabel grimaced when they
announced that we must go with them, that it would do us good.

"We don't want to be done good."

"But you'd love the caves! There used to be smugglers there."

"Well, they sound okay for little kids," Anabel said, yawning the
way her sister Liz yawned, childish things outgrown. I felt sorry
that I had ever shown any signs of interest. Paddy was hopping
with excitement at the thought of smugglers and I did my best not
to react.

"Well, I think you should come anyway, darling," Anabel's
mother said. It was clear that her mother and mine had been

conferring. "So do go and get cleaned up. There are clean clothes on your bed."

"Do I have to?" Anabel rolled her eyes at me.

"Yes, we're going to have a picnic tea afterwards, and maybe we'll go to the shops."

At the mention of shops, she cheered up. Shopping always mattered to Anabel and Liz, even here, even though they lived in London. Shopping was adult, it was what grown women did.

I had an idea that I wanted to follow through, vague yet persistent, so I told my mother that I was feeling sick, and wanted to stay at home. She looked annoyed. "But then someone will have to stay with you. I know, Liz might change her mind, I'm sure she won't mind staying. Then we can leave the babies with her too."

"No, really, I'll be fine on my own."

It seemed a great deal of fuss was being made about this Tilly Whim expedition, even with tea, and shops. I did not like being dragged around shops and took my father's point of view that it was a waste of time and money.

Then my mother looked worried, "Nessa, are you all right? You do look rather under the weather."

"I just probably need a quiet afternoon. I feel a bit tired."

"You've been over-doing it. I knew you were. It's a good thing Jean-Ann has gone home, I'm sure you were keeping each other awake all night."

Over-doing it, in my mother's language, was equivalent to running an unacceptable risk. It was the one thing she always told us to guard against, and this advice would follow me, unheeded, into my life as I went out late, drank too much, worked too hard or travelled too far and finally departed to marry a young man she disapproved of. I yawned again. I even felt, suddenly, exhausted. I too was relieved not to have to look after Jean-Ann, who had gone to Bournemouth to join her family. My mother looked at me with one of her searching looks, and I looked away.

My plan did not include Liz or the babies. I said again, "I'll be fine on my own, really. And I'm sure Liz wants to go; she always wants to go to the shops. You'll only be gone a few hours, won't you? Honestly, I'll be fine."

They were going to have their picnic tea on the cliffs, after the caves. They had already started packing thermos flasks and packets of biscuits in wicker hampers. I thought, who on earth wants to have a tea picnic with babies, and all this stuff? Adults were strange.

"Are you sure, Nessa?"

"Yes, go on, I don't need a baby-sitter, really. I'll just lie down, and read. I want to finish *Nicholas Nickleby*, I've hardly had any time to read it since we've been here, and we're supposed to finish it for school."

This clinched it. My mother looked both relieved and doubtful now, relieved since I had hardly been seen with a book since our arrival here. She went on cutting up sandwiches and cutting their crusts off to fit into a bakelite box that slotted into the fake wicker picnic basket with the thermos flasks. She had already peeled and sliced a cucumber. It all looked like a lot of work.

She said, "Well, that would be a better idea than more Enid Blyton."

Anabel said, "Enid Blyton is for babies, surely you don't read her still?"

I said, "Of course not. I'm reading *Nicholas Nickleby*, I said."

Anabel said, "Anyway, why don't you come? You know that smugglers used to use the caves? Maybe they still do. You should come, Nessa."

"No, I don't feel well—not really sick, just under the weather." My mother's handy phrase. I wondered if Anabel knew that I had a plan that excluded her.

"Maybe you're getting the Curse?" she suggested, slightly more friendly, yet still barbed.

"I'm not even eleven yet! I can't be!"

"Well, maybe you just have growing pains." In her family, this was the accepted ailment. You had growing pains, no questions asked, and had to rest. It was how Anabel came down at last from her superior position, offering me a way out.

"Yes, maybe," I said.

At last there was a lot of slamming of car doors after trips back to the houses to get things they had forgotten. "Take a cardi, it could be breezy!" And they all drove away. I was free.

I went upstairs to the room I now shared again with Paddy, and looked out of the window to make sure that they had all gone. There was the feeling of absolute emptiness that a house has when everyone has just left. An echo of them hung in the air, then faded. I watched the red dust settle back on to the gravel road. I felt light, not exhausted after all, but I flopped down on my bed next to the window for a few minutes, lay on my blue counterpane with my knees up, and thought. The world, the afternoon expanded around me. Everything waited for me to move.

The idea I had was imprecise. I knew I was going to find those two people while my family was out. I would discover what they were really doing, and if they were up to anything. I looked out to the dry mauve-brown expanse of the moor, its bent trees pushed sideways by the prevailing wind; black patches still showed where there had been a heath fire last year, and the bottom parts of some birch trees were still scorched, the gorse-like bundles of black sticks only beginning to put out a few shoots of green. Gypsies, people had said, were the ones who had set it alight, but then people blamed gypsies for everything, and I had never seen them on this, or any other part of the moor.

It was nearly half-past two. My family had taken far too long to get going, and I probably only had a couple of hours. The caves and the tea-picnic would make them all tired and grumpy and there would be some reason to bring the babies home early and even miss out on the shopping, I was sure. Anabel would be in a bad mood when she came back. Liz would complain about the boringness of shops in Dorset compared with London. My mother would say she was exhausted and would want to whisk us all off to bed as soon as she could, and sit down with Aunt Laura and a drink and one of Aunt Laura's cigarettes.

I waited until my mind cleared and then I skipped downstairs, part sliding down the banisters, and out through the side door where the bins were, and down the alleyway. The rough road was wonderfully empty of people and I walked down it, skidding over stones, glad to be unseen. I'd taken a shopping bag from the kitchen on my way out, in case anybody asked. In the village shop, the one on the corner where people went to buy cigarettes, soft drinks, and beach toys, I wandered at the back, looking at tubes of Rolos and packets of Murraymints, postcards that turned this place bright with fake blues and greens; I saw a bunch of fishing nets, a pile of buckets and spades tied together, a rolled beach umbrella, some kindling in bags, a packet of candles. I bought a tube of Rolos— cheap, but a real purchase—and lingered, in case anyone else came into the shop. Outside, the afternoon stung with heat and silence. It was as if the whole village had fallen asleep. The shop had its blinds up, striped green and white. The shop cat slept in a pocket of shade under the counter. I looked at postcards, as if I were thinking of buying one.

"Anything else, love?"

"No, just these, thanks."

"You're on your own today?"

"Yes, the others went to see the Tilly Whim caves. I didn't want to go." It was best not to mention feeling sick, as I'd just bought a tube of chocolates with sticky toffee inside. "Had many people in today?"

"No, it's been quiet."

I sauntered out, and down the hill under the shady trees, towards Roger's dad's hotel. My sandals scuffed up dust. I sucked my Rolo till it was gone, and then another. My mouth was gluey with milk chocolate. When I came to the hotel entrance I stuffed the sweets in my shorts pocket, hooked the empty shopping bag over my arm, and went inside. The darkness in here after the bright outside made it hard to see, and I stumbled down steps. There was an unknown woman at the desk who stared at me. "Can I help you, dear?" There are ways of saying "dear" that don't sound at all friendly.

"I wondered—I wondered if Roger was here."

"No, he's not. He went out with his dad. They may be back later. Better come back tomorrow."

Then I saw them. They were coming down the stairs, their outlines filtered through the dust that danced in the air between us, so that they looked somehow grainy, a little unreal. She came first, he followed. She was wearing a floaty summer dress that picked up air and showed her knees as she came down. Strong knees, small and square and springy like a racehorse's. He slid a hand down the banister and followed close behind, as if he couldn't let any space happen between them. They came down out of the grainy darkness into light from the side window. They were close together as they arrived in the hall. The man put a heavy key down on the desk, a brass ball attached to it. The woman at the desk took it and hung it on a board. The foreign woman stepped back, so she was near me, as I stood between her and the bright square of the open door. She was pretty, with her fair hair and slimness, and her legs were strong and brown in her summer dress, her toenails painted dark red in her open-toed white sandals. We looked at each other.

"Hallo," she said. "Who is this?" Not, who are *you*—but *this*?

The desk woman said, "Oh, a little friend of the manager's son. Run along now dear, why don't you?"

The foreign woman stuck out her hand, and I was stopped in my tracks. "I am Magda."

"I'm Nessa." I took her hand, cool and strong. I never shook hands with adults, or they with me. We stood there together, looking at each other.

"I'm pleased—pleased, that's right?—to meet you. And where is your friend?"

I said, "Oh. He's out. I'm coming back later."

The man behind her said, "Magda, we should go." His voice was deep, and from this part of the country, the sound a little soft at the edges. I thought—she has a name, it is Magda. I am not sure I wanted to know that.

We all moved a little way away from the desk, where the manageress or whoever she was glared at us.

Magda said, "First, can you tell us the way to walk to Shell Bay? We have never been. I hear it has wonderful shells."

I said, "Yes, it does, we go there to look for cowries. There are never a lot, but that makes them special. You have to look in the black patches, where the coal is washed up in tiny pieces; it comes off the tankers; you often find them there. You can find razor shells too, and mother of pearl. Oh, to get there. Well, just go down to the main beach and turn left and walk all along there, past the beach huts, and you'll get there. The best place is just before the point. It's quite a long way, actually."

"What is cowries?" she asked me, bending close to hear. The man waited. I felt his impatience, but I did not want this conversation to stop now, or perhaps I did, because she was too close, too interested, and I had said too much.

"Little shells. Like this." I closed my hand into a near-fist, fingers curled round as if to inspect my nails, to show her.

The man said, "I'll show you. We'll find some. Thanks, young lady." He wanted to go. The woman at the desk wanted us all to go. The hotel loomed behind us, dark and dusty with its shafts of light and she, the foreign woman, seemed too bright and airy a person to be in it at all.

I said, wanting to warn them, "You have to look out for unexploded ordnance, though. You know, bombs and things. There are still some there."

Magda looked at me, a small wrinkle between her eyes, not exactly a frown. "Bombs?"

"Well, probably more likely land mines. Leftover from—you know, the war?"

"Oh. But it is all right to walk there?"

"Oh, yes. Just, you have to keep your eyes open."

We all three moved toward the dazzle of that afternoon's sun. Magda pulled a floppy hat out of her bag and clapped it on her head. "Too much sun! I get red!"

I heard the woman at the desk murmur as if to herself, but so that I could hear, "No better than she ought to be." What did that mean? Who could be better than they ought to be, anyway? I turned and said, "I'll be back later. Tell Roger please." I thought I sounded adult, saying this in a cut-off way, to show her I'd heard. I followed the couple up the shallow stone steps to the road and pointed to the right.

"Down that way, you'll get to the main beach; just walk along to the left and keep going, and that's Shell Bay. It's past the nudist beach. Don't worry if you see some people with nothing on." I thought I should warn them of that too: the nudist beach had been established years ago, before the war, and most of the nudists were quite skinny and old, but they might be shocked.

It was the first time this summer that I'd given anybody the right directions, when asked. Our policy of misleading tourists had been thorough, so that the village must have been filled with confused people asking others which way to go. It was what everybody had been told to do during the war, to confuse the Germans when they invaded. There had been no signposts as they had been taken down. Everybody had been told to lie about where things were. But I told these two the truth, and pointed to my shopping bag to indicate that I had to go the other way, to the shop, or I'd have shown them, and waved them on their way. On my way home I stopped at the Higgins' vegetable shop to buy a couple of apples and a cucumber, just to show. Then I dragged my way back up the hill in the heat. The village clock said a quarter to four. The road past Ted's cottage was quiet, and there was no sign of Ted and his family, just a couple of rusty bikes piled into the hedge, and a winking cat on the doorstep like a striped tea-cozy, watching me in that narrow uninterested way that cats have. It still felt like a village in which everyone had fallen asleep. When I reached our house, I bit into one of the apples, left the other with the cucumber in the kitchen, imagined saying I'd heard that apple and cucumber were good for feeling sick, and went back up to my room. I lay on the bed and imagined I heard time ticking on. The ticks came more and more slowly. I thought of the man and the woman down on the beach, walking along barefoot at the tideline, looking for black patches and tiny striped cowrie shells with their pure insides in which sometimes a small piece of grit lodged, and the way she might count them in the palm of her hand and show them to him, and the way he might smile, and say in that deep voice, "Magda."

When the cars crunched up the road outside, one behind the other, and I heard the voices of them all shouting and calling, and the wail of my baby brother, and then the slam of the door, I think I had been asleep for some time. There was that feeling of waking suddenly and wondering what a new day would bring. But it was afternoon, and the day had brought enough already. I sat up, suddenly panicked, as if I had heard too much. It was like overhearing those things my parents said, when they thought I couldn't hear, or believed I was asleep. Things not meant to be heard, not bad things, only things that opened windows into private worlds I was not supposed to know about, but whose echoed murmur was a kind of reassurance.

I felt like a spy; I was a spy. But I was almost sure that those two people I had met this afternoon were not. What, if anything, was I going to tell the others? Nothing, I decided. This afternoon had been mine—my idea, my visit to the hotel, my conversation, mine to keep, or to forget. I imagined Anabel taking it over, telling me what it all meant. I remembered the firm touch of the foreign woman's fingers as she pressed my hand—as if she were pressing something into it—and the sound of her voice as she said her name. I remembered the way the man's voice caught—"Magda," as if he had a cold, or was about to cry. It wasn't a name I had ever heard before, and it had a resonance that didn't come with Maggie, or even Maya, who were girls at my school. I remembered the stern face of the woman at the desk—usually, there was nobody at that desk—and the strange thing she said. "No better than she ought to be." And how she had told me firmly to run along. Whatever it all meant, I wanted it for myself, to ponder over, and perhaps to find a meaning in my own good time. Not to give it to Anabel, who would probably know what "no better than she ought to be" meant, and be scornful; not even to Paddy, who would not understand. Not to Ted, either, because we had our own small hidden secret, Ted and I, and there was a slight shyness between us these days that neither of us, I'm sure, wanted to examine. It was as if our little group had begun to split just slightly, as we all did things and thought things that we didn't immediately want to tell. I felt the difference: it was like watching cracks spread in ice when you trod on it, when you knew you should go no further, but you crept forward anyway.

Eleven

Out of our separate houses, we met and came trooping down to the village once again, heading towards the hotel. On the way, Ted and Roger came to join us—*Fougasse!*—materializing out of a cottage door, a leafy alley. In through the side door of the hotel and out again before anyone could see us, through the ruined gardens and down through bracken and gorse towards the edge of the cliff. Roger warned us about the woman I had seen at the desk. "She's new, and she's a cow, my dad says, got her nose in everyone's business." We slid out of sight and earshot and outside again before anyone came.

I don't remember whose idea it was to keep on coming here; it was as if we couldn't help it. We met here instead of going up to the camp on the moor. I much preferred our look-out on the moor, where the heather whispered in the wind and the gorse in the sun smelled of hot jam. This look-out—the O.B. as Ted called it—was much grimmer, a real relic of a real war. I thought of the soldiers who had sat here, lived here, hour after hour looking out to sea, aiming their guns, scanning the horizon for German boats, expecting invasion. How hard it would be, to wait and wait and look out, and see nothing. You would want something to appear, just to make up for all the waiting. You might imagine it, or make it up.

Or something might happen, when you looked away. A German ship, an amphibious tank, a secret flotilla of small boats, armed, sneaking round the cliff to come ashore. You would want to be a hero, after all that waiting. You would want to fire, blow something up, sound alarms; you would just long to act. The soldiers who had been posted here had simply scrawled graffiti on the concrete walls, and smoked cigarettes, and cursed as they stared out to sea and nothing came. I knew what it felt like, to wait and watch. Once you were ready to do something, you really wanted to get on with it. You wanted something to happen. You needed it. I knew that now in my bones.

AFTER AN HOUR OR SO OF KEEPING WATCH, we left the dank enclosure, all a little depressed and quiet, and wriggled out on all fours to the cliff edge, to peer over, just in case.

Ted said, after a moment, "Look. Down there. It's them."

He pointed. We wriggled closer to the edge. They were down on the beach, below us. We were lying flat at the edge of the cliff now, looking down on them. We were on our stomachs in the bracken that grew right up to the edge, our bodies had flattened it where we lay, and I sniffed up the bitter smell of its crushed stalks. Around us, beech saplings and hazel grew in clumps, trees beginning to grow thickly again where once they had been cleared away. I inched closer to the edge, feeling my way forward with my fingers till I was level with Ted, close beside him. I saw the woman called Magda down below me put out a hand to her man, as she nearly slipped on seaweed, her foot moving suddenly sideways. I saw the tops of their heads, her hat, his bald spot. The white tennis shoes she wore—not sandals this time—for a stony beach. The pale streamers of the weed, darkening to salad green, left by the recent tide. The rocks and little pools. Everything slippery and unsure, where the tide had gone out. Everything seen from above, as if by God in heaven, or from a plane. They moved slowly closer to the cliff, to walk on firmer sand, where it was marked red and yellow as sandstone crumbled from the cliff itself. At low tide, they could have come around the headland. I saw—or thought I saw—his arm go around her, his head come down to blot hers from our view. The angle of her hat. Then she took it off, laughing. They stood poised on a rock that must have been still slippery. Was he kissing her, or were they simply holding each other up? I wanted to be down there with them, to say hello, to let the others know that I knew them, and they me. I wanted it to be ordinary, in some way that I couldn't define. I leaned as close as I could to the edge, and what I saw was the man easing the woman down on her back into the indent under the cliff, her face hidden from view now as his head came down to block hers, his body moved over her body, his hands on her, only her legs visible now, and her bare feet with their red nails, her shoes kicked off, and her skirt pushed up.

I lay in the crushed bracken beside Ted and Anabel, who was a little behind me. I saw Paddy out of the corner of my eye, to one side of us, hanging back as if he didn't want to go right up to the edge, and Roger, a silhouette against the sky. Above us and at eye-level sea-birds floated, guillemots and gulls. There was nobody out there in the small bay, no boats, no swimmers. It seemed that a great silence held us all still.

I saw that the woman was partly hidden by him now, that he was blocking our view of her, then helping her lie down on his jacket, which he had spread on the sand. Then he was lying on her, and I'm sure they were kissing, although I couldn't see their faces, just the back of his head and the way it moved, like a cat lapping milk. She spread out her legs and her dress came up, showing white flesh, and then he did something to his own trousers, and lay back down over her, and again the movement was catlike, the way cats rub themselves against chair legs, their tails curving above them, and then it was rougher and quicker and then he stopped moving and just lay there. They both lay there as if they had died.

Was it then that a stone skimmed down from the cliff-top to the beach? I felt a movement beside me. It must have been Ted who sent it, as if he were calmly spinning a pebble out over the sea.

He murmured to me, "I dare you."

The next pebble, attached to a clump of earth. Yes, I wanted to impress him. The secret we had between us from that time behind the village hall had attached me to him in a way I didn't like but could not resist. I wanted to tell him, that wasn't me, that tongue-tied girl. This is me, the fearless hero, like you. The one not afraid to chuck stones over the cliff-edge—see me dare.

Then another rock and a bigger clump of earth. We wriggled an inch or so back from the crumbling edge where bracken roots gave handholds and sea-pinks and the roots of small trees held the earth. The turf and stringy bracken stalks beneath our grasping fingers. The land was coming loose beneath us and we scrambled backwards on all fours towards the concrete walls of the gun emplacement as the small trickle from beneath the stone Ted—or someone—had loosed became clumps, falling in a series of thuds, and then a steady sound as if stones were being shot into a barrel from a great height. I hardly dared look at the others, but felt them beside me, flat in the long grass beside the concrete wall, hands flung out as if to hang on to the solid earth itself, that might be about to tip us all into space. A cloud of reddish dust rose from the cliff edge that seemed much nearer than before. I saw Anabel's face turned sideways, her eyes shut and mouth clamped shut too, like a mask. Ted raised his head, looked out towards the edge. There seemed to be a trembling in the air. "Christ," he said.

Roger propped himself on his elbows. "What happened?"

"I dunno."

"Was it us?"

"I dunno."

Paddy said, his back to the concrete wall, his face streaked with earth and maybe tears, "I want to go."

Anabel opened her eyes, resumed authority. "Stay here. Don't move. I'm going to have a look when all that dust's gone."

Ted said, "No, I'll go. You stay here."

He crawled back to the edge, to look over. Roger held one of his feet. We all watched. I saw Anabel look relieved and also cross that he had given the order.

"Can't see a thing. It's all dust."

We were all silent. The reddish dust went on rising against the blue of sea and sky and the sun baked our backs where we lay like a fallen army. Only the sea birds went on moving.

Ted said at last, "Looks like there's a big heap of stuff at the bottom, earth and stuff, that wasn't there before."

"What about the people?" I asked.

"No sign."

"Maybe they heard it and moved out of the way."

"Maybe."

"What were they doing, anyway?"

"I dunno."

I thought I could hear us all breathing, our breath somehow blending in with the earth itself, as if we were part of it. Everything breathes until it doesn't anymore.

"THE THING IS," ANABEL WAS SAYING AS WE ROSE to our feet when safely away from the cliff edge that seemed suddenly much nearer, "This is serious. We must swear not to tell anybody. Ever."

We faced her, solemn with what we knew, or were afraid we knew.

"Swear," she said again. One by one we raised our hands as she told us. "I swear that I will never speak to anybody about this as long as I live, so help me God, cross my heart and hope to die."

I thought: if you swear this, like the Official Secrets Act, then will someone come to kill you if you tell?

Paddy stumbled a little over the words. Ted and Roger stood close to each other, like soldiers. I was watching Anabel, who was enjoying this, I thought, now that she had taken back the lead. Her face was white this morning but her lips closed firmly after she spoke. She was solemn: our general, our leader. Ted frowned. Behind us the red dust still rose, clouding the air. There was a dense silence, now that there were no longer clods of earth bouncing down the cliff face, and the stream of loose soil seemed to have stopped. I felt where the bracken stalks had stung my hands as I'd clung to them, my face down in their bruised milky fronds.

"So, what do we do?" Ted shifted from one foot to the other, itching to take back control, or so it seemed to me. He was often silenced by Anabel, her bossy London voice and quick-thinking suggestions; but he was a boy, nearly her age, he knew this place and he thought he should be the leader. He muttered something and shifted from one foot to the other and scowled.

"We go back to lunch," she went on, "and if anyone asks, we say we were up on the moor all morning. We didn't come down here at all. Ted and Roger had better go straight home. We'll meet up later, to make a plan of action. All right, everyone?"

We all murmured our assent. For what else was there to do? I wanted to look over the edge one more time, to be sure, to see what I would imagine for many years to come. I wanted to ask Ted what he had seen, what had happened. But Anabel shooed us all away from the edge—"It's better"—and we went single file back up through the undergrowth, the narrow path between hawthorn and elder and tree roots, saplings and nettles, up to the hotel where we dived in through one door and out through another, past the scullery, past the boot cupboard and the coal hole, out into the road. We walked back up the road, and I don't know about the others, but I felt exhausted, as if I had come to the end of my strength. Ted and Roger peeled off from the rest of us when we reached the cross-roads in the village. When we reached our houses, Anabel, Paddy, and I separated without a word. I went straight to the bathroom and tried to throw up, but nothing came except a sour string of spit.

We never went back there after that. The summer was nearly over. We waited to see what might happen, and for a day or two, nothing did. We became childish, squabbled with each other, annoyed the adults. My father had gone back to work after a weekend here and we didn't see him again before he came to fetch us home; but I knew that now I would never be able to ask him the question I most wanted to ask and that from now on I was alone with it. It was, how do you know if you were right or wrong, and if you could ever do the wrong thing for a right reason, or because it was simply what happened next and there was no reason for it at all?

The local paper, the *Gazette*, came out, and our grandmother picked it up in the village post office and suddenly there it was, lying on a chair arm in the house next door when I went in to look for Anabel. The room was empty. I looked quickly. I was waiting for Anabel, fidgeting about.

"What's the matter, Nessa? You look as if you've got ants in your pants," Liz passed me by, on her way to the beach.

"Just waiting for Anabel."

"Well, don't bother. She's coming to the beach with Mum and me." Liz, with her hair tied up in a top-knot, her scarf flapping at the back like a little flag, carrying a beach bag with the capitals of Europe printed on it, Ambre Solaire in case there was any sun. Usually, she took no notice of me, her young cousin. Now she stopped and looked at me where I was fiddling with the edge of the curtain, waiting for her to go.

"Oh, all right. I'll just wait. I have something to tell her. Not important, but I thought I'd just see her. See you later."

She looked at me curiously, where I stood in my shorts and T-shirt, barefoot, a scruffy child still—a child just waiting to skim that newspaper story before someone took it away, hid it or put it in the bin.

"Well, Nessa, we're going to the beach with Mum, then she's got to pack; we're off in the morning. She probably won't have time to play with you today. So why don't you go back to your house?"

"I just want to say hello to Gran."

I had a minute, after Liz's lazy departure into the front garden, where she called out to Anabel to hurry up and join her. Their mother was out there with the pram, with little Susie in it, and a selection of beach toys stacked on one end. The morning seemed stuffy and slow, like moving through porridge. It all went on outside me, and I was alone in the room with the newspaper for as long as it took.

I heard someone coming down the stairs—my grandmother, I heard her slow creak on each step—and quickly folded the paper and laid it back on the chair arm. She came into the room.

"Oh, Gran, hello, I came to say good-morning to you."

She caught me by the arm. "Good morning, Nessa. Don't run off. What are you plotting? I wasn't born yesterday, you know. Did you come for Anabel? She's outside with Liz and Aunt Laura; they are going to the beach. Anyway, chick, stay a moment, I hardly see you these days. What are you up to?"

"Nothing. Nothing, really. I just came to see Anabel. And you, of course." Glancing out through the French windows, I could see my cousin cross the scrubby lawn and follow Liz and their mother down the rough road.

"Yes, well, enough about Anabel. I sometimes feel that she might not be too good an influence on you. You mustn't think you have to do everything Anabel says. And, another thing, those boys from the village you have been playing with. Your mother and I don't think it's entirely a good idea."

"Oh, but Dad thinks it's okay," I said, inspired.

"Don't say 'okay,' darling, it sounds so American. Does he? Does he really?"

"Oh, yes, he thinks it's fine. He said so." I knew my absent-minded father would not betray me.

"Well, your mother and I think you might spend a bit more time at home, not out on the moor all day long."

"But it's the holidays! We like being out there. We never touch any ammunition, honestly, and we're really careful about adders; we walk so they can hear us."

"Well, I suppose, if you're enjoying yourselves. But Nessa, darling, don't think you have to copy Anabel in everything. All right?" She looked me straight in the eye, as she held my wrist. She had a way of doing this, her hazel eyes in their nests of wrinkles suddenly hard and bright. I feared that my grandmother knew the truth about everything.

"All right." I nodded, ducked my head, and wriggled away. Smiling, she let me go. The newspaper stayed where it was on the chair arm as we both left the room, and next time I looked, it was no longer there.

TWELVE

IN THE SHOP, THEY WERE TALKING ABOUT the couple from the hotel. I could hear the muffled voices that adults put on when they gossip, their lips like ventriloquists', their eyes stretched wide. I was there with Paddy later that day, having been sent down to buy potatoes before early closing. We lurked near the counter, where a couple of people from the village were talking to Mr. and Mrs. Higgins, the grocers. I liked coming to the shop, where it was always rather dark and the vegetables were kept in sacks on the floor and things like sugar came in blue paper bags. It smelt of earth and greens and floury baking from the back of the building where the Higgins lived, where Mrs. Higgins was usually making a pie.

Today, she was at the high counter, measuring out raisins into blue bags. Mr. Higgins, old and just as white-haired as his wife and only slightly taller, weighed vegetables on the brass scale and handed a brown paper bag to a customer.

I heard, "Yes, but they weren't married. Of course, they put Mr. and Mrs. Smith in the records at the hotel, but then there were their ration books, with their real names. Sandra Dorwood saw them, working at the desk. Seems she was Polish. Came over here with a husband during the war. Mind you, they were good fighters, the Poles."

"But what were they doing at the hotel? I heard they were the only customers. Seems the Colonel or Major or whatever he calls himself isn't doing too well down there."

"Well, he's still giving them war-time rations in the restaurant, letting people go hungry, is what I heard. And the place is a mess, all cobwebs, hasn't been cleaned in years. Why anyone would stay there is beyond me."

I nudged Paddy and we sank back to the back of the queue, to hear more as we waited our turn.

"Seems that the young man was from around here. Wimborne, wasn't it? Somebody said he'd been in the army. But what about her? Not a sign of her. No better than she should be, if you ask me. So what they were doing, well, they were having a dirty weekend, weren't they? She a divorced woman and a foreigner too."

"Ssh, there's children here."

Mrs. Pyle and Mrs. Gould turned round and looked at us, and the other woman, Mrs. Gimson from the farm, just in for a box of candles, thank-you May, and dropped their conversation to whispers.

"Still, it's a shame. He was dead on arrival. We mustn't judge, must we. What will be."

"Maybe someone else judged him," murmured Mrs. Pyle, "up there, looking down."

May Higgins, her brown face, her cloud of white hair, her gnarly hands passing the box of candles—"That'll be one and eleven, thank you"—only smiled, her wide friendly mouth over yellowing teeth. She was one of the friendliest adults I knew, and she was only the size of a child.

I stepped forward with my shilling held in my palm. "Just some potatoes, please."

"Help yourself, duck, fill up a bag, will you? My back's sore today."

Paddy and I exchanged glances, our hands in the earth around the yellowish potatoes. I felt the warm graininess, like feeling for eggs. Our hands grubby as they had been the morning of the cliff-fall, we presented ourselves at the counter.

Mrs. Higgins said, "I hear you've been playing with the Payne boy from the hotel, haven't you, and young Ted Samways."

It wasn't a question. Everyone in the village knew these boys, so of course they knew about us too. We were not as invisible as we'd thought.

"Best take care, mucking about where there's explosives still, dear. And those two are bad boys, you know what I mean? Not your sort, anyway, though I've nothing against their families. I'm surprised your parents haven't told you. Don't want to get into any trouble on your holidays, now, do you?"

"No, Mrs. Higgins."

"Well, on you go now. Is that enough for your big family? Sure you can carry that home?"

"Yes, thanks, goodbye, Mrs. Higgins. Yes, fine. Bye now. Thanks."

We dragged the potato bag between us, and it banged against our legs as we went. I thought about what I'd heard. Not married. Dirty weekend. Divorced woman. Foreign. A local man. Dead on arrival. What did it all add up to? I must ask Anabel what a dirty weekend was, and how you had one. Was it to do with being a spy? Was "dirty" the same as "illegal" or "black market" or even "treason"?

There were so many things I could not ask, now, and it was all because I had met them, I knew them, they had talked to me and I'd told them how to find cowries. They had become real, and nobody knew, apart from me, who they really were. He with the catch in his voice when he said her name—*Magda*. She with the floating dress and the strong knees, and her question, "What is cowries?" and her peep-toed shoes, her painted nails. Real in the way that I myself was real, and my brothers, my family, my friends. There was no way that I was going to doubt that.

I woke with the urgent feeling that I had to tell someone what happened, but by breakfast time, with the ordinary processes of the day, the pouring of cereal, then milk, the smell of toast, its

burned edges, marmalade dripping down the jar, Charlie scream-
ing for more toast fingers, the need faded. My parents seemed like
people at a distance. My grandmother, further away still. Anabel
with her grim, contained expression refused all conversation—
she would kill me if I were to tell. Only Paddy might be feeling
something like this—but no, he was younger, he had started playing with his toy cars again, running them across the wood of the
hall floor, crashing them into the edge of the carpet. Brrrroooom,
crash. I complained of a stomachache and was sent to lie down,
then dosed with Milk of Magnesia. I lay on my bed by the window
and gazed out at blameless blue sky, then clouds, then rain, then
sun again. Then I came downstairs and said I was better, and my
mother seemed satisfied. Life seemed to have become flat, listless,
there was nothing to do. My mother said that the holidays had
gone on far too long. Aunt Laura agreed. Outside the wind of late
August rose and battered the trees, so that they were like wrecked
ships at sea. The sea itself boiled up at its edges. Broken twigs and
branches, some with acorns on them from the whipped ends of
oak trees, littered the road. Everything seemed to be changing. I
wanted to see Ted, to have him tell me that it was not my fault, any
of it. But that was impossible.

WE HARDLY SAW TED AND ROGER AFTER THIS. Perhaps their parents had told them to stay away from us too. There was something
unsaid, to be picked up only by glances, nods, warning gestures.
The sentences begun in French by adults that ended as soon as we
appeared. "Pas devant . . ." The holidays were coming to an end
for us too. It was time to pack up, load the cars, brush sand from
the floors of the houses and close them up again. The beach emptied, the wind grew chill, nobody wanted to sit out on the sand or
bathe in the sea. We went up to the moor, along the sandy path
and up the hill for one last time, "to get our things" as Anabel said.
The holes and tunnels in which we had spent so many hours keeping look-out already looked abandoned. Sand trickled down and

covered the few small objects we'd left there: a rusty kitchen knife, a candle in a jar, a box of stale biscuits. We filled our pockets and left, without saying much—what was there to say? Anabel and her family were leaving by the afternoon train to London and our dad would drive them to the station. Paddy and I kicked about for the rest of the day in our emptied house and waited for the month to come to its end.

I saw Ted once more, in the church choir on that last Sunday, when we stood to see the little procession pass up the aisle, the boys in their white ruffs over blue surplices, hymn-books held high in their hands, as they marched up towards the chancel arch to take their places in the pews there. I saw his feet in dirty sneakers coming out from under his cassock: the same sneakers he had worn all summer, brown-stained with bog water, as were ours. At the end of the service, after the *Nunc Dimittis—Lord, now lettest thou thy Servant depart in peace, oh, what a hope*—the organ burst out its rough music and the choir in blue robes and white surplices processed towards the open door. He didn't raise his eyes from his book; I saw him pass me by without a glance. The organ's sudden thunder sounded like the wrath of God.

PART III
PALIMPSEST

THIRTEEN

THERE WAS NO WAY TO IMAGINE, in 1952, the Manor Hotel as it is now. It is painted yellow, for a start, and so its gables and turrets and small-paned windows no longer have a gothic air, but rather a jolly fairground look. In the nineteenth century, when it was built, it was already known as a sort of folly, the whim of an eccentric member of the aristocratic local family, designed as his sea-side retreat. He and his family used to drive here in pony carts from the family seat inland, and spend their summer holidays in their Gothic seaside house, with grooms to look after the horses and servants for the children. There are photographs on the walls of the children in their bunchy beach clothes, sailor collars and wide hats, and of the groom taking them out on their ponies with picnic hampers and all the trappings of Edwardian upper-class family outings.

In our childhood, it had reached the nadir of its post-war decay. The fierce woman at the desk, the shady Major, even Roger's father have long since given way to a whole new set of people. The place changed hands again a few years ago, and was painted this shade of buttercup-yellow as if for a joke. Its name has been changed to The Hungry Bunny, and there's a human-sized statue of a rabbit holding a menu at its door. The waiters, mostly young Europeans on summer jobs, sashay out across well-mown grass with trays of drinks to set down at tables, or plates of well-cooked food for those who have come to lunch here. They have haircuts that leave their napes bare; they are tanned and smooth-skinned; they are young, having a taste of work in summer-holiday England before going on to something more serious. They have German, French, Australian accents. They set the plates down and say, *Enjoy*.

The sun shines out across the lawn, across the bay, and the people eating lunch sit in the shade under a striped awning in this summer of unusual heat. The sun is still strong, the sky cloudless. The servers wear chic gray T-shirts with the logo of the hotel in white, a picture of an upstanding rabbit, or hare. They wear bright white sneakers with no socks, and gray-green shorts. Across the lawn, a bar is set with bottles of Spanish and Portuguese wine in coolers. There's a wood-fired oven, where a young man is making—not pizza, nothing so ordinary—but thin crackling flatbreads that will be smothered in sun-dried tomato and mozzarella, with good black olives. The scene would be Mediterranean if it were not so English: the big trees, grown to height at the edge of the lawn, shading further lawns where deck-chairs are set for after-lunch snoozing and afternoon tea; beyond that, stretching down to the path that runs along the cliff-edge now, fenced before it reaches the beach. To where a gray concrete building still stands, "Fort Henry" named for the Canadians who built it in 1943, when they were far from home. There is a plaque there, telling of the four men who went down off the Old Harry Rocks in a primitive amphibian tank. Also, two boards provided by the National Trust about this place in war-time, the D-Day preparations, Operation Smash. It's a destination for tourists, now. There are web sites and apps. And next year there will be more of it all, TV and radio programs, as it will be seventy-five years since the actual operation to save Europe.

I stare out at a landscape I know by heart, that is yet utterly strange. I'm meeting Paula, my old friend and London editor here; she liked the idea of a day off by the sea and lunch in a place that has also become famous across the south of England for its home-grown food. She's driving down for the day, crossing on the ferry from Bournemouth, and hasn't arrived yet. I'm happy to wait, sit, think, be astonished at the changes a new century can make, and sip a glass of Portuguese rosé at a rustic table under a bower of roses, sniff up wood-smoke from the oven, nibble the olives that arrive in a little pot. The well-heeled families, the couples, cavort around me. The men wear deck-shoes with no socks and have sweaters draped around their necks. The women are in tight jeans or thin dresses, and wear leather wedge-heeled sandals and have big expensive-looking bags. Sometimes there is a panting dog underfoot, to be led to the dog-bowl full of water at the end of the bar. Everyone, this summer, is being reminded to drink water, even the dogs. But the wine is going down quite freely too.

The shape of the bay is nearly the same. Only the dunes have shifted and trees have grown. The long spit of sand curves out towards Shell Bay, doubles back towards the ferry and the harbor. The white frill of waves spreads in fan-shapes across the expanse of sand. Today, the blue of the water is dotted with the sails of small boats. The car ferry for the Channel Islands, or Cherbourg, crosses the horizon from side to side. The far-off windows of the mainland glitter.

A young server asks me if I'd like to order anything else.

I'd like to order up the past, to glimpse it just for a minute: our young selves in our shorts and grubby sneakers scuttling past the windows of the hotel and dodging between bushes into the thicket that was almost impenetrable, brambles and ivy and scrub, to the place at the edge of the cliff where the gun emplacement was invisible except from the sea, wrapped as it was in foliage. I'd like to say—look, this is what it's going to become. We're going to survive into this time, its glossy appearances, its plentiful food, its growing inequalities, its self-seeking politics. Its charm, its lies, its illusion of permanence. Nothing is permanent, that I can see, except per-haps the earth itself, and the sea that goes on shaping it.

A voice calls, "Nessa! Hello!" from across the grass and I turn to watch Paula coming towards me, her long legs in narrow white pants, her eager leaning-forward posture, her wide mouth and earrings, her sunglasses and wildly waving hand. "I'm here! I made it, finally, I thought we'd be stuck on the other side forever, there was such a queue, but here I am. I parked round the back. Hey, you look great! You're so brown! So good to see you."

"So glad you could come." I stand up and we kiss on both cheeks, clutching each other's arms.

"Oh, good, you got a drink. Sorry to make you wait, but you know how it is, with the ferry and of course everyone wants to come here, in this weather. Hasn't it been incredible? Awful in London, of course."

"It's fine," I tell her, "I mean, I wasn't waiting long. I was thinking about how it used to be. After the war, here."

"Oh, yes, of course, you were here as a kid, I'd forgotten."

"I knew a boy whose father worked at this hotel. It was a rundown place then."

"But how are you? It's been ages. I know, e-mailing and everything, it doesn't seem as if I haven't seen you. How's the writing?"

I let go of my anecdote about Roger, the hotel, Major St. John, the post-war village that was still licking its wounds, emptied of half its inhabitants. What was I going to say? "Well, I came here to finish that piece on emotion and reason; they want it by the end of October, but I'm not sure that I can."

The book is to be about empiricism and prejudice, news and fake news, science and gut feelings, all the polarized notions that we live among. I have written very little of my promised contribution—or little that satisfies me.

"Can't you just expand your original article?"

"Maybe that's what I'll do." It seems like the easiest course—and really, what have I to prove, these days, to the world of academia?

"I think I have writer's block," I tell her. I have been mooning about through weeks of unusually hot weather, casting my mind back to what happened here more than sixty years ago. I have been playing hooky, truanting, messing about. Worrying about those bones and about some foreign teenagers, and pieces of a puzzle I can't yet fit together. Paula is a good old friend—we have known each other for years. Perhaps she will understand.

"The food's good," I tell her. "Shall we order? Those flatbread things are delicious, much better than any ordinary pizza, they have good salads too, and I'll get us some more of this rosé."

"So you came back to your grandmother's place? Why England?"

"The house was free. I thought at least here I'd be able to get some writing done. Also, we're thinking we might sell it. Anyway, there are a lot of repairs to be done, whether we do or not. I told my brothers I'd make some lists of what's needed. As for writing, the weather's been so extraordinary, it's been so hot, I'm thinking I may not be able to do it here anymore than I could in a library back home. Maybe I should have tried to go to a writing retreat, like MacDowell or the VCCA."

She looks at me, curious. I must sound peculiar, excessive, irritable. Perhaps I've simply been alone too long. "What's happened? I thought you were happy to do it. I mean, it's an honor, isn't it, to be asked?"

"I don't think I can go on writing history. Or even any theory of history. I think we've come to the end of it. It may be just my age."

She shrugs and smiles, being my age too.

I go on, "But the current mess seems so far from anything we imagined might happen. I don't want to write about the coming of the barbarians."

A glossy young woman, a blond plait down her back, brings our food—the tomato and mozzarella flatbread with herbs, olives, the works. Herbs from the walled garden, olive oil in a little flask, with rosemary. She smiles. We top up our wine. The day is perfect, the view is perfect, the food is good, the sun is out, people are enjoying themselves; the dingy hotel of my childhood has become this beautifully run, manicured, cared-for place. The walled kitchen garden

with its espaliered apple and pear trees at our backs has every vegetable and herb you could hope for and is warm and spiced with
the smells of rosemary and lavender gently toasting in the sun. We
are alive, we are reasonably successful, we have arrived at this time
and place having known very different ones—she, the daughter of
war-time Polish immigrants, I the returning native from years in
America—and now, surely, all is well. Except—and it is an excep-
tion nobody can overlook, surely—our world seems to have been
taken over once again by criminals and robots, venal politicians,
buffoons and gangsters, and nobody seems to be able to do anything about it.

"You seem depressed," Paula says to me. "Surely, it's not all that
bad. Perhaps it's being alone all this time? I mean, Brexit, yes, it's
insane. Why on earth would anyone would want to resign from the
best club in the world? And the US—God, that man. But something will happen. Something always does. You, as a historian,
must see that."

"Are you quoting Gibbon to me? The Decline and Fall? Or is
it the Whig theory of history, inevitable progress? Or is it Marx,
thesis and anti-thesis?" I feel combative all at once. Is she goading
me into action?

"Well, you know more about all that than I do. I'm just suggesting this is not necessarily the End of Times. Now, drink up, you're
depressing me too. Here we sit, two old biddies going on about the
awfulness of the world. But look. Look around. Isn't this—here,
now—just beautiful? Haven't some things simply improved?"

I breathe deeply, look around me at my familiar place, the place
that has always done it for me, transformed my drab school days
into holiday, made me wild with joy. Where is that joy now? Here,
if I can notice it. In the wide unspoiled curve of the bay, where
nobody is fighting today, nobody defending, and nothing except a
line of mature green trees interrupts the view.

We eat in companionable silence. Then I tell her, "Something
happened here, when I was quite young, and it was unresolved, I

never knew if I—we—had really done a terrible thing or not. And a recent discovery made me think about it all again. Those bones on the beach I told you about. I began to remember some things I'd chosen to forget."

She leans forward, elbows on the table, to listen. She's always had this ability to pay attention, no matter what is going on around her. "Tell me more?"

"Two people, a man and a woman, died here, possibly because of what we did. And I don't know if there's a connection with those bones, but I think there is."

"Nessa, what on earth did you do?" She tips her glasses up on to her head and looks hard at me with her blue gaze. I'm always amazed by Paula's eyes and today they are like chips of sky.

Around us the families, the couples, the thirsty dogs, the young servers carrying trays with glasses of wine. I tell her, "We made a cliff fall on them, because we thought they were spies."

"You made a cliff fall on them? How?"

"We were stalking them. We lay on the cliff top and we threw stones, and clods of earth, and the cliff gave way on top of them."

"Hold on, you said you made a cliff fall? How do you know you did?"

"Well, we started it off," I say. "We began it."

"But pieces fall off cliffs on their own," Paula says. "Maybe you only threw some stones and the cliff crumbled at the same time." She takes a sip of her wine and looks at me, eyebrows raised. "Maybe it was an accident. A coincidence."

I think—history never takes accidents into account, because they provide excuses. There has to be—doesn't there?—cause and effect, and human agency. I have been trained all my life to look for cause and effect. Yet perhaps there are—yes, I know there are—multiple causes, always, and ones that will remain undiscovered. As the detective on the beach reminded me.

Then I tell her, "The bones they found, a few weeks ago, just before I got here, were on the beach where it happened. A woman's skeleton. I can't help thinking that it might be her. I think it's really why I haven't been able to do anything else."

She looks at me, eyebrows still raised, my old friend, my trusted editor over so many years; she who has gently handled my manuscripts, checked my ideas, argued with me, flattered me, challenged me, laughed with me; who has been there, who has made me work in a way that few people have been able to.

"You really think it was that woman? The one you dropped a cliff on?"

"I think it must have been. It was in the same place. They took the man away to hospital, where he died, I knew that, but they never found her, and nobody seems to have known who she was. Somehow, nobody ever looked for her. They must have thought she'd just left, and that he was alone."

She finishes her mouthful of herb-decorated, olive-rich sun-dried tomato and its crust, and takes another sip of her wine. "Did you see at the time what actually happened? I mean, it could have had nothing to do with you at all."

"I didn't look over the edge afterwards, no. I didn't see anybody dead. But what I haven't told anybody, ever, is that they were having sex. Before the cliff fell. I saw that."

"On the beach? Under the cliff?"

"Yes. I saw them kissing, then she lay down on his jacket and they did it. Made love. Had sex."

"You're sure that's what you saw?"

"Yes. I mean, at the time I didn't really know. But later, when I remembered, I knew that was what they were doing. It made it worse."

She's silent for a moment. Then, "Nessa, you really never told anyone? Why?"

"I couldn't. Anabel said it didn't happen. So—I guess I just suppressed it. But this summer, all this time later, I'm having to remember it all over again. The point is, if you didn't know what you were doing—and I don't think we did—can you be held responsible?"

She says at last, "Whatever you did, or didn't do. I just wonder if it's worth feeling guilty about anyway, all this time later. There's nothing much you can do about it, is there?"

"No." Even the therapist I briefly visited at the time of my divorce from Roland never asked, and I did not tell—not out of any desire to hide the story, more that it had sunk so deeply into me that curiously, I thought it hardly mattered. The sessions were mostly about our sex life, or the lack of it, and him having sex with someone else. I never thought to mention the couple making love on the beach—the first and actually the only time I had seen anyone else do it, apart from in films, where you see it all the time. We answer the questions we are asked, so often letting the questioner lead the way.

"The trouble was, there was never anybody who would corroborate it or even talk about it. I don't know if it connects. I can't be certain." Yet as I say this, I'm thinking, it connects the way those bones connected, one beside another, one linked to another, a little imagination, care and science making it all possible. You fit one small thing to another, and another, and eventually it forms a whole. My life since then, marriages, even my career as an academic historian: the choices I have made, what I have expected of life. The times I have chosen Anabel's version over my own.

Paula says, "Well, don't feel guilty about it, for God's sake, it's too late."

"I was the only one of us all who met them; I was the one who knew who they were."

I WAS THE ONE WHO SAW HER KNEES pushing out her floating cotton dress as she came down the stairs as if she walked on air. I told them how to get to the Shell Bay beach, and what a cowrie shell looked like, and about the nudists and the mines. I was there, in that dusty hall of the hotel, watching them go out through the open door into rays of sunshine for a simple walk on the beach. I'd taken her hand, heard her tell me her name and told her mine. When you know somebody's name, they become real to you. I knew her name once, and I have forgotten it. I was the one who betrayed her—because she had trusted me, not the others, with the secret of her unguarded self. I'd known it instinctively as a child and I knew it now: when a person becomes real to you, it becomes unthinkable to wish them harm. Our enemies are always people we do not know.

WHEN WE HAVE FINISHED OUR LUNCH, I take Paula down to the beach, show her where the cliff-fall was, where the trees have been cut away and the raw red sand flattened. We walk across the sand, undress beside the upturned boat and wade into the water. With this summer's heat, even the seas around England have become warm. Pale green weed floats at our ankles, then we reach clear water over sand, and launch ourselves in our discreet swimsuits, out towards the anchored boats. She is a strong swimmer and pulls away from me in a stylish crawl, her pale arms lifting and falling as her stroke carves the still water. She comes back to me smiling, her hair soaked flat on her scalp. "I needed that. You are lucky, to be here, really. London is so dried-out and oppressive, even the trees on the Heath look as if they are about to give up."

"You could stay. Keep me company."

"No, thanks for the thought, but I have to get back to work. I have a stack of manuscripts from agents waiting for me online, and an author from Australia about to show up any minute. But you could come up and stay with me, if you want a change of scene? If this all gets to be too much?"

I'm half-regretful, half-relieved. My solitude, in these weeks before Bruno comes to join me, is important, even if I am not sure why.

We're floating, our heads and toes visible above the water, when she says, "You might ask yourself, what does it mean to you now, that story? Is it important? Is it the coincidence, that the bones came to light just before you arrived?"

"It's important. But I don't quite know why. It's like there's a missing piece, something I don't yet know."

We lie on the water, the huge sky and its few harmless clouds above us. Afternoon heat builds over the land, and at sea, there's hardly a ripple. Silence, apart from a boat engine, a gull cry. Far away, the weekenders on the beach.

"Well, don't let it depress you," she says as we wade ashore. "It sounds as if what you did was a mistake. You didn't intend to hurt anyone. You were a child, for God's sake. Let it go, Nessa. Or find the missing piece and put it in a story. And, come to London, if you can bear the thought in this weather. I'd love to have you."

When Paula leaves and I go back to the house after waving her little white car away down the winding ferry road, I feel more than ever alone. Yet my mind works over our conversation, and the question—what does this matter in the present? Give up guilt, Paula said. You were a child. But I know now that there was more to it than this—something I have not yet understood.

When I was twenty-seven, after my divorce, I went to America to study and later, take up a teaching post. I'd done a teaching degree at London University and taught there after my history tripos, and a lecturer had made the contact for me with a colleague at Columbia. Two years later, I met Bruno. From where I am now, I look back on these choices; nothing about them looks inevitable, or pre-ordained, or even particularly well-thought-out. I seem to have reeled from one thing to another, experimenting with life.

Looking back, I see my departure to the US as both adventure and escape. I hardly thought about what I was escaping from: suffocating Englishness, the rigidities of the class system, lingering questions about my first marriage and early divorce—and what else? We take ourselves with us when we move about the world—of course we do—and yet, I seem to have managed to leave the first section of my life behind. I visited, of course, both with Bruno and on my own. But the tie had been cut, the ship had sailed, I was not the person I had once been.

Until now. It's as if she has been waiting for me in this house, the person I would have been if I'd stayed. Here, my American life seems like a dream. Did I dream my life with Bruno, our house, my work, my American friends and colleagues? Have I been here all along, in this other reality—in the place where those bones have remained buried all this time, only waiting to be dug up? The symbolism appears excessive, even absurd. Yet here it is.

FOURTEEN

IN THE CHRISTMAS HOLIDAYS AT THE END of that year, 1952, when I was just eleven, I went to London to stay with Anabel's family in Ladbroke Grove and entered a life I could never have imagined. I knew my aunt and cousins, of course, we'd spent the summer holidays together, but I didn't know their house, or how they lived in it. I remember stepping in through the front door for the first time and having a sensation of weight above me—all that stone, all those floors and staircases. It was a tall house, large but not as fashionable as it would become later in the century. It was a house of layers: on the top floor, our great-aunt Hermione—our grandmother's sister—had a room, the one I was to sleep in as she was away on a visit to her other sister in Edinburgh. Next down, there were Anabel's and her sister Liz's rooms and a bathroom. There was a room for the baby, Susie, and one for the nanny. Then, going on down the turning stairs, you reached a whole floor that belonged to Anabel's father, Uncle Mark. He had a bedroom of his own and a large study, with a desk at which he sat, and bookshelves full of books; he sat with the door open so that he could see who came up and down the stairs, and I used to hurry past, not to be caught by his accusing stare. Below him, there was a dining room and another room used as a sewing room, with a narrow bed in it, in which I suspected Anabel's mother, Aunt Laura, slept, although nobody ever said so. The basement kitchen was where she, Aunt Laura, sat over cups of coffee and Woodbine cigarettes, while the kettle whistled on the counter top and groceries waited to be unpacked. The basement was below street level, so you could see the feet of people passing on the pavement at eye-level and the wheels of passing cars and the occasional dog lifting a leg to pee.

I had never been in such a stratified house. Everyone seemed to live at his or her own level. We never sat all together in the dining room to eat. Anabel and I ate with her mother at the kitchen table, with the baby Susie in a high chair and her young nanny in attendance. In the evenings, my uncle and aunt sometimes ate in the dining room on the ground floor—on the rare evenings he was in, that was. Mostly, Aunt Laura stayed down in the kitchen with instant soup and Nescafe and her cigarettes. Liz never seemed to eat anything; she was always either out or on a diet—banting as my aunt called it. Young men called for her and she came downstairs in the evenings smelling of French Fern and swishing past us in heels and a flouncy dress, to be whisked away in her current beau's sports car. She was "doing the Season." Uncle Mark never came down to the kitchen, either. He ate mostly at "the Club," and used taxis to get there. I observed all this and couldn't wait to tell someone—my mother? Paddy?—about the strangeness of it all. In our house, everyone ate together, my mother cooked, everyone had bedrooms on the same floor, my parents slept in the same room, and we all shared a bathroom, and till now I'd imagined that this was how people lived. London was evidently different. London was "posh." But it was also uncomfortable, and alarmed me; it was so easy to get things wrong, to be caught in Uncle Mark's critical stare as I scuttled up or down the stairs past his open door; worse, to meet him on the stairs as he huffed his way back to his lair. It was easy to be caught making too much noise, disturbing him or upsetting Liz's afternoon rests that she had to take because she went out every evening to a party or ball. The London season had her in its grip, it seemed. It meant that she spent hours in the bath, ran about the house in her quilted pink dressing-gown all day with her hair in curlers, and at last swept out, trailing the glory of evening dress, with a discreetly dinner-jacketed young man at her side. Nothing had to get in Liz's way. She was going to be *presented*—which meant, to the Queen. Anabel muttered to me that she was also supposed to be catching one of the *debs' delights* as the young men were called, and getting him to marry her.

The most frightening thing was going up to bed at night to my room right at the top of the house, where Aunt Hermione had her lair when she was in London. Even though she was not there, the essence of her was: an old-lady smell, every surface covered in lace mats, photographs in frames, knick-knacks, dried flowers, face-cream jars, and every inch of the walls covered in framed photographs, watercolors she had done, samplers on cloth that looked as if it were rotting outwards from the stitches imposed on it, saying *Home Sweet Home* or *Patience is a Virtue* or some other such motto, stitched by a child—herself, years ago?—with a pricked finger that bled and had rusted the cloth, proof of how painful sewing them had been. The bed was covered in far too many heavy blankets and eiderdowns and even a fur rug that smelled of animals, so that I woke sweating and terrified after dreaming that I had been buried alive. Even in the cold of winter, it seemed to heat me to fever pitch. The worst thing about this room was the bell-pull that dangled near the bed. It was there I suppose so that if my great-aunt needed help in the night, she could pull it and a bell would jangle somewhere in the lower regions of the house and someone—once a servant, now probably Aunt Laura—would run up to assist her. But I had read Conan Doyle's story *The Speckled Band,* which has a poisonous snake in it that slides down a bell-pull, plants its incisors in the flesh of the sleeper, and is used to commit the perfect murder, only of course Sherlock Holmes works it out. I lay awake in the dark, feeling the presence not only of my great-aunt, but of that bell-pull. I even fingered its silky ropiness, to make sure that nothing was sliding down it, no slithery shape was inching its way towards me where I lay. In the near-dark of London, where the street lights filter into rooms no matter how many blinds are drawn or curtains closed, I saw the outlines of the furniture that filled the attic room, and it seemed that it was all coming in on me, the heavy wardrobe, the chest of drawers with its cluttered surface, the little tables with their knick-knacks, the tallboy in the corner that nearly reached the ceiling, even the walls themselves. I would either die poisoned by a snake, or buried under furniture and collapsing walls. I fell asleep at last of course, and dreamed the worst dreams of my life, and woke gasping but not daring to call out, in case I caused anxiety and had to be sent home. I was only there for about ten days at that time, but I wanted those days in spite of the horrors of the nights.

I didn't dare ask if I could share Anabel's room, and it was never suggested. But in the daytime we were free and could go to films, walk in the park, travel on the tops of tall red buses, look at bombed sites still ragged with weeds and rosebay willow-herb, where the sliced-apart houses with their dangling appliances, halfdestroyed bathrooms, and tattered strips of wall-paper still fascinated and appalled me. This was what could happen to a house, I saw: the heaps of rubble that still lay about, all these years after the end of the war, were there to remind us. Life could be buried, people could be entombed in the ruins of their houses. Houses as tall as Anabel's family's own could be ripped open, toppled in a single night. Until now, I had not spent much time in London, apart from trips to the dentist, and I hadn't realized how much had been destroyed, and how long it would take for it all to be put back. My first excursions into the West End were with Anabel and her mother. We sat on the tops of the tall red buses and looked down on ruins where cupboards and beds and bathtubs still hung in mid-air, and torn blinds flapped, and it all looked like a broken-open doll's house, only life-sized. Nothing was safe, these ruins told us; nothing was permanent.

My aunt took us to an Agatha Christie murder mystery in a West End theatre, in which the murderer turned out to be the detective—the last person you would suspect. He tiptoed into rooms and turned the lights off, so that all the guests at the snowed-in house-party were left in the dark. When the lights went up, one more person was found dead. We thought this brilliant, but terrifying. After seeing the play, neither of us would go into a room unless the light had been turned on in advance, and we—or I, at least—was nervous around light switches, and anxious if I saw anyone stand near one. It made going to bed in Aunt Hermione's room an even worse ordeal than it had been before. I made Anabel turn on the lights on all the upper landings before I would go up and she, knowing it was about the play, hissed to me, "Look out, he's probably on the top landing!" or, "Watch out as you pass the bathroom door!"

We went to Madame Tussaud's wax museum, where my mother had warned me about the Chamber of Horrors, but we went to it anyway without my aunt's knowledge, and gazed at wax representations of actual murderers—Crippen, who had murdered women in a bathtub, and had been caught mid-Atlantic trying to escape to America; Ruth Ellis, the last woman to be hanged, having murdered a lover. Then there were the executions: Charles I., in his lace collar that would surely get covered in blood when the axe fell; Sir Thomas More; Mary Queen of Scots in her red dress (practical for bloodstains—too many to count); but each one of them going to meet death solemnly, with the pale complexion that wax gives, and what looked like a warning stare at us, their audience. There were the murderers, and then—worse horror—there were the murderesses. They all had straggly hair, red eyes and haggard faces like witches.

I thought—if somebody knew what we did, that we were actual murderesses, would they make waxworks of us, Anabel and me, and show them in the Chamber of Horrors? Would they arrest us, like Crippen, before we could make good our escape across the ocean?

After the expedition to Madame Tussaud's, we travelled home, rather silent on the smoky metallic-smelling top of the bus to Notting Hill and ran fast down the street in the dark to reach the lit front door of the house, where Liz was tripping down the steps. She was wearing a slinky black evening dress this time, with a fur around her shoulders that had little bright eyes and teeth and dangling paws, and a man was holding the door of a taxi open.

"Where've you been?" she shouted at us in her high-pitched drawl. "Mum's frantic, you were supposed to be home hours ago!"

"Madame Tussaud's," Anabel said, "she said we could. And it's only about six, anyway."

"Well, as long as you didn't go into the Chamber of Horrors."

"Oh, no, of course not."

"Well, all right, I'm off. But watch out, she's in a state. She was even on the phone to Nessa's mother. And Dad's in a bad mood because of the government. Bye, anyway! Be good, and if you can't be good, be careful!"

"Don't say we went into the Chamber of Horrors," Anabel said to me as we went up the steps from the street.

"Of course not." I was wishing that I had not—but you can't unsee what you have seen, I already knew that. I followed her into the house. We scooted up the steep flights of stairs to her bedroom, but on the way heard her father's angry tones on the telephone. There was an atmosphere in the house—but surely it couldn't be because of us and our late home-coming? Anabel's mother was in the kitchen, three floors down. It struck me again that it was hard to know what was going on in a house where everyone lived on a different level, vertically stacked one above another. Her father, Uncle Mark, banged down his telephone and slammed his study door. Far below him, like a person in a different era, Aunt Laura clattered saucepans in the kitchen. Liz had fled in the cab with her young man. We came out of Anabel's bedroom eventually and hung over the banisters, to see what was what. Then her father burst out of his study and shouted, "Oh, it's you two. Well, hurry up and get some supper down you, your mother's in a state."

Anabel asked, "What happened?"

"One damn thing after another. This bloody government, not up to it if you ask me, stock market's on the slide. And your bloody sister chooses this moment to go off with a total ne'er do well, somebody nobody's ever heard of, and she's wearing black, I ask you, your mother's in a state and no wonder, says they're going to some night-club or other, won't even say what time she'll be back."

"Oh, is that all?" Anabel said. I hung back, amazed. Such dramas never happened in my house, my father being a socialist and nobody being old enough to go off with a ne'er-do-well in a taxi.

"Let me tell you, young woman, we're not putting on this show for you when you get to her age. All this effort to find her the right kind of young man, and she goes off with some damn dago to a night-club, doesn't even introduce him. No, you can get out and earn your living, I can tell you."

Anabel said, "I don't want to be a deb anyway, so you needn't worry. Maybe we'd better go down and see Mum. And I'm sure Liz will be fine."

As we slid down the stairs, hanging on to the banisters with our feet only skimming the steps, she muttered to me, "I thought that black dress was rather good, didn't you? But I'm sure the fur was one of Mum's. And I'm sure that man wasn't what Dad said—a damn dago."

"What's a dago?"

"Oh, you know, somebody foreign."

We arrived in the basement kitchen and found Aunt Laura sniffing over the sink, because Uncle Mark had said it was all her fault for letting Liz run around London at all hours with unknown men. I saw Anabel stepping up to her role of peace-maker—something I had not seen her do. "Don't worry, Mum, he's just in a bate because the stock market's going down for some reason. It's not your fault. And Lizzie's sensible, she'll come home okay."

We sat at the kitchen table and ate our baked potatoes, rather wizened from the oven, and minced beef with carrots. Aunt Laura perched, smoking a cigarette. "Well, at least you two are not of an age to get into trouble, that's something." We agreed smugly, it was.

FIFTEEN

I REMEMBER THAT FIRST VISIT TO LONDON as the train takes me past Clapham Junction and on towards Waterloo, in the hitherto unimaginable twenty-first century. I'm going as promised to visit Paula, who has asked me to show her my first draft of the chapter for the book, messy and inconclusive as it is. What looked like historical certainties only a year or two ago now seem to be preposterous and unlikely. Writing about them has begun to feel dangerously pointless. But I have sat at my grandmother's desk in the evenings, and written at least something, putting thoughts of the foreign woman and her lover on hold, as far as I could. I have tried to be rational, not governed by emotion—to do what I was contracted to do. I have also written an e-mail to the archeology department at Southampton University, inquiring about the bones. Opening my laptop to check my mail as we approach London, I see that they have sent me a reply, with an attachment. I skim it fast.

The forensic experts in Southampton have used a new technique for dating human bones. Carbon-14 dating. Radio-carbon in bones remained steady until perturbed by mid-20th century above-ground nuclear testing. From 1954 to 1963 there was a distinct increase, after which there was a decline to former levels. This meant that the bones found were of someone who died before 1954.

The degree of weathering of the bones and their nitrogen content
and that of the nails and tooth enamel suggested that the deceased
died after 1951. The conclusion was that this young woman was
buried in a cliff-fall that took place in 1952, when a local ex-soldier
had been taken from the site to a hospital in Weymouth, but had
died of his injuries on the way. Injuries to the skull of the deceased
woman indicated damage from rock debris, but no single blow.
Foul play was not suspected, and the case has been closed. They
thank me for my interest.

Is she, then, left waiting on a shelf in the university department,
a little pile of bones that have served their scientific purpose? What
happens to the remains of a person found splintered and splayed
on a beach, under tons of sand and rock? I know that there will be
more I have to do, but I close my laptop. One step at a time.

We're coming towards the Thames. I look up to glimpse all
these new buildings, sky-scrapers even, where only warehouses
and back-to-back terraces on narrow streets were before. I see a
big banner pinned against a wall. *Nobody Voted To Be Poorer.* It's
in the colors of the European Union. London is a palimpsest, as is
any great city: here are the marks of earlier poverty still, the workers' houses in grimy brick, and there the shining sharp monuments
to the financial power-house that was. In the fifties, when I stayed
with Anabel, there were still the debutante balls and girls like Liz
going out night after night to meet "suitable," rich, upper-class husbands. There were the bombed sites, and children who had grown
up with rickets in the years before the Beveridge report and the
beginnings of the National Health Service; there were the craters
left with their unnumbered deaths of the poor of London, who had
not had the opportunity or the money to move out. There was Uncle
Mark in his study, growling over taxation and the Stock Exchange
and later, Suez. There was the West End and its theatres, going on
much as it always had, before the war. I remember the fear we had
of shadowy, skinny people in the streets, when we strayed away
from the lit circle of Piccadilly and ventured into Soho. Nobody

talked about the War, only reminisced about Before the War. It was as if a scar had grown across what had happened, hardening and solidifying, until scar tissue was all there was.

I get out of the train at Waterloo, the terminus, and join the crowds rushing towards the Underground. The Tube. Its round-ceilinged white-tiled corridors—the reason, I'd thought, for it being called "The Tube"—had scared me as a child, as did the rushing, roaring sound of the trains' approach, the hot smell of burning metal, as it scalded the rails; dragon's breath, I'd thought, the stink of hell—only I never admitted that I was afraid, as Anabel was nonchalant about it as only a London child could be. Yes, we went around the city on our own, travelling by bus or tube, and nobody, strangely, seemed to think this odd. Perhaps it wasn't. I'd wished that my aunt would come with us, as I never knew, in these days of our explorations, whether Anabel was about to show me some new terror—some hidden, unexplained Chamber of Horrors—that I would not be able to leave behind me.

The still-shabby rattling Northern Line takes me right up past Camden and Belsize Park, and I get off at the narrow station at Hampstead, walk up steep steps to take the elevator the rest of the way, up from the bowels of London. Paula lives, has lived for decades, in this pleasant middle-class enclave up on its hill, near the Heath. Hampstead is known for its intellectuals, novelists and artists, mostly elderly now, as no beginner in the arts would ever be able to afford to live here. For some people, it's synonymous with elitism. For others, it's still where their immigrant parents found refuge. I enjoy the walk from the Tube station on the High Street, past the flower shop and the antique shop, past a newly opened Turkish restaurant, past the pub on the corner where we have often had dinner together, towards the terraced houses of Flask Walk. Paula's house is up a set of steep steps. I knock with the brass door-knocker in the shape of a hand that she brought back long ago from Italy. Paula used to live here with her husband, Mel, but he died ten years ago and she has lived on here alone.

"Nessa! Wonderful. Come on in. I hope it wasn't too awful?" People of our age are getting used to journeys being "awful" and I smile as I remember my mother and her sister and their "ghastly" journeys years ago. Today, the train up from the south-west was on time, and comfortable, and the air-conditioning did not break down, and there was coffee on a trolley to be had, and even a bar. I shake my head. "No, it was fine."

"I thought you might get held up by all the protests. Oh, I suppose in the Tube you wouldn't have seen them."

"Why, what's going on?" I've hardly glanced at any papers in my Dorset retreat, and it is still hard to get online there.

"Huge protests against leaving Europe. They were meeting at Trafalgar Square today, marching towards Downing Street. And of course there are all the others, the Brexiters, trying to stop them. We don't have enough police anymore to control what goes on, since the Home Office cut their numbers, so it tends to get out of hand."

"Would you have gone? If I wasn't coming today?"

"Maybe. Old Hampstead hippy, not sure she's relevant or even accepted here anymore. And, it's so damn hot. But one can always try—and I do think it's worth it. This country—well, I suppose yours is worse. But what shocks me is that people no longer seem to mind being lied to—or lying. This whole mess was built on lies, no?"

I nod. I feel exhausted suddenly; it happens from time to time these days. The knowledge of what is happening to the world we knew—all older people must have felt this since time began to be recorded, the wearying incomprehension of things happening that they could never have imagined. History, I think not for the first time, is very selective.

"I've put you in your usual room. Well, it's the only spare room, as you know. Tea? Or is it time for a drink?"

"Can I have both, tea first?" The journey, although not "awful" has left me with the airless feeling of enclosed spaces, and a dry thirst that seems to inhabit my whole body, as well as the fatigue of thinking about today's politics. It's an unusually hot day for a London summer, and it has been like this for weeks now. The country I came through looked scorched and bleached out, the trees' leaves browning at their edges as if ready for autumn. It has not rained for months. Outside, the sky above London is a hot whitish blue, not the clear seaside blue of Dorset. The buildings seem to shimmer in the heat, and of course all the headlines of newspapers—the *Evening Standard* now free as you came up out of the Tube—have three-inch headlines about Scorchers and Heat Waves, and the exclamations, *Phew!* And, *London Sizzles!* On the Tube, notices warn you not to travel without a bottle of water and remind you to ask other passengers for help if you feel faint. It is almost, people are saying, like the spirit of the Blitz. Now that I live outside it, I notice that England and English people love crises, occasions to rise to, suffering just intense enough to "put a brave face on it" and evoke, once again, that spirit of the long-ago bombing of London. A heat-wave will do, or a demand to tighten their belts: especially if they have never had to tighten them already, and will probably not have to do so now. The recent decision to leave the European Union, incomprehensible to me, seems to have afforded many people a grim pleasure at the thought of things getting effortlessly worse.

"So," Paula puts her bare feet up on a stool and gestures to me to take off my shoes too if I want. She's wearing a loose dress made of almost see-through cotton, and her hair, gray-blond and wiry, is up in a messy bun, away from her face. She fans herself with a magazine. "We're going to need air-conditioning here soon. But I'll resist as long as I can. Meanwhile, I just try to keep the place cool by drawing the curtains till the sun goes down; that's why we're sitting in the gloom. Imagine, in London."

I sip the tea she's made—loose China tea in a pot, with white cups to match. We were both brought up with the belief in hot tea to cool you down—a relic, like many lingering habits here, of the British Raj in India. It works, though most Americans don't believe me.

"How's it going?" It being my life, my time alone in Dorset, the chapter of the book I'm supposed to be writing? "Did you get lonely down there all alone?"

I think, it hasn't even occurred to me. "No. Not lonely. I swim, I walk. I look at trees and squirrels and birds. Yes, I miss Bruno, but he's coming over soon. I've done some on my chapter. For what it's worth. Mostly, in the evenings I've been re-reading Thomas Hardy. *The Return of the Native.* It's wonderful. Everyone is so wrong about everything, and you want to shout out—*No! Don't do it! Don't marry her, or him!* And then they do, and it's all disastrous."

"And it's wonderful?"

"What I love is his sense of the land. It's exactly right, in every detail. He knows what the dry heather sounds like on the moor, and how the wind sounds blowing through gorse bushes, and what it's like to step out in total darkness and only see a light burning, a bonfire on a hill. It's where I am, it's Dorset, and it reminds me—sorry, I don't know why it makes me want to cry— it reminds me of everything that hasn't changed, and everything that has."

I fumble for a tissue. "His people are so little, and so vulnerable. And you see them in firelight and shadow all the time, as if they're hiding from something. And then poor Clym, who's coming home from Paris to see his old mother, goes and falls in love with the country he grew up in again, and can't bear to leave."

"I do vaguely remember it, from school. He falls for a girl who only wants him because he's going back to Paris and she longs to go there. Like in *Revolutionary Road.* And then they don't go. And doesn't she die, too?"

"And he goes blind. I know, such terrible irony. He's remorse-less—Hardy I mean. I've read it before of course, but it's never struck me quite like this. We want what is worst for us, it seems. We fall for people because of our own unfulfilled needs and expect them to fill them and then go crazy because they can't."

"Well, all his characters are pretty young, aren't they? Didn't most of us do that? I don't mean with you and Bruno, of course, but wasn't it like that with Roland?"

"Yes, I thought he was going to take me places. Pretty soon I realized I was going to have to go to them on my own. He had a romantic way of flicking his hair back, I seem to remember, and God knows why, I thought that was enough to entrust him with my life."

She smiles, "Yes, I had a few of those. How's Bruno?"

"He's fine. He went to California to see his sister and her family. He's home now. He's coming over next week." My husband, whose name was Americanized to Bryan, reverted to the Italian "Bruno" when he left high school. Bruno, or Bruin to his grown children, on account of a slight resemblance to a black bear and a bearish shambling gait.

"Do you find that you get better at being alone, at this age? I mean, I know I had to, rather too suddenly, but I find I actually love it. I never thought I'd like my own company so much." Paula gets up to find the bottle of Campari, and orange juice and ice from the refrigerator. It has always been our drink.

"I do, actually. I missed Bruno when I was first there—for, I don't know, some stability he provides. But now I'm quite happy to be alone. It's my place. It's known me all my life. It's easy. It's where I know how to be."

She says, "Here. Finish your tea and drink this. I know I couldn't be anywhere but London now, even England, with all the mess we're in. I suppose it's our mess, we've all helped make it, but still. I've been here far too long to even think about being Polish. And, you must have seen what's happening in Poland these days. At least most Londoners want to stay in, and it's still going to be cosmopolitan. The mayor's good. God knows what the rest of the country's going to be like."

"Well, we're supposed to be the rootless cosmopolitans, aren't we? Citizens of nowhere, as the PM quaintly put it. Too late to change now."

"Here's to us," she says, and we clink glasses, and the ice melts fast, and the light outside the drawn blinds is already a little less intense, and I find myself relaxing into her company, her house, and everything she has made since her parents brought her here during that far-off war, to become who she has become. Paula Jarosz, editor at a London publishing company, known for fifty years for her work in this city, and reluctant to retire, appalled at the xenophobia that has reached even her, but certainly not about to go back to Poland.

"The best I can hope for is that we'll simply drop the whole thing," she says. "You can't turn a bad idea into a good one, however hard you try, and the PM has certainly been trying. People are comparing her to Chamberlain, when he came back from Munich with his peace plan. People who weren't even alive then. The stuff you hear is unbelievable."

I say, "Well, change is the only constant, if that doesn't sound too paradoxical. Something else always happens, usually the thing that nobody has thought of. History doesn't repeat itself exactly, whatever people say."

"Well, you should know."

"Maybe I should, but I don't. We're always facing the unpredictable, don't you think?"

"Tell me," she says, tipping the ice cubes in her glass from side to side, "Where are you with that other story? About the bones?"

I have been longing to re-read the message from Southampton to be sure of its contents, and I open my lap-top to show her. She reads, and nods.

It connects, I know, the way those bones connected, one beside another, one linked to another, a little imagination, care and science making it all possible. You fit one small thing to another, and another, and eventually it forms a whole. Like the boys with Jared and the clothes left in the cave under the cliff. Like the talk in the village store with the stories written up in the paper. Everything does connect, if you examine it hard enough. It's how I've been able to write history. You create a magnet, and you draw all the filings towards it. You hold the magnet, and the pieces come together, across time, across space, to create the bigger picture. And here is the next piece—the piece that Bruno suggested I might find—the science that will hold it all together.

SIXTEEN

BEFORE I LEFT THE HOUSE IN LADBROKE GROVE, in the first week of January, 1953, my aunt beckoned me into Anabel's room and bent to take clothes out of a drawer. She stood with one hand on her presumably aching hip and motioned to me to come closer. I saw a wine-colored corduroy skirt I'd particularly admired, and a cream sweater that looked softer than anything I owned.

"Nessa, come and try these on. Anabel's grown out of them, and your mother mentioned that you might like to take some of them."

I went in, touched the sweater that surely was cashmere although I'd never touched cashmere before. The skirt lay out on Anabel's bed, inviting me. I wished my mother had not said anything about my needing new clothes, as it made us sound poor, but decided not to mind. If I could dress like Anabel, I'd have that glamorous certainty she had, I'd be closer to being her. I took off my gray flannel skirt and put on the corduroy that flared around my hips and came longer on me, but fitted perfectly. The sweater, I knew I had to have; I'd wear it anyway, tight or loose.

"Anabel's bursting out of everything these days," her mother said, "And these should last you a year at least."

So I would go out dressed as Anabel, as if I had grown up to be her overnight. When Anabel saw me, she said, "Oh, so Mum's found a home for those old things." Then, relenting, "Actually, they look good on you." I'd accepted not only the skirt and sweater, but a couple of blouses and a winter coat. Yet, when we went out together to the cinema that afternoon to see a film called *The Kidnappers* about two little boys sent to live with a strict uncle and aunt in Canada, I didn't wear Anabel's clothes, out of some feeling of still wanting to assert my own identity.

"Where's the skirt? You could have worn it. And, the coat, it's going to be cold out."

"But not in the cinema. I didn't want to sit on them and rumple them up."

"Oh, right. Yes, I suppose that makes sense, it's always hot in there, anyway."

"ANABEL, YOU KNOW WHAT HAPPENED IN THE SUMMER?" I asked her later, as we were getting ready for bed—she in her pajamas already, I about to set off on the daunting trip to the top of the house. She had her toothbrush in one hand and her hair coming loose from its slide. I'd been waiting for all this time to have this conversation, and it was nearly time for me to go home, and we hadn't even mentioned it. I had to know.

"What?"

"Those people, on the beach. The cliff fall."

"Oh, that accident. What about it?"

"I don't know—I had a dream about it. I mean, I often dream about it, or something like it. Earth falling, people being buried, you know."

"Sounds like you had indigestion." It was always her mother's explanation, that if you had bad dreams, it was from indigestion. "Too much cake for tea!" She went into the bathroom, and I followed her.

"Do you ever think about it?"

"Well, not really. Not for ages, anyway."

"The thing is, was it us?"

"Was what us?"

"Was it our fault?"

She began brushing her teeth, and I saw her reflected in the bathroom mirror, eyeing me. I stood in the doorway, and my knees felt shaky. As she didn't say anything, but looked at me in the mirror for an uncomfortably long time, I added, "We were there, weren't we? We saw what happened."

She was silent, or rather absorbed in brushing her teeth.

I said, "And when we saw them, they were kissing and everything, weren't they? I mean—you know?"

My daring at asking her this made me shake. What if I were wrong? What if it was not that at all?

At last, after swirling water around in her mouth, she spat into the basin, and looked at me sternly as she dried her face, patting it with a towel. "No, of course not. You didn't see anything, Nessa. It was an accident. It was in the paper, remember? We weren't even there."

"Oh. Okay." I turned to go up my lonely stairs.

"Nessa, you haven't told anybody?"

"No, of course not."

"It was those village boys, Ted and Roger, not us."

"Are you sure?"

"Of course I am. They were oiks, weren't they?" The word, meaning working-class boys, was not one that my father would ever have tolerated.

I flinched. "Oh. I suppose. Well, good night."

"Sleep tight. Don't let the fleas bite."

So, now there was nobody I could ask. Paddy was probably too young to be reliable, and I wouldn't see Ted and Roger till next summer, if I saw them at all. I lay on the edge of my bed, away from the bell pull, and thought of that cliff edge beside the concrete lookout post and the crumbling sandstone of the cliff, ourselves on our bellies peering down until we could see no more, no people, no movement of anything living, just the red dust rising from below.

What had happened in the moments before that? Had Ted begun the tossing down of stones and then clods of earth, almost lazily at first, and had I joined in, because he dared me to? It was hard to remember the order of things, when they happened so fast. There was the quiet moment when I saw them come together, there at the bottom of the cliff. His jacket, his moving head, her white legs. There was the sensation of the earth in front of me giving way, of scrambling back to safety on the rough grass, of lying flat, trying to breathe, wondering what had happened. Anabel said we were not even there, that I must have imagined it after reading about it in the paper. I knew—or had I dreamed it?—that we had all ducked back and then run, towards Roger's dad's hotel through nettles and brambles until we found the path, and that my legs had been torn and were bleeding, and that none of us said anything until we were back safely on the road behind the hotel, looking at each other, not knowing, any of us, quite what had happened. Anabel had made us all swear not to tell. So, what was there to tell? I remembered my glimpse of the newspaper lying on the little table in the sitting room, there and then gone. I remembered the talk of the women in the shop, when Paddy and I went down to buy potatoes. Did I remember lying beside Ted in deep bracken on the cliff-top and copying him as he spun pebbles and then clods of earth over the edge? Was I sure that I had thrown a stone myself? It was puzzling. What if what I thought had happened had not really happened—if I had made the whole thing up? Jean-Ann had asked the question, "Nessa, is this real, or a game?" Going up the stairs to my lonely room at the top of Anabel's house that night, I was still not at all sure.

Yes, I had dreamed *of* it—but not the actual details, not anything that could help me discover any more about what had actually taken place. I dreamed of suffocating, and woke to find it was the heavy quilt over my face. I dreamed of falling debris, rocks, stones, earth, tufts of grass; but in my dreams, debris mixed with the dust and brick of falling houses, and myself lying helpless under what collapsed on top of me.

I never dreamed of *them*; it was always myself who was the help-less victim. I lay awake in my great-aunt's cluttered dark bedroom at the top of an alien house in West London, and tried to get back into the film I had seen—the two little boys with Scottish accents, the baby they kidnapped, their innocent talk, they wanted a dog, would they call it Rover? The older boy was whipped, shut in the woodshed for his crime. If I were to confess that I had been part of that death on the beach, what would be my punishment? Anabel would contradict me, say that I was mad. I would be sent home for lying. My parents would be confused and angry. It seemed that nobody explained anything to children: we were just left to work things out on our own, and often got them wrong.

On my last night in that house, I lay rigid in my great-aunt's bed with the sheet pulled tight under my chin and the bedclothes weighing me down and all the furniture about to topple about me and I had a clear thought, at last. There was another version of what happened, and you could choose that version. In it, my brother and I went to the beach and played there within sight of our parents, and Anabel went to cafés in Swanage with her sister, and we never went near the moor, let alone the gun emplacement lookout. We never met two boys from the village, called Ted and Roger. I never met a woman with a strange name in a hotel lobby and told her where to go to find cowries or saw her summer dress fly up or heard the husky sound of the man's voice as he spoke that name. None of it ever happened. A cliff fell, and we were not there. It was an accident. This was Anabel's version, it was why she could say so certainly that we were not there. She believed it, so it must be true. Or true for her. Could one thing be true for one person and not for another? I didn't think so. Surely what happened, happened to everyone? Did she never dream of that cliff-top, dust whirling up, that sickening edge? Perhaps the only reason that I dreamed of it was that I had made the whole thing up.

I brought my knees up against my chest and hunched there in the cold sheets, held in place by the weight of blankets and quilts. I began to see, at that moment, that you could choose what to remember, what counted, and what was real. The furniture receded, the bell-pull retreated, there was nothing to be afraid of after all. I slept, and didn't even dream, and woke the next morning happy to be going home, but knowing I would return because Anabel was here, and that she could tell me how to live my life from now on.

I put her old clothes, the coveted skirt and sweater, in the bottom of my suitcase and thought, one day soon I will wear them—but not yet.

My visits to the house in London took place every Christmas holiday for a few years, so Anabel and I grew into teenagers together, she always ahead of me, always knowing more, always slightly condescending. I wore more of her cast-off clothes and copied her handwriting, which had become even tinier. We sat in her room one year and made up plays, taking it in turns to write the dialogue. Aunt Laura took us to see Laurence Olivier in *Hamlet* at the Old Vic and we began to write long soliloquies to be delivered front of stage in declamatory tones. We practiced in front of mirrors. She was better at acting, I at writing. We planned to put on the plays we wrote, but they were never finished. We wrote stories about a sinister man called The Shadow, with plots that failed because we could not agree on them. We grew our hair into ponytails, to look like Audrey Hepburn in *Roman Holiday*. We cut pictures of film stars out of magazines. We did all the things that teenagers do, and became exclusive, attentive to the slightest details of others' inferior looks or behavior, a sarcasm-wielding team of two. Liz had started going out with a banker called Geoffrey and no longer went out wearing black satin in taxis with ne'er-do-wells or dagoes, so her father calmed down. She began to show everybody a diamond ring. The stock market had gone up again. There was a new conservative government, a Prime Minister who told us all we had never had it so good.

My own father said, when I returned home, "You seem to be getting more and more like your cousin Anabel. You even sound like her. I hope she hasn't been giving you ideas."

"What sort of ideas?"

"That deb nonsense, for a start."

"God, no," I said, a teenager now, "I wouldn't be a deb if you paid me. They are all such crashing bores."

"Good, well, as long as you don't think that's all there is to life, Nessa. But still, you don't have to swear."

"I'm going to university," I said. "Had you forgotten? I'm going to read history. None of Anabel's friends even know what history is, if you ask me."

"Good," he said, and went back to reading Kingsley Martin in the *New Statesman*. "That's my girl."

Seventeen

Paula knows me well. She's known me ever since we first met and got slightly drunk together at a publishing party, long ago in New York. I remember her running after a yellow taxi, giggling, her shoes in her hand. Somewhere down in the Village, near the Waverley. I remember how we met for lunch in midtown the next day and she told me, if you ever want an editor in England, get in touch. Friendship came before our professional connection. She's as scrupulous an editor as she is a friend—always was, in spite of the drunken giggling that night, that showed me a side of her I rarely saw again.

"Why don't you write it?" she insists. "See what comes up?"

"You mean, as a story? But I don't know what really happened, and I don't know if I can ever find out. Or if I even want to."

"Well, why not give up on the history thing for now—you can do that chapter off the top of your head when you're back in the US—and take to fiction? Make it up. You're at a cliff edge in the story, you said. Literally, I imagine. Well, take it from there. Now, what about some dinner? I've made soup, I thought we could have it cold, and some chicken, and a salad? Will that be enough?"

I follow her into the little kitchen, glass in hand. "I think I eventually agreed with my cousin Anabel's version, because I wanted to stop having to dream about it and be scared all the time."

"What was her version? Simply that it didn't happen? Could you reach that loaf down for me?"

I pass her the baguette from the shelf above the fridge. "That we just weren't there. That we saw nothing. That it was an accident. She said it was the boys from the village that did it. The ones we met that year."

"So you kept that version alive? Total denial that it was anything at all to do with you?"

"Well, it meant I could let go of it." As I speak, I feel how despicable this sounds. She pursues me, non-judging but as always, exact.

"But what else had to be let go of? I mean, if you wipe one major event out of your life, what about all the rest?"

"I know. After that, I think I always had a version of events that let me off the hook—marrying the wrong person, pretending to be in love. Leaving him, never saying why. When I applied for jobs I didn't want. Maybe even deciding to read history, when I really wanted to do English. All sorts of instances, when it was simply easier to believe that what was convenient was also true."

She says, "A lot of people do that, not just you."

"It stopped when I met Bruno, really. With him I didn't have to pretend. I couldn't, in fact. He's also probably the most truthful person I've met. And he's American. It's different."

"I know. What impresses them isn't the same."

"You know, it's more straightforward somehow? Different complications, but you know that." We both married Americans—very unlike each other, but at least not caught up in being English and all that seems to entail.

"Well," she says, "You did become a historian. Aren't they supposed to tell the truth?"

"Touché. Maybe that was why I chose history. Although in historiography, which was what has always really interested me, you get used to the idea that there is seldom one truth." I have spent my professional life examining different versions of history. For the first time, telling Paula, this seems in itself an indictment.

"History belongs to the victor?"

"Well, it often belongs to the person who first picks up a pen."

"And then is challenged, by the next person who gives their version."

"Exactly. So history is not about absolutes, ever, it's shifting ground. But at least you have to try to discover what really happened. It keeps you honorable, in a way."

"Nessa," she says, "You've always been honorable, darling. I've known you all these years. But you know—there is a level of truth that cannot be denied. Take Katyn, for example. The British pretended that it was the Germans who killed all the Polish generals there, while in fact it was the Russians. They couldn't admit that it was the Russians, because Russia was their ally against Hitler. But something really happened there, there were real Russian soldiers who killed real Poles. No amount of rewriting can change that. Anything else is just propaganda."

"That is the level of truth that we try to reach, yes. But often it's overlaid by more than war-time propaganda. It becomes embedded in a society's, a nation's story, and it's hard to disinter. People will believe anything, even against the evidence. I'm sure there must be some Russians who still think that Katyn was a German war crime."

"What I'm saying is that there is a level that is simply truth, whether people believe and accept it or not. People killing people, burying them in a forest. No? Now, I think we need some dinner. Take these plates, would you, Nessa, and go and open the wine?"

PAULA, EVEN AFTER A LIFETIME IN ENGLAND, still does not sound English, as I do not sound American after all my years in the US. Her husband, Mel, always seemed to be trying to be more English than the English, but as she said, the cultural expectations sat differently and you couldn't fake them. It didn't surprise me that they settled here, in leafy comfortable Hampstead, and set up their professional lives without looking back. She had been a reader for Viking, and became a junior editor at Deutsch in the seventies, during which time she escorted a flirtatious young John Updike around London, pursued the elusive Laurie Lee across rural England, and tried to pour oil on the troubled waters of Vidya Naipaul. Mel wrote gory who-dun-its that were set in 19th-century London—he'd been coming here for years to research them—and spent a lot of time in the British Museum and prowling the then-grimy East London docks. He was a man of regular habits—tea at four, drinks at six, dinner at eight—and always wore some version of an outfit he had devised for himself that combined too-short American trousers and knobbly British woollies, with a scarf flung French-fashion about his neck when he went out. Their life had seemed to me admirably uncompli-cated, devoid of drama; they were well-suited, though not evi-dently passionate. They gave parties at which people mostly behaved well and did not outstay their welcome. Paula's own dis-cretion prevented her from ever telling me the intimate details of their life together, as some women friends insist on doing, and I always assumed that this meant she had no need to. But Mel was ill for a long time before anyone ever knew it, and she had known he was probably going to die. He hadn't wanted anyone to know, or to treat him differently, and when he died, it was with the same discretion that the two of them had always practiced: he simply went into hospital one day for an operation, and did not come out. This was ten years ago, more. Paula simply said, "We had so many good times. We had a good life. What more can I ask?"

His royalties, a TV serial, and her position at the head of Unicorn Books allowed her to continue life on Flask Walk as before; and if there was a faint sense about the house of someone missing, someone mourned still, it was in the objects he had left behind—his desk, his typewriter—he scorned computers to the end—and a pervasive scent of something masculine—a cologne; a tweedy, woolly, slightly acrid smell on the stairs; and his old gardening boots and jacket still hanging up on the porch at the back of the house. "I know, I ought to get rid of them," Paula said. "It doesn't make sense to hang on to them, people tell me that all the time. You know, magical thinking, that book? But I don't want to turn him out. Why should I?"

Would I get rid of Bruno's things in our house in upstate New York, if he were to die before me? He is older than I am. It's a complicated thought. Neither of us wanted to get rid of our beloved dog's leash and bowl, when she died; but we glanced at them sometimes, almost guiltily, as we passed them on our way in or out of the house. Surely there is something human about wanting to keep the objects that were part of a loved person's—or dog's—life? The ancient Egyptians believed in objects, in possessions and their power. In so many civilizations, people were buried along with their things. Only in our modern age do we swiftly sweep them aside, empty our houses after a death, in order to do what's called "closure" or "getting on with our lives."

WHEN I MET BRUNO, HE WAS LIVING IN A LOFT on Broadway in lower Manhattan. I remember a trapdoor in the floor, an ancient elevator that came up in the middle of the building. Floors made of narrow ancient boards. Greenish ceramics that looked Chinese. His photographs, everywhere. My first husband, Roland, had wanted to be a photographer, but my second husband actually was one. Was this a sign, or a warning? Bruno's photographs were made through a slow, complex procedure invented in the 19th century in France, a kind of photo-gravure that gave his images blurred outlines and occasional shining haloes and mysterious figures that appeared like revenants from one side of the frame. I prowled, looking at the ones on his walls, genuinely fascinated.

"Doesn't it take a very long time to produce them?"

"Yeah."

"They are like dreams. Or ghosts. Or remains of ancient civilizations."

"They are just images I like, found things, they could be anything. What do you do, Nessa?"

"History. I've just started teaching a bit, at Columbia. I'm sometimes asked to write reviews of people's books, too."

"So we are both looking for evidence?"

I did not know what he meant by that; but he intrigued me: his bulk, his silences, his gestures—a hand coming out to wave in mid-air and staying there like a question-mark, a slight shrug of his shoulders in their worn corduroy—his acceptance, as it seemed to me, of what was.

He had exhibitions, had a book out, was fairly well-known. We met at an art opening, he invited me to lunch, and it was not long before I moved in. We lived together for a year, then for longer, then for what would probably be the rest of our time on earth. Some decisions appear simple at the time, although they may be complex. I think now that the apparently simple ones have been building and spreading their roots as a tree does, out of sight for many years, before you see growth in its branches.

He was already there, waiting for me, as if he'd expected me all along. A long shot, as he put it: divorced man lonely in New York meets divorced woman from England looking for love and food. His wife had lived in the big open loft with him, she was a painter, she had moved out. They had two children, boys, who had presumably grown up here among the ceramics, paintings and photographs, running across the ancient close-knit floorboards, going up and down in the elevator that clanked and groaned. "Not enough room for her art and mine and all the rest, I guess."

This ex-wife, Eleanor, had a stroke long after she and Bruno were separated—not so long ago, in fact, and well after we moved out of the apartment in which I first knew him. He visits her, in a nursing home, once a month. He cuts her nails. It is one of the things that I love and admire about him, that he does this.

Kindness is a rare quality these days—and when Bruno sets off to drive a hundred miles to sit with his silent ex-wife, the artist whose career was so abruptly and unfairly ended, I see him off with a sharp, almost painful sensation—love, admiration, anxiety, gratitude that he will be coming home to me. This kindness moved me when I first met him, when he took my boots, which were soaked, to dry beside the studio stove, having filled them with newspaper first so that they did not curl up at the toes. I'd hung my wet coat on the back of a door, and he handed me a towel to dry my hair, and showed me to the bathroom, before seating me at his table and handing me my lunch. I looked into his brown eyes across the table as he smiled at me for the way I dug into my steaming plateful, and saw that he was offering me more than lunch, and that I could trust what he offered.

I don't think I'd ever have offered to cut Roland's nails, after we divorced, or even before, even if he'd had a stroke.

Our first lunch together that day was fettuccini with a mushroom sauce recipe he had from his mother, who lived in Brooklyn. He would feed me, this man; we would never run out of nourishment. I, the recent immigrant, the would-be historian recently enrolled in a graduate program at Columbia, was permanently hungry; New York made me famished, and I rarely had time or inclination to cook for myself. When his boys, Marco and Ricky, decided to come back and live with us, he sold the loft for what seemed to me a vast amount of money—he'd had it since the 'sixties—and we moved to upstate New York. The apartment in which we first loved each other, in which I grew used to coming home in the clanking elevator and walking in socked feet across creaking boards, was on lower west Broadway, on a street that the planes screamed down on 9/11 before they hit their targets. He saw them from the window—I was away at the time. On the roof, there was—is still perhaps—a pear tree in a wooden box, that was in flower when I first went there, white blossoms against a gray New York sky. The rest, as they say, is history—the solid, real history of daily life, in which what you do is what you are, and you know you are making something together that will bear the weight of narrative, and time.

PAULA ASKS ME, "DO YOU EVER HAVE THE FEELING that as we age, we catch up with our childhoods again? I don't mean the way people say, second childhood, meaning you've lost your marbles. Just, we become more like our original selves? I'm remembering things about when we first came to England, things I thought I'd completely forgotten. Sometimes I think I even get a whiff of Poland, although that might be just from what I've been told. The other day I remembered being given a slice of cake with marzipan all around it. I took one bite, then folded it in a handkerchief and hid it in my knickers, because it was so sweet, I couldn't bear to eat it all at once. Who gave it to me, or why, I don't know. It made me realize that we'd had no sugar for years, so I simply wasn't used to that sweetness, or to having too much pleasure. But the marzipan tasted of somewhere else, somewhere I couldn't remember."

"Poland?"

"And your talking about the war reminds me of things. Things I hadn't wanted to remember, really. You know, I was what, three when we came here? England has always been home. But for my parents, they couldn't forget how this country had betrayed Poland. After Yalta, handing Poland to the Russians after we had done so much to support the allies. It was Roosevelt's idea, and Churchill just caved on it. So they never really trusted the English. They liked them, in a way, but never really made friends that lasted. It was as if they always expected to be betrayed again."

"What about you?"

"Well, it was home for me, as I say. But I was always being warned: don't tell so-and-so something, watch who you make friends with, don't invite that person home."

"More war damage."

"So, these things make us who we are? Do we spend the rest of our lives dealing with them, trying to be different?"

"I think so. You are a good, generous friend though, you always have been." I've noticed her reticence on certain subjects, her wary silences. She is also that comparatively rare creature, a person of complete integrity.

She says, "But, like you with Anabel's version, as you call it, there was always another version. You know? One in which I kept the essentials to myself. I acted as if—as if it were safe. It was a bit like living in a house where the floors have been taken up, so you have to walk on planks, be that careful. Mel knew it, and helped me to trust other people more. So I do know what you mean."

Halfway through the dinner that is lasting into the evening as greenish light comes in from her small garden and the sky darkens over London, she says to me, "There is an absolute, you know— thinking of truth and lies. My parents taught me that. Sometimes you have to realize it, history itself forces you to see it. And once you have seen it, you can't forget it is there."

"I know, relativism can be a slippery slope. But what I'm seeing now is that people really do not know the difference between truth and lies, or care. You know?"

Paula lays down her fork. "They will be made to care. I really think so. Something, one day, will make that happen."

"Like the war?"

"Something like that. But it's never exactly like. Something that we have not yet thought of."

I GO UP LATE, TO SLEEP IN HER PRETTY, SPARE BEDROOM, with the John Skeaping drawing and the photograph of her daughter Penny and the first editions of Beatrix Potter, Babar and Winnie-the-Pooh. Beside my bed she has left a small stack of new novels—Ali Smith and Graham Swift on top and a recent TLS—as if I'll have time to read them. The sheets are tight and clean under a light duvet and the white curtains fit the windows so that only a faint light enters from outside, London with its vigilance, even here in sleeping Hampstead. Or is it the moon? I think of sleeping in Great Aunt Hermione's bedroom all those decades ago, and of the bell-pull and the Agatha Christie play, and the Chamber of Horrors and the ruined houses left by the Blitz—what a cultural diet for a nervous eleven-year-old. I think of getting up to look at the moon—that same moon that shone in on me then—but the memory-foam mattress claims me, and I fall quickly asleep.

In the middle of the night, I wake and sit up, with a name in my mind. Magda. Of course. That was her name—how can I have forgotten it? *I am Magda*. I speak it out loud, and fall back to sleep again almost at once.

"COFFEE?" PAULA HAS A COMPLICATED MACHINE that hisses dark coffee into my cup. She eats cheese and sausage for breakfast, and I eat toast and jam. We ask each other ritually how we slept.

"I woke up suddenly in the middle of the night and remembered her name. The woman on the beach. It was Magda."

"And you'd really forgotten it for all these years?"

"Apparently. But it must have been stored in my mind, only just out of reach. I mean, it happens to me these days, I do forget people's names, I have to wait till they come back to me. But this was different. It was as if she was speaking to me again, in a dream."

"Well, that's wonderful. I'm honored that it happened in my house."

"I think there's a connection, Paula. You talking about Katyn, about Poland during the war, and the marzipan and everything. She was Polish. I think I knew that once."

"Amazing. Isn't the mind an extraordinary thing? Now you know that much, why not write the story? Maybe there's more. Maybe you'll start remembering more of what you once knew."

I spread her raspberry jam and crunch into my toast. "I can't write her story."

"But you can write your own. Reclaim your own memories—the ones you couldn't have if you believed you just weren't there. However it turns out, I think it would lay the whole thing to rest."

SHE AND I GO TO THE NATIONAL TO SEE *COPENHAGEN*, a play by Michael Frayn, that turns out to be about Heisenberg and the uncertainty principle, and we come back discussing it; Heisenberg proposed that two contradictory things could exist at the same time, but life, we agree, makes this appear difficult. We go to the Tate Modern for the Matisse cut-outs. I think of the ageing artist with his scissors, carving out the new shapes, dropping what was not needed to the floor. We cross the new gossamer-thin foot-bridge that trembles above the Thames. We walk about a city throbbing and deafened by helicopters—is there some terror threat?—and we walk on the Heath, dry as old skin over bone, all the grass whitened, the earth hard, the leaves of the trees dry, brown at their edges and even falling. The city lies in a haze of heat beneath us: not exactly smog, but still, a layer of polluted air. We see the monuments that poke up through the layer of murk. Hampstead, renowned for its better air quality, where people came to escape from the plague, from street riots and even from the Great Fire of London, relying on its higher ground. I imagine the city burning, the smoke that would rise from all those wooden buildings, the people trying to get out. How many Londoners were burned alive? How many died in the dreaded bubonic plague that ravaged the city in the previous year? Now, where people used to fly kites, the air is still. Where families and lovers picnicked, nobody wants to sit out in the sun. The great trees stand, withstanding to their best ability a heat-wave that goes on and on. We go back to the house, drink cold water, lie on sofas, switch on electric fans.

When will it stop—when will the rain come again, London rain, reliable as fog used to be, the background of life that we grumbled and complained about but never longed for like this? There is a new unpredictability about the weather, these days, you can feel it everywhere, and it makes the rest of life unpredictable too. The boundaries are shifting; old expectations of seasons cannot hold. Every year seems to bring with it some new extreme of heat, cold, flood, fire or whirlwind. We are living in apocalyptic times—but you can't live every day as apocalypse. Habit drives us even in the face of change. So after a while, we adapt: Paula leaves her curtains drawn against the sun, people buy air conditioners and lighter clothes; we all wait for it to change back to what it was. As it does, eventually. Rain will darken the grass on the Heath and bring the wilting gardens of England back to green life, and everybody will sigh with relief until the next flash flood that will fill the streets and gardens, or the next drought that will bleach it all white again and empty the city streets of air. The next protest will follow the latest absurd pronouncement by the government, the prime minister will run off to Brussels one more time to try to get her plan accepted, the newspapers will print ridiculous statements in letters three inches tall. Villains will wait in the wings. So we live, in this century of extremes.

We don't return to the hard topics of our first dinner together—that evening that slowly darkened, with the white curtains hardly stirring, the food long eaten before we made a move, the wine bottle emptied—but we know they are there. We were made by our childhoods: she escaping with her parents from occupied Poland at the last possible moment, I growing up in the aftermath of war, in a country that gradually relaxed from austerity into comfort, and then into security and smugness, and a general acceptance of the idea that all was for the best in the best of all possible worlds. We met in New York, that re-shaper of consciousness, city of immigrants, of people passing through, casual encounters and swift adaptation. Now, in London, we spend this time together as old friends, aware of time passing, softer with each other perhaps because friendship, long friendship, is precious and increasingly rare—and also because of the world around us that seems to be moving and shifting into unholy alliances, promises made and broken, threats that are both imprecise and alarmingly familiar.

When I leave, she hugs me goodbye on the step and kisses me firmly on both cheeks. I am known—accepted, forgiven, loved. We don't need to say these things. She watches me, I can feel it, as I walk away towards the Tube station, trailing my bag behind me.

"Let me know what happens!" she calls after me.

And I turn and call back, "Oh, I will!"

PART IV
THE HILL

EIGHTEEN

WE CAME BACK TO THE VILLAGE for several consecutive summer holidays in my youth, to stay with our grandmother
and, after her death, to open up the house at weekends and at
Easter to various groups of friends from university, and to visit our
parents, who used to come down here in the summer. The balding
lawn was the place where deck chairs were set out; babies learned
to crawl, then dabble in plastic blown-up paddling pools; people
sprawled with glasses of wine. In the house, vast pots of stew bub-
bled up in the kitchen and beds remained unmade all day. Before
I divorced and before my move to the United States, I spent many
holidays there with my first husband Roland, my brothers Patrick
and Charlie, my friends and their children, various dogs we had,
people whose names I've forgotten.

We were the people who came at Easter and in August. We never
saw Ted or Roger; they lived down in the village, in cottages hidden from view, if they were still here at all. The hotel had changed
hands, been modernized at least inside, as its Gothic fantasy exte-
rior had become something like a landmark. The village hardly
changed, as the heir to the whole estate had given it to the National
Trust in 1981, so no developer could get his hands upon it. It may
have infuriated his own family, but we were glad: the village existed

still in its 1950s state, with only the additions of some new houses on the Glebe estate, halfway up the hill that stretched towards Ballard Down—the only place outside the Trust's domain. The golf course—Anabel's father's favorite escape whenever he came down here—had spread over part of the moor that as children we considered our own domain. Some of the older farm buildings had been pulled down or converted, the old elm trees near the farm were gone, there were no more rusting tractors on view, and the cows no longer came mooing down the path towards their barn beside the church in the evenings. The ancient elm tree at the center of the village had died in the 1970s of Dutch elm disease and had been replaced with a Celtic cross carved in pale local stone. Our grandmother died, and after her nobody went regularly to church to sit in the pew where as a child I had memorized the inscriptions for the dead in their brass plaques on the wall, and the one carved on the chancel arch about entering into the Courts of the Lord. In some ways, the place had changed less than we had—Patrick visiting from New Zealand, Charlie coming from time to time with his young family, Bruno and I on a first visit from across the pond. Time infuses a place with its own rhythms, and this one had been established over a thousand years ago, when a church had first been built here. I sometimes feel my own life as a frail, swift-passing thing when I am here and confront the ancient stones and the sweep of the hill where the Bronze Age kings lie undisturbed. I feel shallow-rooted, easily blown around. Like those tumble-weeds you see rolling aimlessly across scrub-land in the south-western states of America.

I said that we did not see Ted or Roger again, after that one summer. That is factually true—but I did hear something about Ted, that was hard to slot into my memory of him. Village gossip again, probably in the shop—there was only one, the Higgins having retired. People drove to supermarkets for their food now—it was cheaper. The village seemed to be in decline, except for the tourists who flocked there in their cars, clogging the narrow roads in summer, heading for the pub and the beaches. Someone said that Ted Samways had had to go away, and that it was all a great shame, on account of his family, who had always been respected—nice enough people, family's been here centuries, but there you were. I was fifteen, sixteen, seventeen, thoroughly obsessed with the boys I met at dances in the school holidays, only interested in news of Ted in the vaguest way. Like Anabel, I moved in different circles now, or liked to think that I did. At the age I was, girls like to fit in—in fact it's a necessity if you are going to have any kind of social life. I was trying to be as like my peers as possible, and if my father snorted and sneered at the idea of a Young Conservatives dance at the Golf Club, I ignored him and went my own way, with Richard or Henry or Peter or whoever it was at the time. Snobbery is born of fear—of being excluded. It marked me as a teenager, without my realizing it. So, as people only referred to Ted and Roger as "those village boys" if at all, I gradually expunged them from my memory, and danced on.

NINETEEN

I T WAS EARLY SUMMER, AFTER THE END of the university term in 1961, and I had come to the village alone, to open up the house for friends who were driving down later. I came out of the post office having been in to buy stamps, and there he was, older, taller, but evidently himself. Did he blush, as he saw me? He certainly stared. We stood stock still in the road, confronting each other. He was taller than I was, and was wearing overalls and wellington boots. His hair was cropped short and his face just as thin and brown and wedge-shaped—wide at the forehead, narrow at the chin—as it had been as a young boy. He'd looked at me doubtfully as we nearly collided with each other. "Nessa?"

"You are Ted, aren't you?"

"Yup. Never thought I'd see you again. You all down for the summer?"

"I've got friends coming. My parents are coming later. Paddy's away with a school friend, in Greece. Right now, I'm alone."

"Greece! Phew. Lucky sod. How long you here?"

"Just a couple of weeks. I'm down from university, it's the long vac., but I have to go back to study, it's called the long vac term." It must have been like ancient Greek to him, but he only nodded, as if he understood.

We stood outside the Post Office, where Mrs. Pyle kept shop, selling postcards and sandwiches and buckets and spades as well as stamps and postal orders. Traffic passed us, speeding towards the ferry. The vegetable shop, where we used to go to pick vegetables out of the earth-colored sacks on the floor, was now closed and had become a gas station, or garage as we called it in England. The village had changed, was changing; but when you are nineteen, you're more interested in your own changes, and those of your contemporaries than in anything around you. I was quietly sizing up Ted as a possible stand-in for a Lawrentian male lead in my life—a fling only, of course, as I was to go back to university and presumably find a mate there, eventually. I was still a virgin, but obsessed with the idea of sex, as we all were at that time. It was the era of *Lady Chatterley's Lover* and liberation from the habits and beliefs of our parents, and though mine were definitely interested in sexual love—there was a copy of Marie Stopes in my father's dressing-room—it was our turn now. But my first sensation on meeting Ted again was one of extreme nervousness, a tension that seized me as if I were about to be discovered. I didn't know what this was— not guilt, exactly, not a sudden sexual surge, but fear—of what, of being found out?

"You going this way?"

"Yeah, just been buying stamps."

"We could walk a bit, if you like?"

"Okay." We sauntered together down the hill towards the path down to the beach and the hotel, that had changed hands a few years back and now looked cleaned up and ready for the new tourists, the people who came on walking holidays or brought their grandchildren to the beach. I strode beside him, to keep up. We turned down towards the church and the farm and the path up the hill between stunted gorse-bushes and white flint outcrops towards the crest of Ballard Down. Cows were moving out of the farmyard, being herded up on to the hill; the farm had not yet closed down and become a guest house with its outbuildings made into a tea-room, as it would later. Old rusted farm machinery, tractors and ploughs, lay about on the grass verges. The cows shifted along beside each other, splatting their messes on the ground, nudging each other and mooing, tails flicking flies away. Ted and I waited for them to pass. It's so strange to write it—Ted and I—as if we knew each other, as if ten years had not passed since we last spoke, as if we were old friends going out for a habitual stroll. Ted in his wellingtons and blue overalls, with shirtsleeves rolled, I in jeans and sneakers and a T-shirt, walking up the familiar path to the long hill.

What did we talk about as we walked? He flicked at the hedge-rows with the switch of hazel he still carried, I walked in the middle of the road beside him. Flies rose from the cowpats in the fields at our sides. It's easy to remember how it all looked, how it felt: the day hot, nearly windless in the lee of the land, with clouds rising from the hill ahead of us; the smell of elder-blossom—it must have been early summer, I remember its tom-cat scent. Honeysuckle twined in the hedgerows, with bindweed and brambles. Standing green corn in the cultivated fields we left behind us, almost blue in shadow. The uphill climb that made your thighs and calves ache, if you were not used to it. A tractor passing us, so we stood aside, flattened into the woven hazel of the hedgerow. Ted twirling his switch into the air, against the flies. And in the distance, beyond the different greens of the fields and the white line of the cliffs, the dark blue of the English Channel, were the faint outlines of the far high cliffs of the Needles on the Isle of Wight.

But what we said, how we were together—that is another matter. Nobody can remember exactly what was said forty or fifty years ago. We talked in snatches, I can say that. We passed the bunga-lows of the Glebe estate on our right—where I would come to find him decades later—and he pushed the gate open for me that led on to the hill, with its rabbit droppings and sheep tracks, its gorse bushes, its flint stones underfoot. Here, the grass is worn thin as fur over the chalk bones of the hill. It is now, it was then.

I probably asked him what he was doing. I did.

"Oh, just working for my father. You know, he still has the building business but he's wanting to pass it on soon, most likely."

"Why are you wearing boots? It's so dry."

"I was cleaning out a pond, earlier."

"Oh."

"So you're at university?"

"Yes. It's my second year."

Nothing to say about that—it's beyond his reach. People who go to university probably intimidate him.

But he said, "That must be great."

I thought, Jude the Obscure; yes, he would make a Hardy character even more than a Lawrentian one. But I said nothing, assuming he did not know these books as I did. In fact, I was making a lot of assumptions about him. The class divide cast its long shadow between us, as it did not when we were children and ran about together on the moor—until that summer ended, and we didn't see each other again, because the thing had happened that would keep us apart.

As we reached the top of the hill and stood looking down, a little breathless, onto the roofs of Swanage and the white-edged curve of the bay where the Vikings fought and were defeated, and where today a boat heading for Poole carved a diagonal wake, we were silent. I felt him beside me, breathing. He seemed real as few other people seemed real—my parents, my brothers, people who had always been there. I'd found it hard to make friends at university; other people seemed so alien. But Ted, this young man I had not set eyes on for nearly ten years, did not.

"It's a good place," he said finally. "I can't say I haven't wanted to travel, see other places, but then I reckon I'm lucky, to be just here."

"Could you travel, if you wanted to?"

"My dad wants me here. We get away for a weekend, time to time. But not, you know—abroad." He gestured to the wide arcs of the two bays, one behind us, one in front, and the horizon line of the sea. I thought, I can go anywhere I want—but I don't. Or, not yet, anyway. London seemed foreign enough to me. I was a home-body—home still meant safety, acceptance, the things that at nineteen I seemed to need more than others my age would admit to.

"Down to Old Harry, or on up the hill?"

"Oh, let's go on up." I wanted this walk to be longer than the one that takes you straight down to the cliff edge where the sea comes foaming up into little bays and caves, where the Old Harry rocks are like white teeth in the blue. We turned and went on up Ballard Down, and a horse cantered past us, its mane blowing up, its rider neat in the saddle, hands low. The hill seemed to reverberate with its passing. Shod hoofs on white chalk and flint, striking sparks: how many thousands of horsemen had thundered on past this place, during centuries of horse traffic? Time was, is, held almost immobile here, as so little changes, as the green and blue and white of this landscape hardens into permanent geography, as history parades across it—the bronze age men, the Vikings, the look-outs watching for the armada to sail up the channel, the spies out looking for Napoleon, the soldiers braced against Hitler's imminent invasion. Ted and I, nineteen and twenty-one years old, not knowing what to say to each other, were small and flimsy up here, easily blown off course. He took my hand suddenly, as if to anchor me. "You don't mind?" I said nothing. We walked like that, a few minutes, and he let go. My hand stung with warmth. I seemed to be sweating all over. I looked away, my hair blowing across my face.

"I'd like a photo of you," he said suddenly.

"I've got a camera. I'll send you one, if you want."

"I meant, up here, now. Like that, in the wind." Up here, there was a breeze blowing that you couldn't feel on our side of the hill, as it came in from the west, probably to bring rain. "It's really good to see you again."

I said, "Yeah, you too. Funny, isn't it, how we haven't met for years?"

He looked at me oddly, sharply, and then away. For a moment he faced away from me, and I didn't know him enough to ask why. I let the impression go, of his sudden pain. No, he wasn't a character out of a book, or a working-class hero. He was simply himself. He was someone who knew and liked me, whom I had somehow belittled in my mind. We aren't going to talk about that time, I realized with relief. The time when we were not there, as in Anabel's version, when we did and saw nothing. His silence seemed to agree with this notion, so I could keep my own silence too.

We walked on. The hill was a broad green plateau now and we walked into the wind. Sheep ran from us, scattering grown lambs. The rabbits scooted away, tails flashing, and their small paths were littered with rabbit droppings, between the bent gorse bushes pushed sideways by the prevailing wind. The sea behind us, the sky and hill ahead. He had long legs and a countryman's stride, and I marched fast to keep up. We stopped for a moment to watch a hawk hover still on an air current below us, float and then swoop.

"Sparrow-hawk or kestrel," Ted said. "Hard to tell, against the light. Did you see if it had white on its wings?"

I said, "How do they see, from so high up? Do they ever miss their prey, I wonder?"

"The thing about birds is, they know how to do one thing, and they're efficient at it."

I said, daring the question, "I heard that you'd been away. Where did you go?"

"Oh, yeah, I had to leave for a while." He stopped walking, stared beyond me again at the line of the hill ahead. "Then I was in the army. Cyprus. You know, National Service."

"Oh." Was that it?

"We were the last ones to go. They've stopped it now."

"Oh. I see."

I want to write this in the present tense, as if it goes on eternally, in some continuous present. But no, it was just one time, one walk, one conversation, a first time and a last and the only time we would have.

He walked beside me in silence. I thought of what I'd heard in the shop, a few years back, that he'd had to leave, and that it was hard on his family, as if there had been some sort of disgrace involved. It could hardly have been doing National Service, could it? But I didn't want to ask him more, as his whole face had seemed closed against me and my question, as he stared ahead. I saw the jut of his jaw, a muscle moving in his cheek. We were that sharply aware of each other. I remembered how at ten I had wanted simply to be him—and how when I had read *Wuthering Heights* I had recognized Cathy's impassioned declaration, *I am Heathcliff*. Of course, you would want only to be the person you so admired. It seemed to me then that nothing existed that had not already been written about—as if we were all just copying what others had done and felt for centuries, while all along believing that we were unique.

"I should be at work, rightly. But when I saw you, I couldn't resist the thought of coming up here. Don't know why, but I often come up on my own, you know, to get my head clear, get an eyeful of the view."

Whatever we might say, I knew enough instinctively not to mention our childhood past. Since we had no present together, and no future, it was hard to know what to say. I certainly couldn't start talking about books. But I told him, "This place is what I think of often when I'm stuck somewhere—indoors, or in a traffic jam or something. It kind of lifts me out of wherever I feel trapped."

"Me too. It's maybe because it's so old. Nothing much changes. You know, like up here you can feel you hardly exist, and that's freeing, sort of."

So, we shared this. This was our present: this ancient hill, its buried kings, its horsemen, its past, its soaring hawk. We walked on in a close and warmer silence, and he touched my hand again just briefly, took it, swung it and let it go. When he let go my hand felt light, empty. I did not know what it meant, if anything, that he had done that.

The obelisk, a stone finger seen for miles around raised again recently on its old base, had been put there originally in the nineteenth century to mark the arrival of clean water in Swanage and taken down during the war to deprive enemy aircraft of a landmark. We stood still again and looked at the wide view. The huge gray-green bulk of Nine Barrow Down ahead, the far-down narrow road, the stretch of moorland out towards the blue of the inland lake, and behind us the line of the Channel and the ferry going out towards France. Our world, all three-hundred-and-sixty degrees of it—all you could have, all you could take in. We both breathed hard; we were nineteen and twenty-one and there was just one thing to do, so we did it, our mouths finding each other, our tongues feeling their way, our lips stretched and our bodies clamorous. The huge world around us tipped and reeled. We separated, gasping.

"There." Ted breathed out the word, as if after something long-planned, even inevitable. I looked up at him, my neck a little cricked from kissing, my lips wet in the cooler air. What happened now? I could hardly stand upright, my knees were shaking. I thought I might faint. He wrapped me in his arms and we stood on that hill-top for what may have been a long or short time, I don't know, and then he let me go. Neither of said anything. We walked fast down the hill after that, stumbling over flints in the cropped grass, skipping as we went, down toward the road, and the way back to the village.

THERE WAS A NARRATIVE STRUCTURE to sexual relationships in the early sixties that we hardly questioned. Kissing, arousal, talk, sex, relationship, then either marriage or a break-up. Yet I knew, without any instruction, that this was not what Ted and I would have. We would have one kiss, and no more. We would walk together down to the road and back to the village with our sudden secret knowledge of each other intact and unmentionable, to be locked away for the rest of our lives. It was like an echo of something that had already happened, that had ended abruptly—that could not and did not have any development or conclusion, because it was outside of normal life. What I felt for Ted, whatever it was, wordless, almost vexing in its clarity, and what he felt for me—our meeting like a collision on the road outside the Post Office, our deep and inarticulate selves clashing wildly like this on a hill-top—would go unrecorded, unmentioned, with no follow-up possible. We would—we did—walk away from each other into the rest of our lives.

It was almost immediately after this that I got together with Roland, after going to bed with him once after a party in London at which we both became fairly drunk, and then several times more in his Pimlico flat. It seemed necessary, after kissing Ted, to go to bed with somebody—to put that question to rest. I mention this here—do I want to tell Paula? I want to make it clear to some-body, because it occurs to me only now, all these years later, that the version of my life that was laid out for me then, almost invis-ibly, laid out by the rules and expectations of that time, was the one I accepted with no argument in the end: marriage to a middle-class young man, whatever his bohemian fantasies might be, a career in respectable academia. Luckily, we had no children—nobody to suffer from our complete incomprehension of each other. This was the version I'd been given to expect of life. Love—what was it? Not, surely, what Ted and I had felt on the hill, swept up in a sudden physical passion that was—I rationalized—based in child-hood, or to do with hormones, or the beauty of landscape, or what I had read, or what he had done in the army—I didn't know. I did not love Roland Taylor. I said that I did, I married him, I lied, I thought I could keep my uncomfortable truth hidden all my life, tell nobody, never let him suspect. It lasted five years, and then he found Josie. I never told him of my lie, my body's lie, the lie I began upon as we walked down the aisle of that church near my parents' house, I carrying a white bouquet, he with his hair cut and slicked down for once, our parents and families approving. Anabel and her sisters and their husbands, all there. Success, in their eyes, the success I longed to see. I thought I could do it, accept and live out the convenient version, the one that suited everyone except myself.

IT WAS NOT UNTIL I SAT DOWN AT BRUNO'S TABLE in Manhattan that gray chill lunchtime in April, with the rain on the skylight and the flowering pear tree on the roof, that I knew there was a difference. Love, I saw, was nothing you had to hunt for, work at, pretend to feel. It was, or it was not. It's only now, decades later, back once again in the place where it all began, that I see it: you have to choose the truth above the convenient lie, no matter what it does to you or others, no matter how terrifying it feels. When I was a child, I killed someone who was in love—the woman on the beach with her lover. We—I—killed love. We did not mean to, but we did.

TWENTY

I SAW ANABEL FOR THE LAST TIME at my mother's funeral. She came down from London with her sisters and arrived wearing a large black hat that made me feel not only guiltily hatless but not sufficiently in mourning. My mother, I knew, would have scorned black, and hats; but she was no longer there to chat with about how extraordinary people were, and I missed her sharply, sorely. My father, who had died first, would have joked about the people who were beginning to show up—he who detested church events and any kind of hypocrisy. Bruno was with me, amazed at how the English conducted funerals, their shrieking with horror and laughter by turns, telling anecdotes that had nothing to do with anything, gobbling tea and cake and looking avidly around for something stronger. I told him that my family was not representative, but had an uneasy feeling that it was.

IT HAPPENED THAT ANABEL, LIZ, SUSIE AND I shared a taxi back from the church to the house for the reception, if you could call it that. They sat on the back seat and I sat on the little fold-out dickey seat opposite them and listened to them saying how they missed shopping in Harrods and they could have had longer in London to do so if only the train had not been so late, how hopeless British

Rail was, and perhaps they would be able to get something from Marks to have for supper when they got back, if things didn't go on too long. And, where to buy a summer bag.

"Yes, I heard there was a sale on at John Lewis."

"I couldn't find one, though I looked all over."

"Have you tried Harvey Nicks?"

"No, they only had them in brown. A sort of nasty milk chocolate."

I sat and heard them and sharply missed Bruno, who had decided to walk back with Paddy to get some fresh air. I missed America, where even if people would have hugged me too much, and gazed into my eyes and talked about the after-life and being in a better place, at least they would not have talked about shopping. I decided I detested my cousins. But then Anabel turned to me and said, "But Nessa, we're so, so sorry about Aunt Diana, you must be quite wretched, aren't you? I was after Mummy died. We all were. So we know how you feel."

Aunt Laura had died a couple of years before her sister, and I had been in America.

"You weren't at the funeral, were you? I always think that when people emigrate I'm never going to see them again. But here you are. You don't sound very American."

Her gloved hand was on my knee, and I briefly felt the weight of it, that was perhaps the weight of sympathy, or of accusation, that I had been inexcusably absent and in America when her own mother died. Then, thank God, we arrived at the house.

Out on the lawn, a woman was making a fuss about the tea being Indian and having been brewed in an urn. "But Di always had Lapsang! She would never have had an urn!"

I heard someone say briskly, "Well, she has now."

We clustered together as if it would have been unthinkable to stand apart. Paddy was, thank God, about to begin opening bottles of wine—to make up for the tea in an urn? One of Susie's daughters was passing out plates with cake. A fat man in a straw hat under the damson tree was cackling with laughter. I looked for Bruno, imagined him astonished at the English and their levity, their almost brutally casual air. In his family, I knew, everyone would have been sobbing, their arms around each other's necks, the women swathed glamorously in black, mascara running down their cheeks.

I found myself beside Anabel again—her heels digging into the turf of the lawn, her black hat tipped against the furtive late-afternoon sun, her lipstick replenished. She glanced at me, now that we were briefly alone.

"Nessa, remember those holidays in Dorset, what fun we had? We used to run wild, do you remember, we were out on the moor all day, getting up to all sorts of adventures? I often think about them. Of course, it was all quite dangerous, really, with unexploded bombs and everything. I wonder that they let us do it. And, d'you remember those boys we used to play with? Quite rough characters, really."

I look at her, searching for the girl she was, who organized us and egged us on, who was our leader. Anabel has become, as was expected of her, a woman who looks after a rich husband, albeit in an uncomfortable medieval Scottish castle.

"I remember," I tell her, "But it all seems a very long time ago. Can I get you a glass of wine?"

"Oh, that would be lovely. That tea was pretty awful. But Nessa, do you remember, it was all so exciting, following people, thinking we were spying for England? What happened to those village boys, d'you suppose? Did you ever see them again?"

"No," I said. I was not going to give her Ted, even after all these years. I could imagine her mixture of fascination and disgust.

I thought—I am never going to know what she thought about it, or what actually happened on the cliff. I am never going to get an answer from her, any more than I did when we were twelve, thirteen, fourteen. We have agreed, once again, that nothing happened. Nothing *could* have happened. It was not even a possibility. We were not even there.

"And the times you came to stay, and we wrote those plays and stories, and everything?"

"Yes, of course." What else was there to say?

That time with Ted, when we were children. Then, the other brief time when we were young adults. I would never tell her or anybody what had happened between him and me, however slight it had been, and fragile. It was like a door with a secret catch that could swing open and make me unbearably vulnerable. There are things in life that do have to remain secret, secret from any outside view, because otherwise you can't be who you really are. It was then, at my mother's funeral, that I knew that there was a true thing, tiny and invisible at the very center of my life, that was mine and his alone. I poured white wine into a glass and handed it to Anabel, and it was to do with my mother being dead, and my brothers and me being on the front line now, the adults, the people who were responsible for what happened next, and everything having moved on: I decided to confront her.

"About that time in Dorset," I said, "We were there, weren't we? At the place where the cliff fell in. You must remember. It wasn't just the boys, was it? And you told me we weren't there, Anabel. I just wanted to set the record straight." I was shaking as I said it—yes, the old feelings, she's going to be angry with me, I've spoken out of turn. But I held my ground. My mother was no longer here, but I was. Anabel and I were both middle-aged. If there was a moment when I had to take responsibility for the past, it was surely now.

She looked at me curiously for a moment, as if wondering what on earth I was talking about. I caught a flicker of recognition, and I almost had her. But then she shut down. "I honestly don't remember, Nessa. It was all so long ago. Does it really matter?"

She pursed her lipsticked mouth and peered at me with her pale gray eyes, alert under penciled brows. She tipped her hat against the sun. There was a silence between us for a moment, in which I felt she dared me to go further, and I did not. In that moment, as she looked at me, and then away, I glimpsed her vulnerability, and drew back. She knew. She couldn't admit it, but she knew. And in her life, I saw that there were many unadmitted facts, many unexpressed feelings, even many regrets. She was living the life of an upper-class Englishwoman, fenced around with ritual and denial. Who knew the real Anabel? Possibly, nobody. She had had to make sure of that. There was a silence between us, and I felt it, an unspoken admission, her retreat before the truth that lay between us. It would never be said, but I knew how afraid she was, that it might be.

"Is your husband here?" she asked me at last.

"Yes, just over there. The man with the beard and dark hair. I'll introduce you." We teetered together on our heels across the grass, and I reached into my past with her to connect it with my present life with Bruno—my transatlantic life, that invisibility and refuge that I had sought. I saw them shake hands, and Bruno's glance at me said—is this your famous cousin, the one you were so in awe of? And I smiled and nodded and raised my eyebrows just slightly in the semaphore of marriage, and watched him engage her in what he thought was English conversation. I saw her, a middle-aged woman, stuck in a class-consciousness that he as an American escaped—she had no idea where he came from and his accent was merely charming, as in the movies, and he did have those Italian eyes, so—lucky Nessa. I moved away, to pour wine for someone else. It was the last conversation we ever had. Lately, I heard that she may have Parkinson's, and I'm truly sorry. What we shared—what we all share in this life—was a moment, a certain time, something at once irreplaceable and hard to define, that matters whether you like it or not, because it has made you who you are.

PART V
ALWAYS YOU

Twenty-One

I N THE MORNING I WALK UP the familiar path through the heather, to try to find the hide-outs we made in the old trenches of long ago. I remember roughly where they were, on the side of the hill looking back toward the far stretches of the harbor. But my feet won't find their way there as easily as they once did. Gorse and bracken have grown up where heather used to be—they are faster growers—and some of the gorse bushes are as tall as I am. The heat of this summer stills the air and it feels thick with silence. Bees in the heather fumble about. The purple of the bell heather is turning to brown, the ling seems whiter, pale with drought. There's a lizard on the path, darting away. The hill where the trenches were is gorse-topped, with a flare of yellow, the path towards it lost. I watch for snakes—adders and grass-snakes—that like to lie across paths to bask in the sun. I remember how we leapt over tufts of heather and tall bracken to reach our look-out place: how we came up the hill from the south side where there was no path, and the hidden places we had found were just over the lip of the hill, to the north.

Then I know I am there. Today, the trenches are half as deep, and partly covered by gorse. I peer in and see only sand, pebbles, rabbit droppings. Of course, nobody has been here. Children today do not play out here for hours, days, weeks, inventing sto-ries about spies and plots to invade England. The weapons have gone from here, leaving the place to rabbits, deer, lizards, adders, the original inhabitants. I've found the place, but it no longer resonates, it has become neutral, a hillside like any other. Even the double tracks left by tanks on the side of the hill are blurred, duplicated by footpaths, trails for horses, all the traffic of the past sixty or so years.

What did I expect? At least it is not built over, changed out of all recognition, tourist-ridden, obliterated by a century of change. It is inconspicuous still, lacks the meaning we found here long ago, left here for us by the soldiers of that time. War no longer marks this place. Its echo is long gone. History has become geography, a battle-ground has returned to its old innocence. I turn back, go down the rough road and home. Yes, it feels like home, this house. Its curtains drawn to keep the sun out, I live in it as my grand-mother did, and feel her movements in me. Time makes its own way into our bodies, slowing and condensing, drying and wither-ing, sharpening some insights, dulling others. For the first time I think—what will I look like to Ted? I look like an old person, now. An old woman. I don't mind the way I look, and since some people say I remind them of Charlotte Rampling, I don't even mind the sag of my eyelids, the looseness under my chin. But to someone who has not seen me since I was nineteen, the change could be a shock. Of course, he's old too, now. What does it really mean? Do we change, with age?

Inside me still, I know, is the child I was at ten, as well as the girl who kissed him wildly up on the hill.

IN THE HEAT OF AFTERNOON, SHADING MY EYES with hat and sun-glasses, I walk downhill through the village, past the store—the only one left now—past the church, the stone cross, the former farmhouse, and up the hill towards the Glebe estate. The air is rich with the smell of hot nettles, honeysuckle. The hedges grow tall around me, cutting off air from the sea. The house, he told me, is one of the older bungalows built on this land belonging to the church. I remember when the whole place was built in the late 1950's, before the take-over by the National Trust, and my father's fury at the "eyesores" and "gerry-building" that were taking place—that the side of the hill that had been green, wooded and inhabited only by sheep and cattle, was being built on at all. But the local people didn't see it that way: they saw progress, they saw modernity, come at last. I am not surprised that Ted Samways has ended up here, in a brick bungalow with a view that strangers would pay a million pounds for, on the last development allowed in the village.

I'm not surprised that I'm walking easily towards it, either. It all felt remarkably easy, the phone call, the old man's voice in answer, my own belief that he didn't remember my name but was trying to place me, his politeness in inviting me to come for tea the following day. Yes, the village has changed—it has been cleaned up, and the old rusting machinery removed, the banks of nettles trimmed, the grass verges mown. I'm wearing an old skirt, my beach shoes and a wide-brimmed hat that has been in the cupboard in the hall for decades. It's too hot to dress up, and anyway, what would be the point? What Ted Samways and his wife will see is a woman as old as they are, and that is how I will see them. The road is hot and steep between tall hedges of bramble and honeysuckle tangled in among hazel saplings and old man's beard. Before me, the great hill stretches, its skyline pure against the dark blue of afternoon sky. I'm the only walker; it's too hot for ramblers and hikers, and everybody has made for the beach.

I reach the first house, the one he told me about, with its sunburst gate and paved garden path, hydrangeas blooming on both sides. It's brick, evidently 1950s, with an addition to one side that has a conservatory, with curtains drawn to shut out the sun. It must have been one of the first houses built up here, long before the luxury bungalows with their plate-glass windows and curving gravel drives. The front garden has, as well as the hydrangeas like cream puddings, red-hot pokers and dahlias in beds, and a weeping willow tree. It looks like an old person's house—but a fairly prosperous old person, one who decided never again to live in a tumbledown thatched cottage with too many inhabitants, as Ted had to when young. I ring the doorbell and nothing happens. I try the door-knocker, two raps. Silence. Then I hear movement in the hall, as if someone is bending down to pick up mail, or a newspaper. The door opens. A tall, slightly stooping man with silver hair close-cropped and a brown face. Of course, it's him, it's the Ted I knew: you can't mistake eyes, or the way hair grows, or a certain mischievous look that hasn't gone away. I hold out my hand, awkward on the doorstep, the mat with Welcome on it. He peers at me, and I have the impression that he's pretending to be near-sighted, older than he is; in some way, he's having me on. He takes my hand and holds it for a moment, lets it go.

"It's Nessa," I say, in case he doesn't recognize me. "Remember me?"

"Come in," he says, "Don't stand out there in the heat. Nessa. Of course I remember you."

"It's been a while."

"You can say that again." He leads the way down the narrow corridor, away from the light outside into something cooler, dimmer, a refuge from this burning summer.

He ushers me before him in the narrow space that's packed with pictures on the walls, photographs, mostly, and a bookcase with magazines overflowing, and heaps of shoes and several walking-sticks.

"Nessa, well, here's a turn-up for the books. Can't believe it. How are you? Remind me what that cousin of yours was called, I don't remember."

"Anabel."

"Yes, Anabel. I remember. Bossy, she was. And a younger brother. Or two, were there?"

"I didn't know if you'd remember. Ted—can I call you Ted?"

"Well, it would be a rum day if you didn't. Come in, come in, we're letting the heat into the house. I've laid tea in the sitting-room, it's the coolest."

There seems to be no sign of a Mrs. Ted Samways. He's laid the tea himself. I notice his hands go out to touch the banisters, the wall, the doorframe as he leads the way down the corridor. As if he isn't too steady on his feet? His hands are large and brown, with dark spots, but well-kept. He straightens a photograph as he goes. "Nessa," he says, as if to himself, "Well, fancy that." Then, "I Googled you, after your call. Saw all the books you've written. Quite a list, eh."

I follow him into the low-ceilinged, cluttered room, where a sofa and two armchairs take up most of the available space, and a tea tray with cups and saucers, a milk jug and a plate of Jaffa cakes awaits us on a low table. I sit down in an armchair, to avoid the sofa that looks too intimate, somehow, as if we'd be tipped together in its lap. He tidies boat magazines and a local newspaper from one end of the table.

"I didn't know if you'd remember me."

"Well, of course I do. Of course I remember you, Nessa. We were just kids, eh? Long time ago now. Funny thing, life."

A small fear lodges itself in my gut as I sit there: that I am about to be blamed for something I have not yet thought of. That sharp uncomfortable feeling, of being known and therefore vulnerable. I have felt this before with him, surely, but now I am old and did not expect it. He goes off into the kitchen and puts the kettle on to boil, and I have time to look around the room, that is silent and though cluttered, also empty with the peculiar emptiness of a person living alone after a lifetime with someone. I see from the photographs that he married young—yes, at the church in the village, a young Ted with long hair, thin-faced as ever, clean as a choirboy and not much older, and a dark-haired plumpish young woman wearing a springy white veil and smiling hard. It must have been not long after I last saw him. I see that they have children, and that the children have children. I see faded rosettes that someone must have won at a gymkhana, years ago. I see paintings of boats, a blown-up photograph of the bay, another bookcase with some thick books on it, including a recent biography of Churchill, a desk in one corner with papers piled under a nautical-looking brass weight. Then he comes back with the pretty teapot that matches the cups.

"Got out the best china, see," he says, "It's not every day that I have a visitor for tea. I couldn't give you tea at the kitchen table, now, not after all these years. Pat would never forgive me." He puts down the teapot and lets me off my awkwardness about his missing wife. "Pat died a year ago. My wife—there she is, see?" I look again at the smiling bride and at his younger self. Pat and Ted. Ted and Pat Samways. Their children and grandchildren: evidence of this man's long life.

"You must miss her. I'm so sorry."

"Aye, I do. Life and soul of the party, she was. Never a word of complaint, though she was ill for a good while. Yes, I'm on my own now, have to make the best of it. What about you, did you marry?"

Perhaps he is wondering, as I did, why I am alone here; perhaps he fears to ask the question too. I say quickly, "Oh, yes. My husband's American, he's over there at present; he's coming to join me. I came on my own. No children, no. But Bruno has two, so he shares them with me. He has a big family. Italian."

"Still have the house up on the heath, do you? Your grandmother bought it after the war, if I remember right?"

"Yes. We kept it; we used to rent it out. My brothers and I thought we'd hold on to it, for somewhere to land." He raises his eyebrows, as if this makes us sound like migrating birds or helicopters. "We most of us live outside the UK now." I add, "It needs a lot done to it, if it's to survive another winter. We've been thinking about selling."

"Sounds like the rest of us, eh? Going downhill. Maybe you just need a good builder. Maybe my son could help you there; he's in charge of the business now. So, you all went off to foreign parts."

"Yes. I live in the US, Patrick in New Zealand. Charlie's in Germany."

"I see." Silence. I see him thinking—or imagine I do—about the strangeness of not living in the country, even the specific place, in which you were born. "Never really thought about leaving, myself. Apart from a spell in the army, of course. We were the last year to do National Service. Then I took the business over from my dad, and so it went. Married a local girl, Pat was the daughter of Mrs. Pyle in the post office, remember? So, no reason to leave. And now, I wish I'd seen more of the world." He pours the tea in a thin brown stream, his hand steady—nothing doddery about him—and hands me milk. "Your lot put milk in after, right?" I decline sugar but take a Jaffa cake, a curious reminder of childhood teas, with its chocolate coating and gooey jam inside.

"If Pat'd been here, she'd have made you scones. But I haven't got round to that, yet." He seems not to wonder why I've come, but sits there tranquilly with his saucer raised high so that he can sip his tea easily. His gray hair is cut in very much the same style that he had as a young man, short back and sides and wavy on top, and he seems to have lost none of it. His face is lined and brown, with a few moles on his temples. He's a lean man still, with hardly a noticeable pouching at his belly as he sits there. So, here we are. What now?

I watch him slurp his tea, and catch a quick sideways glance. Yes, he does wonder what I am doing here, why I have come. Are we going to make each other wait, leave the subject we have to talk about while we exchange pleasantries, deny that there is anything between us at all?

I say, "I went up on the moor, earlier. I thought I'd see where those holes were that we used to play in."

"Oh, aye. The old trenches. Did you find them? Must be all covered up by gorse now. I haven't been up there in a while."

I open my mouth to speak, thinking—well, that's a dead end,
then—but he preempts me. "I'm glad you came. You don't want to
come to the end of life with things unsaid. Since Pat went, I know
that. It can happen to any of us, any time."

I wait. The room is still, and behind the partly drawn blinds, I
see the line of the ancient hill that hasn't changed in millennia, and
will not.

He smiles at me, and it's Ted's smile, with wrinkles. "You haven't
changed."

"Oh, come on! Of course I have." I laugh, but feel stricken. "You
look the same."

What we see, I think, is part memory, part longing. That face,
those eyes. The person inside who does not change looking out
from the shape of the one who does.

He says, "Still the same way with your hair, that way you pushed
it back off your face. I remember. If that isn't too personal."

"No, it isn't." I push my hair back, where my forehead is sweating. We both laugh.

He says, sounding abrupt and effortful, "I've something to say,
to get out of the way. I've always felt sorry about it, Nessa. I should
never have done it. I couldn't talk about it when we—well, when
we last saw each other. Any of it. I just wanted to be up there on
that hill with you, that day, and nothing else in the way, then. You
know?"

I wait to see what he means—any of it? My heart seems to be
beating overtime.

"Of course, these days it would've been seen in a worse light than
it was then, and we were only kids. But it isn't too late to say I'm
sorry, I hope. We're old now, but we're still the same people. I've been
hoping maybe I'd get the chance, but I never really thought I would."

I still have no idea what he is talking about. It seems to have
no connection to me, or what I have come to ask. I hope he isn't

going to apologize for kissing me on the hill. That memory, that one moment, I want us still to have together—a shared story, a knowledge deeper than words.

"I'm sorry. Maybe I shouldn't have mentioned it. You've only been here five minutes. It's been on my conscience, that's all. You have time to think, when you're suddenly on your own. About life, about things you have done."

I say, and it comes out almost as a whisper, "What?"

"You don't remember?"

"I don't understand."

"Well, maybe, least said, soonest mended. But that time, behind the village hall? When we were kids?"

I'm silenced by him. I try to remember the village hall. Behind it, what was there? Oh, yes. That.

"Something I asked you then. I'm embarrassed to say it, now." He pours boiling water from the kettle into the teapot, fumbles the lid back on. I can see that he longs not to go any further with this apology about something I have not even remembered.

"I asked you to show me something. You know, I'll show you mine if you'll show me yours." He's trying to make light of it. But it was light, wasn't it, at the time? "You know how boys are curious about girls. And we were all so ignorant. I had no sisters. But I shouldn't have asked you, just the same."

"Oh. Oh, I see." I begin to see it, the scene in which Ted, the boy Ted, asks me to lift up my T-shirt and show him my chest. I'm only ten. I have nothing to show him as yet, just tiny nipples nearly as flat as his own and a discreet little slit where I pee. And as for what he has to show me, I've seen my brother in the bath countless times, and running naked about the house, and my baby brother squirting pee up from where his nappy was being changed on my mother's knee. I've seen boys and what they have for as long as I can remember, and I'm not curious about what's between their legs. But I remember the sudden warm press of his mouth on my cheek.

The request he'd made was so strange to me that I almost didn't remember it. And he, this elderly man, has been feeling guilty about it for his entire life? I don't know what to say. Memory makes and also distorts our lives.

"Yes, I do remember. But really, it didn't matter. Not at all."

I have never told anyone, apart from that therapist, about being in that close dark place with Ted, when he asked me simply to show him my childish body. I never thought to—at the time, it seemed such a straightforward request. Yet, in my fantasies, I have to admit, it has lived on, merging in retrospect with the kiss on the hilltop and the unfocussed desire of that later time. Two episodes. Our story, our secret.

"Well, people are saying these days, it can wreck a girl's life. All these men coming out of the woodwork with things they did years ago, that they didn't ought to. So I'm glad to have the chance to say I'm sorry. Yes, we were just children. But, all the same, I should have known better. I was older than you. I just liked you, Nessa, that was it, and I was curious."

"I think we all remember things differently," I say, "According to our feelings about them. I honestly didn't think much about the time when we—did that. I mean, it wasn't a big deal. It's what children do. It certainly didn't wreck my life. In fact—" I am about to say I'd forgotten about it, but that seems vaguely insulting.

He looks back at me—relieved, puzzled, I can't tell—and then says, "Well, that's a load off my mind. All these blokes recently—you know?"

He's told me what he's had on his mind, that small scene from so many years ago. Now I feel less shy about asking him what I need to know. "Yes, I understand. But really—there's nothing to apologize for. No, I wanted to ask you about the cliff fall. About the bones they found on the beach this summer."

A fly buzzes against the pane. Outside, a couple of young women pass on horseback, going up the road; I hear the sharp clop of hoofs, voices calling.

"Oh, did you, now? Well, did you see last week's paper?"

"No? I was away, in London."

He sorts through a heap of papers on the low table and turns up the copy of the local Gazette. "Look."

I take it, and recognize what I read. The forensic experts in Southampton have used a new technique for dating human bones. Carbon-14 dating. Radio-carbon in bones remained steady until perturbed by mid-20th century above-ground nuclear testing. From 1954 to 1963 there was a distinct increase, after which there was a decline to former levels. This meant that the bones found were of someone who died before 1954. The amount of weathering of the bones and their nitrogen content and that of the nails and tooth enamel suggested that the deceased died after 1951. The conclusion was that this young woman was buried in a cliff-fall that took place in 1952, when a local ex-soldier had been taken from the site to a hospital in Weymouth, but had died of his injuries on the way. Injuries to the skull of the deceased woman indicated damage from rock debris, but no single blow. Foul play was not suspected, and the case was closed.

It's the official version of what was sent to me by e-mail from the University of Southampton. I hand the paper back to him. "It was her. The woman we followed. That time, remember, we were there, you and I and Anabel and Roger and Patrick." Those people. That couple. "Anabel wouldn't talk about it. Paddy was too young to remember. There was only you and Roger left, and me. I'm right, aren't I? It must be her."

"I thought so too," he says.

"And it's taken all this time to come to light."

He watches me, sets down his plate. "Things take the time they take, I reckon."

"What happened after we left, that summer, Ted? I really want to know. Where's Roger, is he still around?"

"Roger's away in Bournemouth, managing a hotel. He hardly ever comes back. He got off scot-free, thanks to his dad and that

Major bloke that owned the hotel. It was me that copped it. You never knew? We were seen, that day. There was someone saw us."

"How can they have? Who?"

"Someone told the police that I had started the landslide. They told on us. The cops came to the cottage, talked to my dad, and Roger's. You never knew?"

"I didn't know any of this."

My tea is too hot to drink still, and I put my cup down. Tea, the ritual of it, is no longer the point. "I knew nothing. They wouldn't let us see the papers. All I heard was in the Higgins' shop. Then we left, and didn't come back till the following year. But we weren't allowed to see you, I do remember that."

He says—this man who is also young Ted, the choirboy, the boy in ragged shorts I knew, and the young man who gave me my first real kiss, and the bridegroom in the photo at the wedding I never saw, "Well, as I say, I was the one that copped it. Roger's dad talked to old St. John at the hotel and he got him off. I got three years' Borstal. Reform school, you know. They were tough with kids in the old days, I can tell you. Didn't do me much good. Except we did a load of bricklaying, so my dad was pleased about that; I was a dab hand when I came out. When we weren't cutting up pipes for the lead and copper."

"Oh, no."

"Oh, yes. And—I'm sorry to have to say it, but you all went off back to London and wherever and nobody accused you of a thing, I shouldn't wonder." His Dorset accent gets stronger, as he stares back at me across the ruins of our tea.

"Oh, Ted. I never knew." I am really horrified. "You never said. That time we walked on the hill."

"I couldn't. I didn't want to. I was ashamed. I was still angry, too. You all get off scot-free, and I'm clobbered." He looks down, and I feel the wave of his old shame and anger. "I didn't want you to know. I guessed it would be the only time we had together, you and me, and I didn't want to ruin it—so, I just let it go. I'm glad I did."

"I am too. It was perfect, that time."

He looks at me sharply, to check my glib response—then sees that yes, I mean it.

"Well, it's water under the bridge now," he says.

Water, time, a whole lifetime. Days spent thinking of quite other things. Time is a spiral: we come back to what we already knew, and see it differently.

"Her name was Magda." It matters, to know that and to tell him, and I am glad that I can.

He looks up sharply. "You knew her name? How? Nobody else knows who she was."

"I met her," I tell him, "I talked to her. She was with him, at the hotel."

"I didn't know that. Tell me more. You went to the hotel?"

"Yes, on my own. I went there one day and I saw them both. I told them how to get to Shell Bay. She shook my hand. She told me her name, and I told her mine. And then—I forgot it. Until the other day."

"Jesus." He rubs his hand across his face. "It's all so long ago, but it's like it was yesterday, what with seeing you again."

It's as if she's in the room with us—her floating dress, her blonde hair, her accent. Or, I'm in the dusty hotel again, fidgeting at the desk, holding out my hand in the shape of a cowrie, to show her.

I say at last, "You hardly think about something for fifty years or more, and then there it is, right in front of you."

"I had to think about it," he says, "I was made to. It changed my life."

"Ted, what happened? To you, I mean? I can't believe you didn't tell me."

"I'm telling you now because we're old and it doesn't matter anymore. You think I was proud of myself? It damn near wrecked me, and there you were, fresh as a daisy, that day on the hill, just out of university and all. I would've been mortified. Damn, if it hadn't been for the army, I wouldn't have been able even to ask you to go for a walk. In some ways the army did make a man of me."

Here it is, at last—his life, spread out before me. It's the last piece of the whole story, the piece I have needed to find. And I have given him his—her name, our meeting, that long-ago scene in the hotel.

"It's all a long time ago," he says, "But it was hell at the time, let me tell you. I did my time in remand school—I was too young to be up for manslaughter, but they reckoned I was out of control, a danger to society. Then I came home and worked for my dad. He kept me on a short rein. I'd had dreams, plans to study, get away, go abroad, work—go to America, even." He shoots me a hard look. "Yes, I wasn't going to spend my whole life in one place. I got away to do National Service, though, because you had to. Went to Cyprus. Loved it. We were meant to be peace-keeping, you know they were at each other's throats. We saw a lot of bad stuff. You couldn't love that, not the trying to stop people killing each other, no, more the just being away, out of the country, and nobody knowing who I was." He pauses. "That was just before you came down here and we went for that walk, like I said. Then I thought, what the hell, no point even trying to get in touch with you, might as well marry and settle down since I can't go anywhere else, and Pat was willing."

I say, "And you apologized to me. It should be the other way around."

"It wasn't you, Nessa."

I feel shy to tell him that I'd seen that they were having sex, our couple. Had he seen that too?

He says, "It wasn't exactly an accident though, was it? Whatever they say now."

"But if we didn't know what we were doing?"

"That was the excuse people made during the war. They didn't know. Or, they'd been told to do it. Obeying orders. It doesn't work. They drummed that into me in the reform school. Oh, they made us feel guilty there, but it was somehow all right because we got our punishment, they beat us and starved us and I remember thinking, even though I was still really a kid when I came out, I've done my time now, I'm clear. You know, getting a beating, it lets you free in a way. But the other thing—nobody else knew except you, Nessa, and I never thought to see you again, so I was, like, stuck with it. Then when we did meet again, I had some of the same feelings, but of course, I was a man by then, not just a little boy."

"But who could have seen us? That day at the cliff? How can anyone have seen you clearly enough to accuse you? Do you know?" We'd been lying flat at the cliff edge, surely protected from sight even from the back windows of the hotel by the gun emplacement's concrete wall.

"I do know who it was. It was her. Your cousin."

"Anabel?"

"Yes."

I have always known, of course I have, since first she told me, it was those boys, those oiks, not us, we were not even there. Until this moment, I have never connected what had to be true. "Oh, God. Of course." The last fragment of the mosaic—Anabel. Her evasiveness, her lie. Her turning away from me at the funeral. Anabel, who was terrified of what we had done and had to blame it on someone else, a working-class boy who would never be able to find her to exact revenge or even apology.

We are in at the deep end, now—because we have to be. I'm beyond embarrassment, and I think so is he. I'm shocked at what I've just realized, but he is calm—of course, he's known all along. Nobody else could have seen what happened. It had to have been one of us, who was there. It had to have been her, Anabel.

"Oh, God, I'm so, so sorry."

"It isn't you who should be sorry. Anyway, it's old history now."

I tell him, "I knew, but without really knowing. She told me, over and over, now that I think of it. She insisted that we weren't there, that it was you and Roger."

"And that is what she told her parents, and then the police.

Look, would you like a drop of whisky with that? I think we could do with it." He gets out a half-full bottle and drops some into my tea. We clink teacups. I think—were we in each other's lives all along? Are we still?

"Why did it happen? Do you know?"

He says, "You mean chucking the stones down on those people? I think it was because we were all filled up with propaganda from the war still. Without understanding it, really. The whole country was full of it—what's the word, paranoia, and a sort of excitement, as if we couldn't bear it all to be over. A bit like this nonsense that's going on now, come to think of it. Nationalism. Suspicion of strangers. And, it was true, there were still spies about, and people looking for retribution, and there was also a sort of stupid thinking that was suspicious of anyone foreign. I was deep in it, from boys' comics and films and TV, and everything, and the fact of all that having happened right here in the village. I was sick that I'd missed it, the war I mean, that I was too young. So, when I had the chance to do something, I jumped at it. I thought it was patriotic."

"It's so strange, that they found her, just this year."

"Yeah. It was all about the anniversary of D-day, clearing the site. I went down to find out but as I say, they wouldn't let anyone by. I wanted to know, or I half wanted to. I didn't feel good about it. Pat had died, and I reckon I didn't want to think about bodies and skeletons and what's coming to us all."

"It was just before I got here."

"End of June, wasn't it? Just before the tourist season really got going, and they wanted to clear the way to that beach. And next year, it's going to be crowded with all the anniversary stuff."

"So the anniversary was the reason for it, why she turned up this year. But I couldn't help thinking it was more than a coincidence. It felt like a message, for me."

Ted looks doubtful. "Well, I think it's a coincidence, myself. I don't go much for messages from bones. But nobody knows who she was really, though they say she was from Eastern Europe. He was a Dorset man, from Wimborne. They were lovers, here at the hotel just to get some time together."

"The woman at the hotel said something about a dirty weekend. I didn't know what it meant, then." I like the way he's said it—lovers—a word I haven't thought he'd use.

"Poor buggers, probably only wanted a bit of peace and quiet."

"I saw them, what they were doing. I didn't understand it at the time."

"Having sex on the beach? Yeah. I couldn't get enough of looking at them, horrible kid that I was, and then—well, I wanted to chuck something at them, I couldn't stand it, somehow. It was exciting, in a way I didn't understand at the time. There, now you know."

"I remember. I felt weird about it too, but I didn't know what it was. I didn't know if anyone else saw."

"Well, I did. And then I killed them."

"We killed them," I remind him.

"All right. We."

I tell him, "Anabel kept telling me that we weren't even there. I couldn't talk about it, not to her, not to anyone. I began to believe maybe I wasn't there at all. It was easier. But I remembered it, deep down, the way you remember parts of a dream."

I was a child who had recurrent nightmares, that fear of suffocation—as if I, not she, were the victim.

"Well, you didn't dream it, Nessa. You were right there beside me, and I dared you to chuck a stone over too."

I remember, I'd wanted to impress him. I feel that stone in my hand. I feel the earth beneath me as I lie flat at the cliff edge. Does the body remember what the mind wants to forget?

"And then a sort of avalanche began, that we hadn't expected. Right? I had to tell about it so many times myself, I couldn't even be sure of what had happened and what I was making up to save my skin. But you know, we do know what's true, really, in our hearts. We just do. If we let go of that we turn into monsters."

I see his own hand shake a little as he refills my cup and his, splashes in more whisky. I think, he went through it and came out the other side, the accusations, the punishment, and I did not, and it gives him an authority that I have to respect.

I say, "You did time for his death, all that time ago. But what about her?"

"You can't blame yourself now, Nessa."

"But I was as much to blame as you were."

"We were all of us carried away by the idea of protecting the country against foreigners. Everybody was. We were told to be suspicious of people. Not just Nazis or real criminals. Everyone. Remember? All those films about heroes. The Dam Busters. Remember the Dam Busters? Everybody cheered when they dropped all those bombs. Bloody Douglas Bader. And men being brave on sinking ships. I was crazy about it all, when I was a boy. Collected all the model planes, German as well as English, had little kits for making them, sticking them together with glue. Messerschmidts, Heinkels, Dorniers, as well as Spitfires and Hurricanes. I used to have dog-fights with them, one in each hand."

I can see him, a plane in each hand, making the kind of noise that boys make to sound like war-planes. Paddy used to do that, too.

I say, "What a strange time it was, when we were growing up. There was so much I didn't understand. The war being over but somehow not. Everything people had felt and believed was all still there, all covered up by the flags and cheering and congratulating ourselves."

We have made our confessions to each other, and now, talking about the bigger picture, the England that we grew up in, we can say it—it wasn't just us.

"We couldn't stop telling ourselves that story. Right? Churchill and Monty, brave little England, doing the right thing." He says, "I've read a lot. I started reading when I got out of Borstal. I know now it wasn't all like that. We have to try and understand the times we've been living in, even if we get to it too late."

The people being deported this year, from this country. And the people who have lived here all their lives—from Europe, from

Jamaica, from India—being sent away because they don't have the right papers. The ones refused entry, left to drown at sea. The ones locked in cages in the country I live in. He's right; we become monsters, if we don't admit what we know to be true.

The sun moves away from the window, and the sky between the blinds is a darker blue. The end of afternoon. How long have I been here with him? An hour, two, half a century? I have been waiting to have this conversation all my life.

I taste the bite of whisky in the dregs of my tea. "Did you see Roger much when you came out?"

"They didn't want me going around with him after that. His folks, I mean. I was a bad influence. Well, I mean, I was." He chuckles. "We were bad boys."

I'm relieved that he can laugh. "We weren't allowed to see you, either. So, I never knew."

You saw nothing, Nessa, nothing at all. We left Ted to carry the whole story alone—a burden he could not put down. I knew what Borstal was all right: a prison for children. It was what we were threatened with, when young, if we did not behave, but it never came anywhere near our sheltered lives.

I have to ask him, "Ted, you've done time for it. Can you forgive me?"

"Forgive you for what? Not knowing I'd been shipped off to Borstal? Not coming there with me? Chucking that stone or lump of earth or whatever it was when I dared you to? Don't be daft. There's nothing to forgive."

"It was so unfair that it happened only to you."

"Well, that's the class system, ain't it? Doesn't look like much has changed, since. Toffs get away with it, always have. But it wasn't your fault, Nessa, none of that. You didn't know."

"I wish I had."

"Really? What could you have done? Come and kept me company? Look. Here we are, two old codgers—though you look pretty good, Nessa, if I may be so bold." He gives me that sudden grin.

"Don't be sorry," he says, "I've had a fine life, really. Good marriage, good kids, grand-kids, good health. My own house. I'm still here. What have I got to complain about? The odd aches and pains, but I'm mostly good. Still walk out to the end of Old Harry most days. I miss Pat of course, but in a way it's good not to see her suffer. Life. You have to take it as it comes."

"You said you'd wanted to go to America," I remind him.

"Well, yes, I had wild dreams, didn't we all? I used to read—what was the man's name? Zane Grey. Of course, you got there. But America's not what it's cracked up to be, is it? Nowhere is, really. I'm happy here, always loved the place, and since the whole estate went to the National Trust, I'm going to enjoy it till I end my days here, with nobody building on my view."

The boy Ted has become this philosophical aging man, who sips whisky from a rose-patterned teacup and tells me, it's all right. Nothing is what it once seemed. We were young, and now we are old. Ted was someone who could have done anything, led people anywhere, and the army could have allowed him that chance. In wartime he could have been a hero—or dead. I remember him watching the hawk float on its layers of air, just below us. His attention to detail. A sparrow-hawk or a kestrel? I remember the quick grasp of his hand in mine, his long-legged stride. He has missed what he could have had, yet he has remained, in his essential self—the eye on the hawk, the passion of that kiss—who he has always been. You have to hide that part of yourself, sometimes for decades, until it is safe to bring it out again. In his seventies, it shows as a gleam of humor, a flicker of pride, and regret.

I say, "There must be something I can do."

"You're here. You're still alive and so am I. That's enough."

"I still need to do something. I just don't know what." Talking to him now is like talking to myself. There is something—a truth, a decision—that I have to get to, and I'm feeling my way.

He says, a slight edge to the question, "You mean, to make yourself feel better about it?"

"More than that. You know what I mean. To right a wrong."

I'm tempted to accept what he says—take the obvious explanation, let it be simple. Life goes on. Too much time has passed for it to matter anymore. Magda's broken bones are like all the bones in the churchyard, the bones in those bronze age burial sites high in their barrows on the hill. They are just bones. Her life was over long ago. The body disintegrates, and the person is gone.

Ted looks at me, bright eyes among wrinkles, the tufts of his eyebrows. His brown hand on the chair arm, with its loose gold ring. He's waiting for me, as he waited at the crest of the hill, for me to catch up. How odd, and yet how right: we were children together, and then nearly lovers, and now here we are again.

He says, "I reckon she belongs back here. Now that she has a name."

"You mean, I should go and get her?"

"I think you could do that, Nessa."

There's a moment when we say nothing, and simply look at each other, and it feels to me like a long time. Tea, the room, the present are no longer relevant. His eyes are on me—still waiting for me to catch up with him. Time hasn't happened—or it's turned in a circle, a spiral, bringing us back to this point. I'm back on the hill, nineteen years old, feeling his thin young body pressed against mine as if mine was all he ever wanted. Layers of life—like the invisible air currents on which the hawk rises.

"All right," I say. It's a promise of fidelity, the one I couldn't make to him years ago. I have no idea how to set about doing what he suggests, but I know that I must try.

He gets up. The moment has passed. "Excuse me, I just have to go down the corridor. All this tea—and I'm an old man now."

In his absence, I examine the wedding photograph on the shelf again: the two of them against the ancient stone of the church, flowers clutched in her hand, his stance rather stiff, as if holding himself in place. Love or convenience? Resignation or joy? His eyes in shadow, hers uplifted to glance at him. Doubt or confidence?

Impossible to tell. It's a public photograph of a private moment, an inscrutable blueprint of what will unfold over the years.

When he comes back, he grins—*excuse me*—and flops down in his armchair again and a movement of his hand towards the window, the day outside, lets me know that it's nearly time for me to leave.

"Seems like it's the present-day stuff we have to deal with now," he says at last. "You heard about what's been going on here? People dropped off boats, onto the beaches. Kids, mostly. Teenagers. They all say they're from Iran, but it's likely some are from Afghanistan."

"I think I have seen some of them." I feel for my bag, that's on the floor at my feet. I too will have to visit his bathroom.

"First door on the left," he says. "Only door on the left, in fact. Be gentle with the plumbing; if the chain doesn't pull, leave it."

"People smuggling," he says, when I return, having washed my hands in a shallow basin, looking at my own face in a spotted mirror. "That's what they call it now. As if people were just things to be moved around."

"It's going on here?"

"Boats have been coming across from France, mostly ports in Brittany, Paimpol, St. Malo, small places with harbors where there isn't much surveillance. Some fishermen got paid to bring kids across, earlier this year, dropped them off along the beaches here. They hid in the caves till the coast was clear."

Ah, the shirt and the tin. Water entering twice a day to wash away the traces. A small lithe person, a few small lithe people could crouch down and hide far up in one of those caves, and watch the tide, and wait for it to go down, and come out under cover of night. Teenagers; children, too young to know much about what had happened to their country, only aware of the need to escape it.

"My son went down and found some of them," Ted says, "You know, you want to help where you can. He took them home, three lads and a girl, fed them, got them in the bath, cleaned them up, sent them on their way. Eddie told me they were good kids, spoke a bit of English, they'd learned enough. Their parents, or some-one, must have paid for them to try to get here. It was after the camps at Calais closed down, it started—people got the idea that it would be much easier to come across from the Brittany and Normandy ports. Some of them French skippers got fined a lot. But yeah, they came in, here and at Brand's Bay, and down near Weymouth, Ringstead Bay, you know? Eight people were picked up at Brand's Bay in the spring. They landed anywhere there were small beaches, where a boat could come ashore at night, and caves to hide in."

It's the story of this present time and I hear his voice quicken as he tells it. I think about those dark teenagers smoking roll-ups with Jared. The foreign bus ticket. The blue T-shirt and the bean can in the cave. The evidence is left everywhere, if we can notice it; most of the time we simply aren't paying attention. Refugee Afghan teenagers, Iranians, hiding in smugglers' caves. Boats coming in at night, dropping them off. The defenses of this coun-try raised against the defenseless. Ted's son finding them, taking them home.

"Eddie, that's your son's name?"

"Yes, Edward Samways like me, only we couldn't have two Teds in the family."

"It was good of him, to help them, give them food."

"Only what any decent person would do," he says, "But you know, it's become illegal to help them now. What do you think of that?"

"I saw some of them sitting out on the moor, smoking. Then, coming out of the shop one day. Then they went for the bus. What happens to them when they leave here?"

"They get a chance to apply for asylum if they've made it to land and they're underage. At least, up till now they can. Eddie gave them a bit of cash, to start them off. Eddie and Eric are pals, see eye-to-eye. Of course, there's people in the village who'd just want them all arrested."

The iniquities of our time. He drums his fingers on the chair arm, frowns. He was that teenager, arrested, jailed, with nobody to listen to him, nobody to hear his version.

"Ted, I should be going." I begin again to make a move, though it's an effort to do so. I could sit talking to him for hours, filling the gaps that time has left us. "Thanks for the tea."

"Already? I never offered you any cake. I bought one specially. Battenberg cake—do you like marzipan? Well, maybe you don't eat a lot of sweet stuff. I'm afraid I do."

"Well, you know, we've said a lot. And thanks for the whisky, too."

"Will you come back? It's good to see you."

"Maybe." I think then, that I probably will not. We missed the moment in our lives in which we might have been more to each other. There's that wistfulness, that incomplete knowledge of each other—that unspoken question. That unlived story, in which I might have come back once again to the village as a young woman, and he might have found me again, and we might have—but, no.

"My husband, Bruno, is coming tomorrow to join me. We'll probably be—you know—doing things together. He likes all the walking we can do here."

"Ah well. I'm glad you came."

I turn to say goodbye. He says, "I always liked you the best, Nessa. I can say it now, maybe. I fancied you something rotten. Even when we were little. Even then."

"Not Anabel? I always thought you admired her."

"I was scared of her. It's not the same thing. No, it was always you. You were steadfast, like a little pony. You were brave."

I lean forward to kiss his cheek, and he seizes me by the hand— to steady himself or me? "Goodbye, Ted. Take care."

He stands at the open door and watches me go back down the slant of the steep road at the end of afternoon. I can feel his eyes upon me, but I don't turn around. I walk on, not looking back, until

I've reached the bend in the narrow road that runs between hedges of bramble and holly, the road we took going the other way when young Ted strode with young Nessa up on to the hill. I go past the farm building that is now the tea-shop and turn up towards the village, the corner store that sells wine and local cheeses and the *Guardian*, and up the rough road to where our house still stands and the path goes up on to the moor like the white crease at the fold of an old canvas-backed map that no longer quite fits the terrain it describes. Perhaps the land itself remembers, as people come and go—armies, generals, smugglers, refugees, tourists. The couple on the beach. Ted and me, on the hill. The sea set on fire, so that the country might survive invasion. Foreign children, Iranian or Afghan, crouching in caves, listening through the wash of the sea for the voice of their possible futures, far from home—these are the people we can try to help, now.

ALL THIS TIME IN ENGLAND, I've been asking myself, what was my responsibility here? What effect did these events have on my own life? Listening to Ted, I had to realize how self-centered this was: his life was changed dramatically, cut down to size, his future entirely tied to what happened on that day in 1952. My own life— well, it was an escape, an evasion, one wished upon me by Anabel, but accepted easily enough.

Yet: *It was always you.*

How many times in a lifetime do you need to have that said to you? Once may be enough. Once gives me courage this afternoon and carries me lighter of heart into the future. Not exonerating myself, no, but remembering that other people hold the key to what's important in life, and our loves are there to inform us of this. The chain of human connection—the linking of bone to bone—must not be broken.

THE NEXT DAY, THE DAY BEFORE Bruno's arrival in this country, I clean the house and get groceries in, to make it as welcoming as I can. The telephone rings. A man's voice says, "Eddie Samways here. Dad said you might need some help with the house, that you're thinking of getting work done. I said I'd get you an estimate, if you want. Don't want to let a house go, not with another winter coming, he said."

"OK, well, why don't you come and take a look? You know where we are?"

I imagine the two of them, the two Edward Samways, father and son—grinning at each other over the inability of the middle class to keep their houses in good repair. There are tears in my eyes as I think of young Ted with his hazel switch and his pocket knife and his dirty knees, long ago, leading us all around. Ted in Wellington boots and shirtsleeves, striding up the hill. Ted's one long impassioned kiss. Ted yesterday, a suddenly shaky hand pouring whisky. "It was always you."

Then my husband, his soft deep American voice welcome to my ears, calls to say he is boarding his plane; he is on his way.

I CALL PAULA IN THE EVENING, my last evening alone here in the cocoon of my grandmother's house.

"Paula, I saw Ted. The boy I told you about—the man he is now, of course. My age, our age. He was sent to remand home, a sort of children's prison, for what we did, because he was the one who got caught. It stopped him from doing what he wanted to do in life, his father made him stay here, and he's been here in the village ever since. It was real, for him. He couldn't make up an alternative version, the way we did, Anabel and I." I pause, and my voice cracks. "It was Anabel who told on him, so that he got into all that trouble. He said she told her parents, and then the police. She as good as told me that, years ago—but I never took it in. We betrayed him."

"Nessa, are you all right?"

"Well, I'm probably better than I was. He didn't seem angry, only accepting of what happened. But the point is, he paid for what he did. We—I—never have. I've only ever had half of the story. If that. All I could see was like a sliver of the whole. Like looking at part of the moon. Paula, it was awful, what we did to him. But he wasn't angry, he said he'd done his time."

"So, Nessa," Paula says in her dry, slightly accented voice, "you know what you have to do, now you have the other part of the story? The whole of the moon?"

"You mean, write it?" I don't tell her, not yet, that Ted has told me what, practically, I must do. It lies between him and me now, a pact. Whatever it takes. What those poor bones have been asking me to do, all along.

The following day, in the morning before Bruno is due to arrive, I go down to the beach where she was found and sit on a rock with my feet in the sand and think of her, the woman who died here. I think of what Paula has told me about coming from Poland during the war. I think of the obligation that comes from being still alive. I think of Ted, and his instinctive honesty. Are some people simply born knowing what is true?

I'll do it however I can—get Magda's bones back, talk to the police, the forensic scientists, talk to the vicar here, tell the whole unexpurgated story. Arrange for a burial place for her in the churchyard here, in among the monuments for the Great War and the children who died young, maybe even next to the centenarian who'd fought Napoleon, and his wife who was born in a village in northern France. Give her back her name and the likely dates of her birth and death. Restore her to the place and time in history where she belongs. Who knew if there were people still alive in this world who would want to know, even to mourn her? It will be at least a first step.

I can make amends, but I can't change the past. It's over, all of it. The voice that speaks to me now is my own. You can have her buried but nothing you do will change what has already happened. You can however write the story about that summer. What you do next, moving into the future, is the only thing you can change. Pay attention to the present moment. Go on from here.

It was 1952, just seven years after the end of the war that convulsed the world . . .

THE TIDE IS COMING IN; I hear its changed voice as its register shifts and the little waves begin to unfurl. So many boats are moored in the bay now: any one of them could have brought scared teenagers over from France and simply let them come ashore unnoticed— this other story continuing, its roots in a far-off war. I watch a child in a dinghy with an outboard motor skid across the surface of the water, planing easily between yachts at anchor, the tiller in a careless hand. There's the rattle of halyards in the wind from the sea.

In my mind's eye, alive and vivid as today, a young blonde woman in a summer dress and sneakers and a cotton hat steps with her lover down a beach. I see her smile as she kicks off her shoes and reaches up for him, in the moment before the cliff falls.

Acknowledgments

I would like to thank my kind and brilliant agent, Kimberley Cameron, for her tireless encouragement and good advice and my editor Jennifer McCord for her persistence, patience and dedication to excellence.

To those who have read and re-read this novel at various stages: Jessica Argyle, Sue Roe, Ellen McLaughlin, who have all provided consistent writerly friendship over the years—profound thanks.

I would also like particularly to thank Phyllis Rose, Annie Dillard, Alison Lurie (posthumously) as long-time mentors and friends, as well as all the writers who have welcomed me to the writers' community in Key West since I first landed here 30 years ago. Also, my 'present-day' group of writers who keep me going: Katrin Schumann, Jessica Argyle, Brooks Phillips.

As always, I am deeply grateful to Kathryn Kilgore for the Artists and Writers house, tucked away behind the gumbo limbo trees in Key West.

And of course, thanks to my husband of 30 years, Allen Meece, for all the lunch-times spent discussing the ups and downs of writing fiction, and for his constant support of me and my work.

Betsy Osha

ROSALIND BRACKENBURY WAS BORN in London, England, grew up in the UK and has lived in Scotland and France. She has lived in Key West for nearly 30 years with her American husband.

She has been writing all her life and has published novels and collections of poetry, as well as award-winning short stories. She was Creative Writing Fellow at the College of William and Mary, Williamsburg VA, in 2006 and 2012. In Key West she has run yearly poetry and prose workshops at The Studios of Key West and she has been featured both as panelist and moderator at the Key West Literary Seminar. She was Key West's second Poet Laureate in 2014–15. She has a daughter and a son, both living in the UK.